CW01426345

EXECUTION
LULLABY

EXECUTION LULLABY

NIGEL LATTA

HarperCollins*Publishers (New Zealand) Limited*

First published 2000
HarperCollins*Publishers (New Zealand) Limited*
P.O. Box 1, Auckland

Copyright © Nigel Latta 2000

Nigel Latta asserts the moral right to be
identified as the author of this work.

All rights reserved. No part of this publication
may be reproduced, stored in a retrieval
system or transmitted in any form or by any
means, electronic, mechanical, photocopying,
recording or otherwise, without the prior
written permission of the publishers.

ISBN 1 86950 364 3

Typeset by Chris O'Brien
Printed by Griffin Press, South Australia on
50 gsm Bulky News

Acknowledgements

To everyone at HarperCollins I owe a huge debt of thanks. In particular thank you to Ian Watt for first opening the door and inviting me in from the cold. Sue Page for all her work in making this book what it is. Lesley Marshall, for taking my twisted little story and straightening out the kinks.

A special debt of appreciation is owed to Michael Butler. During the often hellish process of writing this dark tale he was my sounding board, my adviser, my shrink, and my friend. Most of all my friend.

Les, Marieke, and Michelle Simmonds, for providing such a quality demographic. My brother Craig Latta, who I can always depend on for straight shooting. Neville Kippenberger, for being the utterly unique soul that he is.

Vivienne Thompson helped me to stay true to the path, even when it got hard to see. Anna Ritchie from Active Physio kept me going when my hands were threatening to give up. The irrepressible Dr Lambie for being more of a friend than anyone could ever deserve.

Three final but very important thanks: The Doors for providing the soundtrack (the last fifty pages should be read with 'The End' playing over and over). Neela, my first and most valued critic. And lastly, Rohan, my wonderful son, for providing such a compelling reason to finish the manuscript.

For Neela
This dark tale of love

Beware, there is one more step inside the door.

-Isak Dinesen

1

The last really happy memory I have is of a sunny Sunday morning in March. It was still quiet back then, and the air was still sweet. It was nearly a week before the dead girls started talking to me, and a couple more days again before I began to smell them.

Rot takes its own good time.

Just like love, I suppose.

I woke up and Juliette was already kissing me. She amazed me like that—I've never known a woman as passionate as she was. Sex was like an art form to her. Some people paint, some write. Juliette made love. She had this way of making you forget everything, forget yourself even.

'Hey, sleepyhead,' she said between kisses. 'I couldn't wait so I started without you.'

She has the most divine voice, soft and very feminine but with just a hint of something raw underneath.

I remember moaning quietly as her lips and hands worked away at me. The line between sleep and arousal is whisper thin for men. Her skin brushed mine and she smelled like honey and sex all rolled into one.

We made love for what seemed like hours. No talking. Just touching and moaning. Secret sounds. Pleasure upon pleasure, each new sensation building on the last until it felt as if the whole world was warm wet skin.

Afterwards we lay next to each other, the sun streaming in through the large bay windows of the bedroom, and talked. Juliette loved to talk about sex too, she loved to tell me what she'd felt as we'd moved together. She knew what that did to me. We went another round.

I remember that morning so clearly now. It wasn't the last time that we made love, there were many more times before it was over, but it was the last time that I made love to her free of fear.

'Do you love me?' she asked later.

The blankets were cast aside and I could see her body stretched beside mine. She was beautiful. I could feel her breasts pressed into my side and her leg wrapped around me. She loved to push herself up against me when we were finished so I could feel how wet she was.

'Of course,' was all I could say.

'No,' she said as she raised herself on one arm, suddenly serious, 'do you *really* love me?'

She was like that, she could go from light and playful to the depths of intensity in moments. It was dizzying sometimes.

'I have always loved you.'

'Would you die for me?'

Her breasts lightly brushed against my chest as I looked into her pale blue eyes. 'I would die a thousand deaths for you, my Juliette.' It was corny, but that always seemed to please her most of all. It was almost as if she wanted me to overplay my hand. She loved that, and I loved her for it.

'Good,' she said.

We had our breakfast together and talked some more. It wasn't anything in particular we did, that last morning. Just the two of us together, no doubts, no fears. It was bliss.

Later that day I went to put a box in the trunk of

the car. No big deal, nothing special—just taking out some junk.

And then I found the dead girl's watch.

And nothing was ever the same again.

2

I met with my lawyer today. His name is Gerald. He hates coming on to the row, though he never says it. He doesn't need to, I can see it in his eyes. They let him meet with me in my cell. I sit on the narrow bunk and he sits on a small steel chair that the guards bring. I knew it was bad news the moment I saw him. Gerald has a lousy poker-face.

'I've got some bad news, Simon,' he said as he rummaged about in his briefcase.

'Uh huh,' I said.

'The state has set an execution date. October fourth.'

'Uh huh.'

He couldn't bring himself to look at me. He's young, only in his thirties, and it's all pretty frightening for him. I think he feels responsible for me.

'I know this feels like a setback, but you have to be strong.'

I smiled at him then, at his weakness and his fear. Not in a nasty way—I like him, don't get me wrong— but it was just so goddamned ironic that this boy was telling *me* to be strong.

You're probably thinking it's pretty arrogant for me to call Gerald a boy, when he's at least a couple of years older than me, but you'll understand once you know more about the path that I've walked. Sometimes

I feel like I'm a thousand years old.

'Is she okay?' I asked him. I knew he would have gone to tell her in person. Gerald takes his job very seriously. He reminds me of a priest in many ways.

He stopped and looked up. Even after all this time he still didn't understand how I could love her so. 'This is the no-bullshit phase, Simon. We're going down to the wire and you need to focus on saving yourself.'

'Is she okay?'

He sighed. 'Yes, Simon, she's okay.'

'You went to her?'

'Yes.'

'How did she take it?'

He paused for a moment, studying me. 'She laughed, Simon. She looked at me and she laughed.'

I smiled. 'Good. I'm glad that she's happy.'

'Can we talk about your case now, Simon?'

'Sure.'

He talked for an hour but I didn't really listen. This is all weighing heavily on poor Gerald. It's his first death penalty case. I'm sure he's lost weight in the last couple of months. He has a wife and two kids. I have this picture of Gerald in my head that I can't seem to shake. He's sitting in his kids' room late at night, watching them sleep, and worrying about them. Worrying how they might turn out.

He's read all the trial notes, you see, and I've told him some other stuff as well, some of the things that weren't in his neat little files. He wanted to know—or at least he thought he did. Now he knows what I was, and he sees what I've become. It's such a short ride from the top to the bottom, such a very short ride.

I'm not a bad person, despite what you may have read about me. I've done some very bad things, I won't deny that, but I'm not a bad person. It seems odd to be saying that, sitting here in my ten-foot-by-ten-foot slot on death row, but I believe it to be true. I have to, that's all I have left.

I know you want to hear about the bloody stuff, all the sordid little details of the killings, but you'll have to wait. People always want to see the nasty stuff, it's not their fault, it's just the way of things. The publisher even asked me if I wanted to put any photographs in the book. Apparently it boosts sales if you have pictures.

'Pictures of what?' I asked her. She's a nice woman, her name is Kate.

'Oh, you know,' she said, 'the usual stuff. Pictures of you, your wife, some of the victims. We could even get some crime scene photographs from the cops.'

'I don't think so, Kate.'

'Oh, okay. Well, maybe just think about it then, okay?'

'Okay, Kate.'

They're going to wait until after the execution to publish the book. Then they'll be able to put in whatever pictures they want. I guess there's not much I can do about that. I can't speak to Gerald about it—he finds the whole idea of me writing a book distasteful. He's never said it but I can see it in his eyes.

If they have put pictures in, I'll make one prediction: I bet you've already looked at them. I bet you looked at them before you even bought the book. I bet you stood there in the shop thumbing through them like some dirty old man with a skin magazine. Nothing draws the flies like a box full of dead girls.

It's erotic, isn't it? We don't have to pretend with one another, you and I, not here anyway. Sex and death—what else is there? I can hear your questions even now as I'm writing. Were they pretty girls? Did he *do things* to them before he killed them? *After*? Don't pretend you're not having these thoughts, we all do.

Sex and death, that's why you picked the god-damned book up in the first place.

But you'll have to wait for all that. I'll give it to you, don't worry, you'll get your peek under the sheet, but you'll have to wait. This is my only chance to tell you, and so I have to tell the story in my own way and in my own time. I want you to get to know us first. You have to—otherwise what comes later makes no sense.

3

You'll have to forgive me if I jump around a bit. I'm trying to keep it all in some kind of order, but it's hard. The problem is trying to tell a crazy story in a way that makes sense to people on the outside. I can understand it all, but then I lived through it. Whether the insanity makes sense to you is another matter.

4

I met Juliette when I was only twenty-three. It almost seemed an accident at the time, but looking back now I think she'd always been waiting for me. It was in a bar in New York City, just off Fifth Avenue. I'd come to the Big Apple with my first novel, trying to find the break that never came. I'd been walking the streets for a couple of days, plodding from publisher to publisher. None of them would even see me. Eventually I got tired and gave up. My feet hurt and the boundless certainty that I'd be discovered was all but gone.

'You look lonely,' she'd said as she sat down on the barstool next to me. I turned and was instantly stunned—quite literally stunned, she was that beautiful.

She smiled at me. 'You're not from here, are you?'

'No,' was all I could say. Women terrify me. I'd only ever had sex once in my life—three years before with a skinny, pimply girl called Sylvia Larson. Now here I was in New York City sitting in a bar next to a woman who was too beautiful to exist in real life.

'So . . . ?' she asked.

'So . . . I'm . . . uh . . .' I stammered back.

She laughed this time, and the sound was like roses. 'So where are you from?'

'I'm from Nebraska,' I said as my brain finally caught up.

'You're a long way from home, soldier.' She studied me with her pale blue eyes.

I looked around the bar. 'It sure feels like it tonight.'

'This place stinks of smoke,' she said. 'Would you like to walk with me?'

'Yes.' I smiled. 'I would very much like to walk with you.'

So we did. I floated through the streets of New York with this strange and beautiful creature for hours, my tired feet suddenly feeling like it was their first day out in the world. She was interested in everything about me, when I told her why I was in New York she squealed.

'Oh, you're kidding?' she said, grabbing my arm. 'You're a writer? For real?'

'For real.' Not that I was thinking anything about writing just then, I was thinking how wonderful it felt

15

to have her body pressed against mine.

'I've *always* wanted to meet a real writer.'

'I don't know how *real* a writer I am. I haven't managed to sell the novel yet.'

'But you will,' she said, as if it were already decided, 'and then you'll become famous and forget me.'

'I swear this to you,' I said to her, standing on the street with snowflakes falling all around us, 'I will *never* forget you.'

New York faded away, all I could see were her eyes. 'Would you like to make love to me?' she whispered.

I couldn't speak. I wanted to speak—God knows if there was ever a question that begged an answer it was that one—but I just couldn't find the words in me.

'Come on,' she said. I guess the question had been answered before it was even asked. She took me by the arm and led me deeper into the city. I couldn't believe this was happening, that soon I would be lying naked with this achingly beautiful woman.

Eventually she led me down an alleyway and we climbed up a fire escape. The window to her apartment was open.

'I hate using the stairs,' was all she said. At that moment she could have told me anything and I would have thought it was okay.

Her apartment was empty except for a mattress on the floor and a few dirty cups in the sink. It didn't look like anyone actually lived there, more like someone was waiting there.

She kissed me. 'Do want me to take off my clothes?' she whispered.

I nodded—at least I guess I must have because she started to undress. It was the most magical thing. As she shed each layer of clothing she began to glow brighter and brighter. Her skin has this wonderful translucent golden hue. I've never seen another human being like her. Standing in that small apartment watching her was the defining moment of my life. When she finally stood naked before me it felt as if the world had stopped.

There was nothing else except her and me.

And when she came to me, when my skin touched hers, I felt like I was going to die. There have been times since then when I think maybe I did. Sometimes I wonder if my body isn't still lying upstairs in that little apartment in New York City. It'll just be bones by now if it is.

Much later, after we'd finished, we lay on her mattress. I remember steam rising off our skin in the cold air of the apartment.

'Take me with you,' she said.

'Where? Back to Nebraska?'

'No—you're never going back there. I mean take me with you to wherever you're going next.'

'I have to go back there, that's where my family is.'

She turned to face me, and her eyes were so goddamned intense I nearly had to look away. She bent and licked my chest, long and slow, like a very old cat drinking milk. 'We're family now.'

She was right, I never went back to Nebraska.

5

I wouldn't want you to get the idea that it was only sex, although the sex was beyond imagining—there was so much more to it than that. I think it's that our

17

souls are joined, linked in a way that's hard to understand. I had never really believed in the concept of 'soul mates'. As far as I was concerned that was the stuff of fanciful novels and corny Hollywood movies, but then I met Juliette in a bar in New York City and the world was never the same again. Three years was all it took to get me from that barstool to this bunk on death row. Like I said, it's a short ride.

I know this all sounds like so much cliché, all this talk of souls, but it's true. It probably also sounds like a justification, that I'm trying to build a case to somehow excuse what we did. I'm not. I can't justify what we did. I don't want you to forgive us, I just want you to understand us.

It was the feeling of connection far more than the sex. Right from that very first moment it felt as if she was inside me and I was inside her. I didn't need her to talk to know what her thoughts were. I never needed to ask what she wanted to eat or drink, or when. I just knew. And she knew too. Soul mates? I guess no one can ever really know that, but we sure as hell know more about each other than any other two people I've ever seen.

6

Seems like everybody wants to get to know you when you're a serial killer—the title brings its own kind of celebrity. A shrink from the FBI came to see me a few weeks ago. He wanted to know if I'd be willing to talk to him about the murders. He looked like something out of the movies, with his dark suit and careful eyes. But I had nothing else to do so I said okay.

They put us in the interview room, although it's really more of a box than a room: plain gray walls and a stainless steel table in the center. They shackled me to the chair. I guess that's fair enough, me being a convicted killer and all.

'What do you want to know?' I asked him as the fibby was laying out his pens and questionnaires.

'I'd like to ask you some questions about your crimes,' he said in an obviously practiced manner.

'Is this work or fun?'

'It's part of an ongoing project that the FBI has to build up our knowledge of men who have committed a number of homicides.' He had all the spontaneity of a textbook.

'You mean serial killers?'

He paused for the briefest of moments. 'Yes.'

I couldn't help but smile. 'So that would make me Hannibal and you Clarisse, wouldn't it?'

'I guess so.' The agent smiled, but his eyes never changed.

'I'm afraid you may be disappointed, Agent Hanson.'

'How so?'

'I'm not that interesting.'

'You don't have to be interesting, just answer the questions as honestly as you can.'

'Do we get to do the quid pro quo thing, Agent Hanson?'

'Sorry, Simon, this isn't the movies and I don't do the quid pro quo thing.'

I laughed. 'That's okay, I wouldn't know what to ask anyway.'

He asked the kinds of questions that you'd expect, and that was fine for a while. I told him about my family and my growing up. My parents were pretty normal people, farming folk from Nebraska. I was never beaten or sexually abused, and most of my memories from childhood are happy ones. I went to school, had some friends, all the usual stuff. Not too many friends, not too few. I was never cruel to animals as a child. I didn't steal things or burn things down.

He thought I was lying, but too bad. One of the bright sides of being on death row is that you soon lose interest in other people's opinions of you.

It was okay until he started asking me about the girls. I hate thinking about that stuff.

'Tell me about Carol Keenan,' he said.

Carol Keenan was seventeen when she died. I saw pictures of her family on the television after she'd disappeared, her mother crying and her father rigid with fear. They pleaded with whoever had their daughter to return her safely. I knew that was never going to happen—I'd been the one who pushed her body out the back of my station wagon at the bottom of some shitty little dead-end road.

'What do you want to know about her?' I asked him.

'Why did you ring the police and tell them where to find her body?'

'I saw her parents on the television, the appeal they made for her return.'

'How did you feel when you saw them?'

I sat looking at him, the memory of that night like poison in my mind. It felt like a hundred years ago and yet somehow it was still going on. I remember watching them, seeing that poor mother's tears, seeing how desperately she wanted to believe that her daughter would be coming home—raped maybe, but alive. It nearly pushed me over the edge that long-ago night, knowing the poor woman was praying her daughter, her precious child, had *just* been raped and not killed. I could hear her prayers in my head:

. . . Please, God, let him only rape her. Please, please don't let him kill her . . .

And underneath that the other prayer. The darkest one, the one she doesn't even let herself know she's praying:

. . . but if he does kill her, God, let her die quickly, don't let her suffer, please don't let her suffer . . .

The sound Carol's body made as it hit the ground kept playing itself over and over in my head. I couldn't stay in the room and watch her parents, but I couldn't leave. I ran in and out of the room, tears and snot streaming down my face. I remember hearing this terrible sound, a pitiful, heartbreaking wail. I'd thought it was Carol's mother on the television, but it turned out it was me. After a while I couldn't even run. I collapsed on the floor and curled up into a ball, screaming and sobbing as the horror of it all swept over me.

It was only Juliette's hand on my cheek that saved me. I had been so close to the abyss that night it would have been easy to just slide into it. Sometimes I wish I had.

'Simon?' Agent Hanson's voice brought me back into the room. 'How did you feel when you saw Carol's parents on television?'

I searched for the words, but there were none. 'I felt very sad,' was all I could finally bring myself to say.

7

Juliette and I left New York and traveled for a while. I had a few bucks saved up from my job back in Nebraska where I'd worked as an usher in our town's only movie theatre. It hadn't paid very well, but it gave me time during the day to write so I didn't mind. We soon burned up my puny savings and had to work odd jobs as we traveled around. Juliette has always been a restless soul. Too long in one place and she starts to feel trapped.

We stayed in the smaller towns. Juliette said she was sick of big cities and wanted to be in out of the way places for a while. We never stayed anywhere longer than a couple of weeks. I'd get a job pumping gas, and she'd work as a waitress. There seems to be a permanent shortage of gas jockeys and waitresses on the East Coast.

We'd stay just long enough to get to know the place. Juliette's favorite thing was to watch people. It was a kind of game with her. She used to love to try and work out who was sleeping with whom, and who wanted to sleep with whom. We'd sit for hours watching strangers getting on with their daily grind.

'See that guy?' she said to me one day as we sat drinking coffee in a tinpot little burg four weeks out of New York.

'Who?' I asked.

'That big fat guy over there.' She pointed to a bloated, red-faced man sitting on a park bench. He looked about sixty but was probably only forty-something.

'Yeah, what about him?'

'He wants to hurt that red-haired woman who works in the grocery store.'

I laughed. 'How the hell do you know that, Juliette?'

'I can tell, I've been watching him for a couple of days now. Can't you see it?'

I looked at the man again, but to me he just seemed

like a fat guy sitting on a bench. 'No,' I finally said.

'Sure he does, he hates her. He wants to tie her up in his trailer home and hurt her. He wants to put a whisky bottle in her.'

'You can't tell that just from looking at him.'

'I can.'

'How?'

'Well, look at him.' I did as she said. 'He's the fat kid who grew up here and never did anything with his life. All the locals know him, but he resents them terribly, has done his whole life. He's displaced trailer-trash.'

I shook my head. 'What do you mean they all know him? Nobody even looks at him.'

'That's how you can tell he's local. His big fat ass has been sitting on that bench so long now nobody even notices him anymore. If he was a stranger he'd get at least a few nervous glances.'

I watched for a bit longer and realized she had a point. Creepy-looking fat guys always get a few glances. This one could have been a rock for all the notice anyone took of him.

'Okay, but how do you know he has a thing for the redhead? And how do you know he wants to tie her up and hurt her?'

'It's obvious,' she said. 'He always sits on that bench even though there are lots of other benches, so there has to be a reason. This one looks straight into the grocery store. He can watch her all day. Look, here she comes now, you watch his right leg.'

The red-haired woman appeared in the window of the grocery store. I looked across at the fat man's right leg. It jiggled ever so slightly. 'Holy shit,' I said.

'Now look at her,' Juliette continued. 'She's in her forties, pretty, also local. Everybody knows her. She's friendly and well liked by the whole town. I bet she was probably a cheerleader or something at the local high school, and I bet they were in the same year.'

'So how do you know he wants to tie her up and use a whisky bottle on her?'

She looked at me then, genuinely puzzled. 'I thought writers were supposed to be observant, Simon?'

'Clearly not this writer.'

'It's obvious that he hates her. He's probably had a crush on her since high school but he's never acted on it because he's always been the fat kid. So he sits and watches her every day with this burning desire for her and this terrible resentment. She's too snooty for him, that's what he thinks, and so one of these days he's going to show her.'

'Yeah, but what about the whole tying her up and bottle thing?'

'How long do you suppose he's been sitting there watching her, Simon?'

I looked at him. 'Years probably.'

'So you think he's been sitting there for years, hating her and lusting for her, and the only thing he's ever come up with is a common old meat-and-potatoes rape? No way. He does all kinds of things to her in his head. He'd want to tie her up because that way she'd be completely powerless. That would be important for him, that he was in total control and she knew it.'

'But how do you know specifically that he wants to use a whisky bottle?'

'He tells her all the time. Watch,' she said as the fat man pulled a bottle of whisky from his coat and took a long slug. He swallowed and then put the bottle back in his mouth. He didn't take another drink. He just left it there, sucking on it. I watched him looking over the road at the red-haired woman. His eyes said it all.

'Jesus.'

'Told you,' said Juliette.

She was incredible like that. She could see things in you that you thought were hidden from the whole world. It was like she had these old eyes that had seen everything there was to see. Nothing was hidden from Juliette.

A month later we were having breakfast at a truckstop just outside of Philadelphia. We were watching the news when a picture of the red-haired woman came on. Her naked body had been found weighted down in a river. The police believed she'd been sexually assaulted and tortured and they were holding a local man in custody. There was a picture of the cops leading him into the station, and despite the blanket over his head it was clear he was a very large man.

I remember feeling sick as I watched it.

'Told you,' Juliette said. 'You want the rest of that pancake?'

8

It bothered me, thinking about the red-haired woman and the fat man. I felt like we should have done something, warned her at least. I sat on it for two days and then I had to talk to Juliette about it. It was late. We'd made love and then I'd lain in the dark for hours thinking about it.

'Juliette?' Nothing, just blackness. 'Juliette, you awake?'

'Mmmm?'

'I keep thinking we should have told someone.'

'Told someone what?' Her voice was fuzzy with sleep.

'Back in that town, about the fat man.'

She sighed then, and I felt the bed move as she rolled onto her back. 'What do you mean, Simon?'

'I mean we should have told someone about him. We knew he was thinking about doing that stuff to her and we didn't tell anyone.'

'It was just a game, honey. We didn't know the guy was actually gonna do it.'

'A game? He killed her, Jules, just like you said he would. That's no game.'

'Who would you have told, Simon? What would you have said?'

I thought for a moment. 'Maybe the sheriff? Maybe we should have at least told that woman?'

'Do you know how crazy that would have sounded? We're strangers in town and we go up to these people and start making all kinds of crazy allegations. How exactly do you think they're going to respond to that?'

'I just feel like we should have done something, that's all.'

'Look, baby,' she said as she stretched one arm out and touched me, 'there was nothing we could have done. We didn't know he was really going to do it.'

Even in the darkness it felt like a lie. 'You knew,' I said. In my mind I could see Juliette lying there—eyes open—staring into the blackness.

'Bad things happen, Simon. Sometimes it's just as simple as that. You try not to stand too close to it, and you protect the ones you love as best you can. The world's too full of hurt to save.'

That didn't feel enough, but then she rolled on top

of me and kissed me. I suddenly found that I wanted her more than ever before.

Later, as the orgasm was taking her, I kissed her cheek.

It was wet with tears.

9

The layout of death row at the Eden Hill Penitentiary is grimly functional. It's pretty much what you'd expect of a place that's been specially designed to kill people. We call it the Garden of Eden, or just the Garden for short. There is no original sin here, just the same old wretched ones that seem to go round and round. I don't know who first started calling it the Garden—some ironic soul would be my guess. In any case, the name has obviously stuck.

The Garden is housed in a separate building to the rest of the prison. To get to it you have to go down a long razor-wire corridor. I remember that walk. I remember trying to suck in as much fresh air as I could, trying to burn the sight of the cold blue sky into my brain. I didn't expect to be seeing it again.

You come on to the Garden through a pair of large gray steel doors, then the guards walk you to your cell past all the other dead men. The place has been set up so that the inmates can't see each other, with the cells opening onto a single wide corridor that runs the length of the row. Way down the bottom there are two more doors. To the right, through the gray door, are the infirmary and the interview rooms. To the left, through the pink door, is death. Everything in the place is gray—everything except for that one door.

There are thirty-five cells in the Garden of Eden. I was given cell number twenty-three. Funnily enough, that's the same age I was when I first met Juliette.

It used to be that the condemned would sit on the Garden for years before the State finally got around to killing them. Just lately though, the good people of this state have decided that they want their killing done faster. Now the average stay is about two years. I'd been here only five months when I got my date. Seems people want me dead even quicker than most.

It takes a while to get it sorted, all the ins and outs, but you do sooner or later. I'd thought it would be just like the movies—you know, with a big tough guy called Bull who runs the place, and all the butch gay boys raping everyone else. It's different in the Garden. Here they're much more careful about who has contact with whom.

I guess it's no different to anywhere that you collect the dying together in one place; you have to keep everyone separated in case the virus spreads.

We don't really have anyone in the Garden who's the designated boss, but we do have the 'connected' guy, the one who knows everything about everything. His name is Wendall Gates. He's an odd character, a serial killer convicted back in 1996 for the murder of twelve women. Privately Wendall has told me that the number is actually much closer to thirty. He and I seem to have a strange affinity for one another, which puzzles me. I've never been one for killers. That may seem oddly hypocritical, but it's true. I used to be the guy who muttered 'hang the bastard' at the end of the news story. I supported longer prison sentences, and I supported the death penalty. The Chinese were right, you do have to be careful what you wish for.

Wendall had my number from the very first day I arrived.

'You know the current only flows one way here,' he'd said as he sat down beside me in the small exercise yard. I was staring down at my shoes and hoping no one would talk to me. They only let a half-dozen of us out at any one time. God knows what they think we'd do, there's more concrete and razor-wire here than any place I've ever seen. The yard itself is little more than a small concrete box with a door and a thin wire grill between us and the sky.

I tried not to sound scared. 'Pardon?'

'The current,' he said, 'it only flows one way.'

Wendall is the stereotypic death row inmate. He looks like the only reason he was put on the earth was to kill, get caught, and be executed. He's tall, just a little over six feet, white, and totally bald. He has a tattoo of a skull and crossbones on his forehead, and predator's eyes. Wendall looks so much like a serial killer it makes you wonder if he's some kind of sick practical joke.

'What do you mean?' I asked him.

'There's a current flows down the row,' he said as he picked at a scab on the side of his nose, 'in through the big door and then out through the pink door.' He smiled, but it touched nothing good inside him. 'Ain't no going back through the big door. Ain't no comin' back from the pink door. Sooner or later the current gets us all. It'll get me, and it's gonna get you too.'

I didn't want any trouble so I looked down at my shoes again, hoping he'd get the hint and move on.

'I know you didn't do it,' he said.

'Do what?' I asked, still looking down.

Wendall leaned in real close, close enough for me to feel his wet breath on my cheek. 'I know you didn't kill those girls,' he whispered.

Startled, I looked up, but he was already walking away.

10

It worked. Wendall got my attention. Juliette's trial was still going on back then. There'd been one mistrial because the jury couldn't reach a unanimous verdict, and the second trial was drawing to a close. So when Wendall whispered his little piece in my ear it frightened me. I wasn't scared of my own death—I could live with that, so to speak—but *her* death was incomprehensible. If she died it would all have been for nothing.

It was another four days before I was put out in the yard with Wendall again. I tried to play it cool, but he wasn't interested in those kinds of games. Finally, when there was only five minutes left before they put us back in our holes, I walked over to where he was standing. I felt sick.

'Hey,' I said.

Wendall could see straight away that I was bullshitting him, but he was polite enough not to mention it. 'Hey.'

'Cold this morning, isn't it?' I said as I rubbed my hands together theatrically.

'Sure is,' he replied. 'Might rain later on.'

I felt like screaming, but I kept up with the banter. My biggest fear was that he was an undercover cop, planted here to get some information out of me about Juliette. I couldn't help myself though, I had to know what his game was. 'What did you mean the other day when you said you knew I didn't kill those girls?'

Wendall looked up at the sky. 'You think it's gonna rain?'

'I don't know, and to be honest I don't give a shit. But I do want to know what you meant when you said that.'

'I meant I know you didn't kill them.'

'Are you a cop?' I asked him. I'd read once that if you ask an undercover cop straight up then he has to tell you. I didn't know if that was true, but I had nothing to lose by asking

He laughed. 'You sure are scared of something.'

'Are you a cop?' Now I was really frightened. If he wasn't answering my question he must be a cop. And that would mean they were still trying to lay the lot on Juliette.

'Settle down, Simon,' Wendall said. 'I'm no cop, just a concerned citizen wanting to see justice done.'

'Yeah, well, justice has been done. I killed them and now the government is going to kill me. An eye for an eye, just like the Bible says.'

Wendall chuckled. 'You didn't kill all those girls, Simon, you're not the type. But that pretty wife of yours, I seen her on the news, she's the type. I think *she's* the one murdered all those poor little girls. What do you say?'

I felt as if Wendall had sucked the spit from my mouth. 'You're full of shit,' I said with a thick tongue. 'I killed them all and I goddamned loved it. I looked into their eyes as I did it and I had the biggest hard on of my life. Then when they were done I jerked off into their cold, dead faces.'

Wendall just chuckled again. 'Man, you're the one who's full of shit.'

'And how the fuck would you know?' I demanded.

'Simple,' he said, 'takes one to know one aint.' He winked and walked off.

11

Wendall wasn't the first to volunteer that theory. They'd all tried to pin it on her, but I'd been too strong. I'd had to be—the cops had pushed hard when they first arrested us.

'Your wife said that you killed the girl and then you tried to kill her when she attempted to stop you.'

I nodded my head slowly. 'Yeah, I did it. I killed the girl, and I stabbed Juliette as well.'

It was a little over three hours since they'd found me and Juliette with Theresa Wright's body in our basement. Detective James Goodlow sat across from me with blank eyes. I learnt as time went on that when his eyes went blank he was thinking. Goodlow did the first interviews. If you watched my trial on television he was the distinguished-looking black guy who made a statement to the media after the jury came back with the death sentence decision.

'I think that maybe Juliette was more involved in this thing than you're telling me, Simon,' he said.

'No, she wasn't. It was just me, it was all me.'

'Well, I think your wife was more a part of it than she let on. I think that's why you stabbed her, because she knew too much about the other girls.'

'Is she going to be okay?' I asked, feeling oddly numb.

'She's in surgery now. The doctors say they don't know if she's going to make it or not. You did stab her in the chest, Simon, but then'—he leaned across the small table—'I don't need to tell *you* that, do I?'

I remember feeling colder than I'd ever felt in my life. I've often wondered if they did that on purpose to aid in the interrogation.

'What about the other girls, Simon?'

I didn't answer. I couldn't.

Goodlow opened a manila folder in front of him and began laying out photographs on the desk. One after another. Young, bright, smiling faces. Pretty faces. Ghosts.

I knew them all.

'What about these girls, Simon?'

'I can tell you about these two,' I said, pointing to Milly and Lisa, 'but I can't tell you about the rest yet.'

'Did you kill them all?'

'Yes.'

Goodlow sat there for a moment. I didn't want to look at him. It was all I could do to look at the photographs.

'Their parents want to know what happened to them, Simon, so they can bury their children in peace.'

'I can't tell you about the rest yet.'

'Why not, Simon?'

'I just can't.'

He paused, and I realised he knew why I wouldn't tell him.

'Will you tell me in a few weeks, Simon?'

I swallowed. 'Yes.' My voice was almost a whisper.

'Oh, Christ,' he said, and I could hear the revulsion in his voice. 'Are you waiting for them to decompose, Simon? Until whatever physical evidence is left rots away?'

There was nothing I could say.

33

'You cold bastard,' he said, his voice shaking with rage. 'You cold, murdering bastard.'

He left the photographs on the table and went to get coffee. Goodlow was a very professional man. He'd know it was better to beat the hell out of some locker than to beat the hell out of me.

12

I know that Goodlow still thinks the only reason I worked at Bedford College was to hunt for more girls, but he's wrong. Towards the end Bedford College was the last place I could still find the old me. It was a sanctuary, somewhere I could hide from the monster I'd become.

I got the job the year before we were arrested. After months of drifting she'd finally had enough.

'Here,' she said as she sipped a Coke in Will's Diner the day we hit Bedford.

'What?'

'I want to stay here.'

'Okay,' I said, 'let's stay here.'

'No, Simon,' she said, putting down her Coke, 'I want to *stay* here.'

'You mean *stay* stay?'

She smiled. I can still see it now, she was so beautiful.

I looked out the window. Bedford was one of those odd places halfway between a town and a city. Quite but not quite, if you know what I mean. It lay on the coast, with a small natural harbor marking one end of town and a hill marking the other. It had nice little tree-lined streets, with nice little green lawns. Kids on bikes. Antique stores. All that hokey stuff. It was as good as anywhere else.

'Okay, we'll stay.'

Within a month we had a small house on the edge of town and I had a job at the local high school teaching English. Juliette set it all up. We'd stayed in a motel for the first week. One day she went out for two hours and when she came back she said she'd arranged a job interview for me.

'Which gas station?' I asked.

'Not a gas station, at Bedford College.'

'The high school?'

Her eyes were sparkling and I could see she was excited. 'Yup.'

'They looking for a janitor?'

'Nope.' It was like watching a little kid trying to keep the world's coolest thing secret.

'Well . . . ?'

She practically threw herself across the room at me. *'I got you a job teaching English,'* she squealed as we fell backwards onto the bed together.

I couldn't believe what she was saying. 'What do you mean?'

'I mean,' she said in between kisses, 'I talked to the head of the English Department and he's agreed to hire you. He has to interview you first, but I don't think that's going to be a problem.'

'Juliette, what the hell are you talking about?' I said. 'I'm not even a *teacher* for God's sake.'

She giggled as her hands fumbled with my belt. 'You've taught me a few things,' she said.

'I'm serious, Juliette,' I said, grabbing at her hands. 'I can't teach English.'

'How do you know if you haven't tried?' she asked, and went back to working at my belt again. I tried to stop her, but not *that* hard.

'This is crazy,' I muttered as she unzipped me. 'I can't do it.'

'Oh, you can do it all right,' she said, and kissed her way down my stomach. 'You can do all kinds of things if you just set your mind to it.'

Then she took me in her mouth and I stopped caring what I could and couldn't do.

13

Bedford College was a large co-ed school with about four hundred kids. It sprawled over a large area with several grass quadrangles giving it some form of structure. The central feature of the school was a large stone building called the Hall of Memories, a memorial to the young men from the school who had died in the various wars America had fought. All the buildings were stone, but the Hall of Memories was made of a particularly hard looking stone.

Being new to the place I got lost almost straight away. After five minutes of bumbling around corridors that all looked the same I finally realized if I didn't ask someone for directions I was never getting out.

'Excuse me,' I said to a group of girls standing by some lockers. They looked about seventeen and were all very pretty. That wasn't why I'd asked them, but a man can't help noticing these things.

They turned to look at me. 'Yeah?' said a tall blonde girl.

'I'm looking for Mr Mack's office.'

The girl smiled. 'You're really lost, aren't you?'

'Yes, I guess you could say that.'

'You go down this corridor, turn left, go all the way down to the end, and then through the glass double doors. His office is the third or fourth on the left.'

'Thanks, Carol,' I said.

'How'd you know my name?' she asked, looking puzzled.

I pointed over her shoulder and smiled. 'It's on your locker door.'

'Oh,' she said, and giggled. 'So it is.'

Eight months after that conversation I drove deep into the woods and dumped her body out the back of my station wagon like the dirty secret she'd become. Just like that. The first time I saw her, though, standing in the hallway with her friends, she looked more alive than anyone I'd ever seen.

'C'mon, Carol,' said one of her friends that day, 'we should get going.'

'Okay,' she said, and then she turned and walked away.

Her directions were good. I found a typically bland wooden door with *Mr M. Mack* stenciled on the door. The *M* stood for Mervyn—Pervin' Mervyn the kids used to call him. Of course I knew none of this as I knocked on his door that day.

'Come,' a voice called.

I opened the door and went in.

Mr Mack looked up at me from behind a stack of papers. He was overweight, balding, and his complexion suggested high blood pressure and not enough fresh air. I never liked Mr Mack. Right from the start there was something about him that I just didn't take to. Maybe it was his piggy little eyes that seemed to look at everything as if it were a trough.

'Yes?'

'I'm Simon Chance,' I said as I walked over to his

desk and extended a hand. He reached up and shook my hand with a grip that was warm and wet.

'Ah, Mr Chance,' he said. 'I've been expecting you.'

We exchanged the usual social pleasantries for the minimum amount of time and then got down to it. I suspect he knew right from the start I was bluffing.

'So where have you taught, Simon?' he asked.

'Mostly in the mid-west.'

He smiled and rolls of flesh peeled back to reveal bone underneath. 'I see.'

'Yeah, mostly smaller schools—semi-rural places mostly.' It felt like the only word I knew was mostly.

'And I assume you have taught this level before?'

'Oh, yes. I taught high-school English for three years before we began travelling.'

'We?' asked Mr Mack, his piggy little eyes sparkling in a way that made me feel distinctly uneasy. 'Oh yes, of course, you and your delightful wife. How is Mrs Chance?'

'She's just fine,' I said. There was something about the man's tone that made me feel angry, and I hadn't the faintest idea why.

'You're a very lucky man, Mr Chance, having such a beautiful woman to come home to each night. A very lucky man indeed.'

'Yes,' I said, 'I am.'

'She was extremely persuasive when she came to see me yesterday.' He smiled again. 'Ordinarily I don't hire teachers without extensive references, but in this case your wife convinced me to make an exception. She was *very* persuasive, very persuasive indeed.'

I didn't say anything.

'Mrs Chance managed to convince me that you would make a fine member of the staff, Simon, very fine indeed. So much so that I'm prepared to waive the usual red tape and let you start next week.'

I couldn't believe he was hiring me. He'd only asked me a couple of questions that I hadn't even really been able to answer. 'Well, I . . . thank you.'

'Of course,' he continued, 'this is highly irregular and quite at odds with school policy, so I'm really taking a bit of a chance with you, Simon.' He chuckled. 'No pun intended, of course.'

I smiled politely. 'Of course.'

'It might be best if you didn't share too much of this with the other staff members. That kind of thing can only produce ill-feelings. I'm sure you understand, Mr Chance.'

'Of course,' I said again, equally polite.

He stood up and went to a filing cabinet. He took a small silver key from a hook behind the cabinet, unlocked the top drawer and pulled out a thick brown folder.

'This is the senior school syllabus,' he said, sliding the folder over the desk at me. 'You'll find everything you need in there. It's quite funny—' he chuckled as he sat down again '—it's all just paint by numbers stuff really. Anyone could walk in off the street and teach this stuff.'

'You think so?' I said.

The piggy eyes sparkled at me again. 'Oh, yes,' he said. 'You could be a total fake and no one would ever know.'

I had no idea what Juliette had said to this man, but it must have been good because he obviously knew I was no teacher. 'You're very kind to give me this job,' I said.

'Oh please, Mr Chance, you don't have me to thank—it was your lovely wife who did all the hard work of persuading me.'

There was something in the way he said it that made me feel even more uncomfortable. I could see he was about as impressed by me as he would be by a bug. I felt like I wanted to be away from Mr Mack. Partly because I didn't like him, but mostly because I couldn't stop myself from wondering what Juliette could have done to get him to hire me.

She's a beautiful woman.

Mr Mack said it himself.

14

Juliette was out when I got back to the motel. I sat and watched television—Jerry Springer talking with transsexual hookers who were dating their own mothers. It filled in the time.

It was after ten that night when she got back. She jumped when she saw me sitting in the darkened room. 'Jesus,' she said, 'you scared me, Simon.'

'Did I?'

Juliette could always see right through me. 'Are you jealous, Simon?' she asked quietly as she dropped her handbag on the floor and knelt in front of me. She rested her arms on my knees and I could feel her breasts against my shins.

'Why do you ask?'

'Because you look like a man who suddenly doubts whether his wife has really been working late.'

'I can't help the way I look.'

'Did you get the job?'

It was an innocent question. Sincere. I felt the hook in it as soon as it was out of her mouth. 'Yes, I got the job.'

'Do you think that I slept with dirty old Mr Mack to get it for you?'

My mouth felt suddenly dry. 'I didn't say that.'

She smiled. 'Men don't need to say these things, Simon. Women see things in men before they even think it most of the time.'

'How did you persuade him to give me the job, Juliette?'

'You really want to know?'

I didn't want to say it. I didn't want to know. 'Yes.'

'Sex.'

And there it was. One little word.

It was a long time before I could speak. 'Just like that?'

'Just like that.'

'You slept with him to get me the job?'

'No.'

'Don't play with me, Juliette,' I said, trying to control myself. I wanted to be impenetrable. I wanted her to break herself against me. Unfortunately I'm too soft for that. She makes me cry like a little kid.

'Oh, baby,' she said as she jumped to her feet and hugged me. 'Don't cry, of course I didn't sleep with him. I teased him a little, I even flashed a bit of thigh, but I didn't sleep with him.'

She smelt so goddamned good. Even when I was being ripped apart at the thought she'd betrayed me, she still smelled like heaven.

'I went into his office and talked to him. I teased him a bit and I did unbutton my blouse a little, but I didn't sleep with him. He's a revolting old lech. All it took was a few giggles and a bit of skin and he was sold. I swear I didn't sleep with him, okay?'

It hurt. Just the thought of it hurt.

'Come on, baby, you don't really believe I'd do

41

something like that, do you?'

I said that I didn't, of course. What else could I say?
I could see that a part of her was enjoying the scene
though. It was as if it pleased her to know how much
even the idea of her betrayal hurt me. I thought I knew
her back then, and so I thought I understood what
her pleasure was about.

I have been wrong about so many things since I
met Juliette.

15

As I was writing this I remembered a conversation I
once had with Juliette about death. We were sitting at
a Greyhound terminal in Philadelphia. I can't remember where we'd just come from, or where we were
going. She was leaning her head against my shoulder.
It was late at night, and we were both cold and tired.

'Do you ever think about death?' she asked me out
of the blue.

'Only when I'm waiting for buses.'

'No,' she said as she swatted me lightly on the leg
with a mittened hand. 'I'm serious. Do you ever think
about it?'

'I try not to.'

'Why?'

'Because I don't like to think about death.'

'Why?'

'Just because.'

She laughed. 'Just because is not an answer, Simon.'

I could see she wasn't going to let this one go. 'Well,
I guess I don't like to think about it because it scares
me.'

'What scares you about it?'

I paused for a moment. 'I don't like the thought of being dead.'

She sat up and looked at me. Her eyes had lost any sign of fatigue. 'Why? What do you think happens when you die?'

'I don't know, I guess we just blink out.'

'You mean like a broken bulb?'

'Yeah, something like that.'

'That's very bleak, Simon.'

'I suppose it is.'

'You don't believe in an afterlife, then?'

'My little brother died of cancer. That pretty much cured me of any belief in a benevolent God.'

'Oh, Simon,' she said, taking my hand. 'I didn't know. I'm so sorry.'

Except, looking back now I'm not so sure she was sorry. I think maybe it kind of excited her.

'It's okay, Jules, you didn't kill him.'

'How old was he?'

'He was ten, I was thirteen. He'd been sick a long time. It wasn't a bad thing that he died. It was sad, but it wasn't bad.'

'Did he suffer much?'

I felt the old memories stirring. The pictures, the smells, the little noises.

'Yeah, Jules, he suffered.'

'I guess you don't like to talk about it, huh?'

I shook my head. 'No, not a lot.'

'I know how it feels—I lost my father when I was the same age.'

'He died of cancer?'

'I was only a teenager.'

I put my arm around her. 'Oh, Jules, I'm so sorry.'

It felt like we were playing with the sympathy

boomerang; I got a whack and then she got a whack.

'He suffered when he died, he suffered terribly. At the end he was screaming. I remember lying in my bed and pulling the pillow down over my head so I couldn't hear him. He just kept screaming and screaming.' A smile flitted across her face. 'I even remember the pillow. It was red, with these large white polka dots. I used to call it my ladybug.'

'Oh, my God,' I said to her. 'That must have been a nightmare. Couldn't they give him anything for the pain?'

It felt stupid to say that—like it wouldn't have occurred to anyone at the time to try pain medication—but I'm a man, and men need to fix things.

'There was nothing anyone could do for him. When he died I cried, but not because I was sad. I cried because I was happy. I was happy that he'd finally stopped screaming.'

'You were just a kid, Juliette. It's not bad that you were happy he wasn't suffering anymore. No one wants the people they love to suffer.'

'No,' she said, looking up at me with tears in her eyes, 'that's not it. I didn't care about him—I was happy for me. I was happy that I didn't have to listen to him screaming anymore. I was happy it was finally quiet.'

'It's okay Jules,' was all I could say. 'You were just a kid.'

'I believe in an afterlife,' she said, her voice breaking apart under the weight of the tears, 'and I believe we're all judged for what we've done. All of us. My father, me, you, all of us.'

She cried then, and I held her. I didn't know what else to do. A little while later we got on the bus and left Philadelphia. She never spoke to me of her father again.

44

16

And so we made Bedford our home. We set down our bags, planted our roots, and let the rest of the world go on without us. Bedford was the end of the line for Juliette and me, the very last stop on the end-of-the-world express service to hell. I didn't know that then, of course, and even if I had I don't know what difference it would have made.

In the beginning it was like we'd found heaven. I started my job, she found us a house to rent, and we set about building a life for ourselves in suburbia. The house was on the outside of town in a quiet little street, single-storied with solid red-brick walls, and tiles on the roof. It had a view of the hills out the back, and a garden with roses and a lemon tree. The only thing I didn't like was the clay floor in the cellar. I thought it would make the house feel damp.

'I don't know about this dirt floor thing,' I said to her as we stood in the cellar with the Realtor.

His name was Chuck. Who the hell is called *Chuck*?

'Most places around here have a clay floor in the cellar,' chipped in helpful old Chuck. Chuck was the kind of guy who did that—he didn't talk like a normal person, he *chipped*.

'I don't think it's bad at all,' said Juliette. 'It gives the place a homely feel.'

I raised my eyebrows. 'Dirt is *homely*?'

'Oh, come on,' she said. 'All we'd use it for is storing stuff anyway, and the house is lovely.'

'It sure is, little lady,' said Chuck cheerily from behind us. 'This is one of the nicest little places I got on my books at the moment.'

All I could think of was that Chuck rhymed with fuck.

45

'Please, baby,' said Juliette, 'I *really* like the place.'

I could never say no to Juliette. Not about houses, not about dirt floors, not about anything as it later turned out.

'Okay, then. If you like it, we'll take it.' I turned to Chuck, whose eyes were gleaming with the thrill of the kill. 'Sign us up.'

'Yes, indeedy,' he said, rubbing his hands together in the murky gloom of the cellar. 'I can just tell you two are gonna be *real* happy here.'

I saw an article in *People* magazine where they interviewed a whole bunch of locals from Bedford. Good old Chuck recounted his own version of that conversation in the cellar; he said we spent an hour down there poking around. He even said I brought my own shovel with me and dug several small holes in the clay floor. He said I told him I wanted to see if the ground was soft.

'I didn't think much of it at the time, other than the fact that it was a bit odd,' lamented Chuck in the article, 'but when I heard about all those poor little girls they found buried down there—well, it just made me feel sick to my soul.'

The truth is we were down in that cellar for less than ten minutes and I didn't poke at anything, but then, what does the truth have to do with a good story?

Right, Chuck?

He wasn't a part of it, at least not the bad stuff, but he felt the need to make himself part of it after the fact. Worst of all, he felt the need to push his way down into the cellar, which is pretty much the dark heart of the whole damned deal.

Think I'm sick? Take a good look around, then tell me who *isn't*?

Someone torched the house three weeks after the

police removed the last of the bodies. I watched it on television in jail. It was strange to see our little house going up in flames on the evening news. Although I guess that would be a pretty strange experience for anyone.

A crowd of locals stood around with the firemen and watched it burn, their faces bathed in the flickering orange pulse of the fire. It looked almost pagan, which I guess isn't that far from the truth.

Before all that, though, before I actually did start poking around in the cellar, things were good. Juliette made the house a real home. She loved it. We painted the walls of the living room a soft green, and the bedroom a delicate blue. We bought pictures to hang, and cheap furniture from yard sales. Within a month it looked like we'd been there forever.

I had an office off the short hallway. Juliette made me set it up so I could write. She was still determined that I would become a best-selling writer. I guess she's going to get her wish. From what the publisher is saying, this book is going to sell a huge number of copies. Only problem is I'll be dead by then.

I did start a new novel in Bedford, a fanciful little piece about a demon who falls in love with a mortal woman. The demon is sent to destroy her, but he falls for her and can't bring himself to tear her down.

For the first time in my life it was easy to write. Usually it's a struggle for me—settling down into the story can sometimes take me an hour or more, and then I'm easily distracted away. Yet in our home on the outskirts of Bedford I found that the words would come flying out, almost as if there were something tearing them from me.

The irony of the story is, of course, not lost on me. A demon and a mortal woman. Love in dark places.

47

But I don't think there was any conscious thought behind my choice of story. It just seemed to choose me. I had written four chapters by the time I found the watch in the back of the station wagon. I never got any further. Events seemed to take over at that point. The only copy of the novel went up with the house, which is a shame because I think it was actually pretty good.

Who knows, maybe we could have had it all?

17

I thought teaching was going to be a nightmare, but actually it wasn't that hard to do. Old Pervin' Mervyn was right, any fool could do it once you had the instruction book. I put in a few late nights to make sure I had a good head start on the kids and then I was fine. I managed to stay about three weeks ahead of them right up until the very end. In the last few weeks I was flying by the seat of my pants, but by that stage I didn't really care.

Many of my students saw English as an inescapable part of the whole school dirge, but a few were different. Theresa Wright was one of them. She was a senior and had her sights set on bigger things than Bedford. Theresa wanted to be a writer. She approached me one day after class, soon after I started.

'Excuse me, Mr Chance?'

'Yes, Theresa?' I said as I looked up from the papers on my desk. She was an attractive girl—long blond hair, striking blue eyes, and a figure that took a great deal of effort to ignore. It's one of the things I think all high school teachers struggle with, at least all the men anyway—the thoughts that come unprovoked when you're surrounded by such youthful beauty all day. Try as I might to keep myself focused, there was always a background level of self-conscious guilt. Bodies are bodies. It was impossible not to notice them.

'I heard that you're writing a novel.'

'Well, yes I am.'

She flashed me a shy smile. 'I've written a couple of little things myself.'

'That's great, Theresa. What do you like to write?'

'Fiction—mostly just short stories so far. They're not that good though.'

'Don't be so sure. Have you let anyone look at them?'

She squeezed out another shy smile. 'Well, that's kind of why I wanted to speak to you.'

I put down my pen and sat back in the chair. 'Fire away.'

'Well, I was just wondering if you would mind reading one for me?' She looked down as she asked me, and I could tell she was painfully anxious. I knew what she was feeling. Showing someone your work for the first time is about as naked as you can get. It's something people who don't write will never understand.

'I'd be honored, Theresa.'

She looked up then, and her eyes were still anxious, but there was a bloom of light in there as well.

'I have this one that I wrote last year,' she said, fishing a bundle of pages from her backpack. 'A kind of love story. It's a little rough, but see what you think anyway.'

I took the paper from her. 'I'll read it tonight and talk with you about it after class tomorrow if you like?'

She smiled again, and this time the smile was more relaxed. 'That'd be great, Mr Chance. Thanks.'

I wanted to read it quickly for her. For writers, waiting is almost as bad as the rejection itself. Rejection is the death, but waiting is the thousand imagined deaths.

Waiting is when the demons come.

'You're welcome, Theresa,' I said.

She smiled at me once more and turned to walk away. There was a skip in her step that I recognized. It was the same skip I'd brought with me to New York when I'd first met Juliette. My big trip to the city where I would sell my novel and become rich and famous.

I'm on my way, the skip said, *I'm on my way.*

18

I did read it that night, and I was genuinely stunned at the depth and maturity of her writing. The story was called *Shrapnel Tears* and it was about a wounded soldier in Vietnam, dying alone in the jungle surrounded by the bodies of his friends and enemies. He knows he's dying, and the story recounts his love for his high school sweetheart back home. The soldier tells it all to a small monkey who sits with him and listens carefully to his tale.

The end was so moving I cried.

'What's wrong?' asked Juliette, coming in with some coffee for me.

I passed her the story. 'Read this,' I said.

I watched her as she read, and when she finished she turned to me with tears in her eyes. 'This is such a beautiful piece,' she said. '*So* sad, but so beautiful.'

'This girl writes better than most people twice her age.'

'How old is she?'

'Seventeen.'

Juliette shook her head. 'It's hard to believe a seventeen-year-old girl could write something . . . well, something like *that*.'

'I know.'

'I can just imagine that poor boy, lying in the jungle, dying all alone. It's so sad.'

'I wish I had half her talent,' I said with just a touch of bitterness. That's what it's like when you're a writer—you read everything with either scathing contempt or an almost palpable envy.

'Don't say that,' said Juliette as she came over to me. 'You're a very good writer.'

'I'm a very unpublished writer.'

'When you finish your next novel they'll be falling all over themselves to publish you.'

I smiled, putting Theresa's story on my desk. 'We'll see.'

She took my head in her hands and held me to her chest. 'We *will* see,' she said. 'You're good, Simon, and one day the world will see that.' It was some comfort to me in my frequent moments of despair that even if I had nothing else, I had her. 'You are a great writer, and one day the world *will* see that.'

'I hope so,' I said, but the words felt a little empty. I knew that Theresa was already a better writer at age seventeen than I would be at seventy.

'Come to bed,' she said and kissed me on the forehead. 'Let me love you.'

And as always she made the darkness seem not so bad.

19

I could see that Theresa was nervous when she walked into class the next day. I could have waited till the end of class to talk to her, but that would have been cruel. Like I said, for writers waiting is the thousand imagined deaths.

'It was very good,' I whispered to her as she walked past. She flashed me a smile that was one part pleasure and nine parts relief. I knew the feeling well. After the class was over she took her time getting her books together, waiting until everyone else had gone.

'So you liked it?' she asked, clutching her books to her chest.

'You have a real talent, Theresa.'

'Really?'

'Really.'

'Oh wow,' she said, and breathed a huge sigh of relief. 'I was so worried that you were gonna say it wasn't very good.'

I smiled at her. 'This is one of the best short stories I've ever read.'

Her face flushed red. 'Really? You really mean that?'

'Absolutely. There are a few grammatical errors that I marked, but I think that once you correct those you should send it out to some magazines.'

'So it was believable, the monkey and the soldier?'

'It was very moving, Theresa. You're very talented.'

'I didn't know if it worked or not. Him talking to a monkey as he died. I thought it was maybe a bit dumb.'

'In the hands of a less talented writer it might have been, but what you did was *very* good. My wife read it as well, and we both cried.'

She let out a whoop of joy then, a fresh clear sound in the staid confines of my classroom. 'Thank you, thank you, thank you,' she gushed.

I smiled again. 'Why don't you rework the grammatical stuff I've outlined and then come back and see me. I can give you some addresses of places to send it.'

'That would be fantastic,' she said. She turned to go, and then suddenly spun round and gave me a small kiss on the cheek. She had tears in her eyes. 'Thank you, Mr Chance, I'll never forget this.'

'You're very welcome,' I spluttered. I was a little taken aback by the kiss, but I knew what an intensely emotional moment it can be when someone says you have talent. 'Now you'd better get going or you'll be late for your bus.'

She smiled once more, and was gone.

20

Shrapnel Tears was published in *Time* magazine six months after she died. I have the copy in my cell. It was part of a piece called 'Death of the Maiden' which recounted the tragedy of such a blazing young talent dying in such a terrible way.

It is inconceivable, the article said, *to think that a writer as young as Theresa Wright could have produced a work of such striking emotional resonance. Yet it is so much more inconceivable that she should have died in the way that she did. We are left to wonder what might have been possible if Simon Chance had not made Bedford his killing ground.*

But perhaps the last word in this terrible tragedy should come from her father, David Wright. His eyes are sunken now, and his body looks somehow thinner than that of normal people. Not skinnier, but thinner, as if a layer of reality has been peeled away from him. He stares out through his kitchen window as he speaks, at the garden where Theresa learnt to walk, and run, and ride her first bike. His voice sounds as empty as the eyes which roam restlessly over the small suburban back yard.

'All she ever wanted to do was write stories, ever since she was a little girl . . . and the thing which I just can't seem to get past is . . . is that she had so much left to say.'

And that is perhaps the most horrific thing of all, the fact that all the young women who fell victim to Simon Chance's evil hands had so much left to say.

21

'Did you get the milk?' Juliette called out to me from the kitchen.

I stopped in the open front door. 'Oops!'

'Oh, *Simon*.'

'I'm sorry,' I said as I put down my briefcase and took off my coat. 'I just clean forgot about it.'

She came out of the kitchen, her hands covered in flour. 'I told you *three times* before you left this morning.'

'I know, I'm sorry,' I said, and kissed her powdery cheek. 'I'll go get some now.'

She put her arms around me and kissed me back. 'I missed you today,' she said.

'What have you been doing?'

She smiled, and kissed me again. 'Go get the milk.'

'Your wish is my command.' I pulled myself away from her.

That's what it was like. Going to work, coming home, buying milk. Just like normal people.

22

Milly Brown was a good girl, all sweet Miss America and apple pie. She was an honors student at school, she did volunteer work at the ASPCA, and she was, from all accounts, a gifted cello player. She was so pretty and so full of promise it was almost inevitable that someone would kill her.

Killing girls like Milly has become an American tradition.

When she failed to return home from her after-school cello practice her parents weren't that concerned at first. She was a popular girl and would often stop off at a friend's place on the way home. But when there was still no sign of her by eight o'clock that night they began to get worried. At ten o'clock, with still no word, they called the police.

I imagine that must have been an awful call for her parents to make. Calling the police was the first step down a long, dark road. It means you have to let that terrible thought in the door: *something's wrong*. There's no going back from there. You call the police and you have to entertain the idea that someone's got her. And if there's a chance someone's got her then there's a chance she's already dead.

It was all over the news the next day. People don't go missing in Bedford. Bad things don't happen here. Except, of course, that they do. Bad things happen everywhere.

A strange air settled over the town. People wore

hope and concern like a mask, but deep down everyone knew she was dead. It's always the first thought that comes into your mind when you hear about some missing kid: she's dead.

They organized search parties and canvassed people on the streets. Nobody had seen anything. The last time Milly had been seen alive was when she left music practice. This was pretty odd in a smallish town. The place is big enough so that you don't know everyone you see, but you know most. It stood to reason that someone would have noticed her walking home. She was a pretty girl.

No one came forward though, at least not with anything useful. Milly had apparently walked out the door of her music teacher's house and disappeared into thin air.

I followed the case like everyone else. Milly was a senior at Bedford College, and while she wasn't in any of my classes I remembered seeing her about the school. In the days following her disappearance Milly became quite a celebrity at school. Everyone had their theories. I preferred not to listen to the gossip. I just hoped that she would turn up alive, but as the days wore on it became increasingly unlikely.

People in town wanted an answer about what had happened to Milly Brown. When they didn't get one from the police they began to generate their own, and by the end of the second week the nastier theories started to surface.

She was into drugs, and was killed when a deal went bad.

She had a secret life as a prostitute and one of her clients killed her.

She was being sexually abused by her father and he'd killed her when she threatened to tell.

I've always hated the human race's tendency to cannibalize itself. Three weeks ago the Brown family had been liked and respected. Now their daughter was gone and the town was tearing the remaining family members apart in some kind of bizarre feeding frenzy.

I remember seeing Milly's dad in the grocery store the day before I found her watch in the back of our station wagon. If a scream could take on human form it would have looked like Patrick Brown did that day. He was standing in front of the milk, staring at it. He stood there for ages. I tried to imagine what horrors were filling his mind as he stared at the rows of white milk cartons. Knowing she was out there somewhere. He was buying milk and his baby was out there somewhere, lying in a ditch, or maybe buried in a shallow grave, dirt in her eyes, dirt in her mouth. I couldn't even begin to understand that kind of horror.

Eventually he shook his head, as if he were shaking himself awake, or pulling himself away from something. He took a carton of low-fat milk and shuffled up to the cashier. He walked like an old man.

The next time I saw him was over a year later at my trial. He sat in the public seats and stared at me throughout the whole trial.

I still couldn't begin to understand what it must have been like inside that poor father's heart. I felt like saying something to him, telling him some lie—like she didn't suffer, or she never knew. I didn't, of course; they would never have let me. And he would never have believed me.

But I wanted to.

23

Like I said, the last really happy memory I have is of a sunny Sunday morning in March. We made love, and then we had breakfast together. Later that day I took a box of soda cans out to the car. I was going to take them to the recycling yard. An ecological good deed. No big deal at all.

But I then found the watch, and the whole world changed.

We'd bought the station wagon when I got my first pay check. I'd never liked station wagons much, but Juliette made a big deal out of how practical they were. Of course, her definition of 'practical' didn't fully reveal itself until much later.

Juliette liked to recycle. She said it made her feel good to know that other people would be drinking from our old cans, even if someone did melt them down and make them new again. So I took this box of cans out to the garage and opened up the back of the car. For some reason it always smelt of dog—old wet dog. It was a hot day and when I opened the trunk the smell hit me like a warm moldy hammer.

It's funny the things you remember.

As I lifted the box into the back I caught my hand on the latch and scraped the skin from my knuckles. I dropped the box and the cans went everywhere, making a huge din in the small space of the garage.

'Fuck, fuck, fuck, fuck, *fuck*.'

I remember that it *really* hurt, but after a few moments the pain started to lose its edge.

With my knuckles still stinging, I scooped up the cans from the ground and out of the back of the car. There was one last can wedged in the tire well. Why

58

is it always the last one that's the problem? Doesn't matter what it is—last bolt, last screw, last box, last door, last laugh—you can always guarantee the last one is going to be the problem.

The can was slippery with old soda, and it was hard to get a grip. I grabbed it and gave it a yank. There was a brief moment of resistance, and then the can shot out of the gap, my knuckles grazing the lip of the trunk again in exactly the same place on the way past.

As I stood there, sucking my knuckles and cursing through the blood, I noticed a glint of gold from the tire well. I bent down and could see that it was a gold strap, like a watch, and I thought that Juliette must have dropped something in there. It was clear that I wasn't going to get it out without lifting out the whole tire, which also meant undoing the nut that held the wheel in place.

What the hey, I thought, I've got the time.

Getting the nut off was a bitch; it had taken a beating over the years and was pretty worn around the top. I'm sure there's some technical word for that, but I never bothered to learn much about cars so I can't tell you. Suffice to say it was tricky getting the damned thing undone without turning the nut into a completely spherical—and thus completely undo-able—piece of metal. After a brief period of me grunting and groaning, it finally gave.

When I lifted the tire out I got my first good look at the little object that was to completely change my life. It was a woman's watch. The gold strap had been broken at the side of the watch, and as I picked it up I could see that the metal was all twisted, like it had been wrenched.

It felt cold in my fingers. Dead metal. I didn't recognize it, which struck me as odd, because I couldn't imagine Juliette having a watch that I didn't know about. In fact she had very little jewelry, and her own watch was a tired old Casio with a black leather strap. This one was very nice, or at least it had been. It was Swiss and looked expensive. The strap and casing were gold but the face of the watch was jet black.

I turned it over and saw there was an inscription on the back in small flowery engraver's writing:

To M.B.
Sweet sixteen
Love M & D

And suddenly, just like that, the world tilted.

24

I know that this is all out of order. Milly Brown was actually number four in the line, but she was the first girl from Bedford. The rest of them had been runaways who'd disappeared from truck stops and roadsides around Bedford—all the usual places girls like that go missing from. In the broader scheme of things they don't count for much—let's face it, if all of America's dead runaways stood up at once there'd be no room left for the rest of us.

America, land of the free, and home of the unmarked grave. A little patch of dirt to call your own. A home for the homeless.

In the months before Goodlow arrested us I used to feel them all calling out to me, all the dead kids. Not just the ones Juliette had killed, but all of them. It was like a constant muted cough, the dull sound of clay in open mouths. I sensed them all around me, bodies buried and long forgotten in secret places. I tried not to listen to the things they whispered, the sadness and the fear, but it got harder and harder as time went on.

They are so lonely out there under the dirt, so scared and so dreadfully lonely.

Milly was different. Milly was town. She wasn't some trailer-trash runaway turning up dead in a ditch, she was flesh and blood. She was one of our own. So when the killer plucked her from the quiet streets of Bedford, people woke up. We don't mind so much when the wolf feeds on strays, but when he feeds on our own, on the flock, that's very different.

Milly Brown was where it all started for me as well. I'd read about the other girls in the paper, but I have to admit I took precious little notice. The stories started about four months before Milly was sucked from the sidewalk. Except they weren't really reported as disappearances, more as last sightings. There were a couple of articles in the local paper about the girls who'd gone missing, but like I said, they were runaways. Trailer-trash passing through. A few paragraphs on page four kind of stuff. Maybe a few parents told their daughters to be careful, but most let it slip by unnoticed.

I don't know what it is about our national psyche that makes us so loth to believe that it actually *does* happen to us. You've only got to turn on the television to see a dozen tragic stories about homecoming queens found butchered in dumpsters or strangled in parks. I don't think it's ever been more dangerous to be young and pretty and full of promise.

I was the same, of course. I never believed that it happened to us—or, more accurately, I never believed that *we* were the ones who did it. I believed in monsters, I saw them on the six o'clock news almost every night. I just never believed that the monster would be me.

Who does?

25

Standing next to our old Ford station wagon, amidst the stink of old wet dog, and holding that little gold watch, *M.B.'s watch*, I felt the world turn around me.

Milly Brown had been missing for two weeks. Her face was all over the news, her name all over the radio. She was the subject of every conversation. It was almost as if the ground itself had started to ooze her name.

Milly Brown.

To M.B.

I remember the sounds around me as I stood there. A lawn mower somewhere off in the distance. A dog barking farther down the street. The brief clear spurt of a child's laughter appearing from nowhere and disappearing just as fast. Birds. Breathing.

Sweet sixteen.

And the sound of a beating heart, counting out the moments like an executioner's drum.

I don't know how long I stood there for, it could have been seconds or it could have been hours. Hell, it could have been *days*. It just seemed to go on forever. I didn't want to do what I had to do next. I didn't want to ask. I was too scared. Not of what Juliette would say—I was sure there would be some rational and logical explanation for the presence of M.B.'s watch in the back of our dirty old Ford.

Love M & D.

I was scared of whether or not I'd believe her.

It didn't occur to me until much later to wonder how come I reacted the way I did. How come, in the middle of that bright Sunday morning, I suddenly found myself fearing the most unimaginable horror. Too great a horror even to name. There were reasons, things that with the benefit of hindsight led me to feel the way that I did. In that moment, though, it was too much. I wasn't ready to acknowledge any of that. All I knew was that I was more scared than I'd ever been in my life.

I didn't want to turn around and see what was following me. I didn't want to know. I wanted to just keep doing what I'd been doing from that very first night at the bar in New York. I wanted to pretend that it all made sense. I *wanted* to pretend that, but the screaming panic inside me that had started the very first time I saw Juliette wouldn't let me.

It *was* too good to be true, and inside I'd known that from the start.

And all the while I'm just standing there, bathed in the warm stink of the car and holding M.B.'s little gold watch dangling in front of me like entrails ripped from a corpse.

Maybe you should just eat it then, I whispered to myself, in that crazy way we do sometimes when we're alone. *Maybe you should just swallow it down, get in the car, and keep moving.*

I giggled and it sounded forced, almost contrived. That's when the moment broke and I knew I had to go back inside and ask her about the watch.

Juliette was leaning over the kitchen table reading the paper. She was wearing only a T-shirt and her perfect naked bottom peeked out from under it. In the sunshine she looked like a photo from *Playboy*, the kind of photo which makes you ache to turn the next page.

'Juliette.'

She looked up from her paper and smiled. 'Hmm?'

'Did you lose a watch?'

'No,' she said, holding up her wrist for me to see, 'it's here. Why?'

I handed her the watch: 'I found this in the car.'

I felt as if the world was grinding to a halt around me, as if it were all coming into some kind of dreadful gritty focus.

She looked at it for a moment, and then passed it back. 'How odd,' she said, and turned back to the paper.

'Did you read the back?' I asked her.

'No.'

I turned it over and read out the inscription.

She looked at me in her sleepy, sexual pale blue-eyed way. 'You think it belonged to the people we bought the car off? Weren't they called Baxter or something?'

And of course they were. The man's name was Barney Baxter and he'd sold us the car for a steal because he was leaving town to take up a new job out west somewhere. Los Angeles or San Diego or something. He just wanted to get rid of the car and didn't really care how much we gave him for it. Big, sweaty Barney Baxter, computer engineer, and father of four. Two little boys and two girls. The oldest one must have been in her late teens and she'd looked almost as big and sweaty as her dear old dad.

To M.B.

What was her name? Mary? Molly? Mindy? Mandy? *M. Baxter*.

'Are you all right, baby?'

She was next to me and I hadn't even noticed. I felt sick with relief. There was a reason for M.B's watch being there. And better still, I believed it.

'I just felt a bit faint,' I mumbled.

She put her arm around me and led me over to the chair. I felt as if my legs were about to give out on me.

'Sit down, baby,' she said, cradling my head into her breast. I could feel her nipple through the thin cotton. It felt hot and hard against my face.

'I'm okay,' I said.

'You looked so pale. You scared me.'

'It's nothing, really. I'm okay now.'

She looked down at me. 'I love you, Simon. You know that, don't you?'

I nodded. 'I know.'

She bent down and kissed me, and her tongue slid gently into my mouth—warm and deliciously sweet. My hands slipped up under her T-shirt, up over her hips and stomach, cupping her soft breasts as she moaned.

Then she pulled back. 'You'd better go,' she said, her voice husky with sex.

'Uh huh,' I said.

It was only when I was driving to the recycling station that I remembered something else from the day we bought the car. I remembered Juliette making me take the spare tire out of the back of the wagon and inspect it before we bought the car. Barney huffed and puffed at that. I think he felt like we didn't trust him, which I guess was true. I also remembered putting it back in the tire well once we'd had a good look at it. Back into the empty tire well. Straight after that I'd given him a check and we'd driven off in our new car. We took a bit of dust and mud from the Baxter's place, but we didn't take any gold watches. If Mary-Molly-

Mandy had a watch it was still on her wrist when we left.

Driving through the quiet suburban streets of Bedford, amidst the sunshine and weekend ramblers, I felt very cold.

26

I knew I had to get rid of the watch. I didn't stop to question my motives at the time, I just knew I had to get rid of it. So after putting the cans in the recycling bin I drove out to the Bedford Municipal garbage dump, a sprawling wasteland outside of town. I bypassed the main track and drove down to the back corner of the dump. I didn't want to be surrounded by people; I wanted somewhere a bit quieter, out of the way.

When I got out of the car the smell hit me at once. The stink of rot and ruin. Dumps are the places where we see ourselves revealed. Dumps are where you find the truth. The truth about Bedford wasn't to be found amidst the clean well-tended streets—that was only the façade. This was where the truth could be found, here amidst the old condoms and empty boxes. All the broken and spoilt stuff that we tried to push beneath the ground and hide.

The problem is that rot floats. You can push it as far down into the ground as you like, but rot floats.

So I stood on top of a garbage hill, holding M.B.'s golden sweet sixteen watch, and felt the rot seeping up from the ground. I felt it leak through the soles of my boots and into my feet, into my blood. I felt it flow through me, filling me with dark thoughts. Filling my heart.

Love M & D.

I knew it couldn't be Milly's watch. I knew that. But I also knew that I had to get rid of it.

I held the watch up and looked at it one last time. I thought of the day that M.B. must have opened the box and seen it for the first time. How shiny and new it must have looked then.

Sweet sixteen.

Taking a deep breath, I threw it as far out into the garbage as I could. There was no sound when it hit, and I imagined the garbage opening up to receive it, swallowing the little gold offering in one gulp, sucking the watch down into its putrid heart.

'I'm sorry,' I whispered, not really knowing why, or at least pretending I didn't.

'Help you?'

I only just stifled a scream.

'Mister?'

I turned and saw an old man wearing a pair of filthy gray overalls. I assumed he was old, anyway— he was covered in dirt and wrinkles and could have been any age. There was a faded orange patch on the left breast of his overalls that said Bedford Municipal Council. He was chewing something and staring at me.

'I, uh,' I stammered, 'I was just getting rid of some junk.'

The man's eyes were milky gray as they stared at me. 'Shouldn't be dumping here. Not allowed here.'

He had a thick New England accent.

'I'm sorry,' I said. 'I didn't realize.'

'Dangerous wandering around outside the designated areas. All kinds of dangerous things in here.'

He studied me with those milky eyes, chewing like an old buffalo with a piece of cud.

'My apologies,' I said, trying to sound relaxed, 'It won't happen again.'

He nodded. 'Uh yuh.'

I turned and got into the station wagon. I had trouble starting the car because my hands were shaking so much I could hardly get hold of the keys.

As I drove away I looked in my rear-view mirror. He was still standing there, chewing, and watching me.

27

The sex changed after that.

'Hurt me,' she said.

'What?'

It was night. I'd come back from the dump, showered, and spent the rest of the day trying to forget the little gold watch with the jet-black face. Trying to pretend that it wasn't important. I'd been quiet and moody, but if she noticed she said nothing about it. That night she came to me when I was brushing my teeth. I could see her in the mirror, wearing only a white cotton bra and briefs. She looked like a goddess.

'Hurt me.'

I rinsed the toothpaste from my mouth and turned to face her, water still dripping from my face, cold droplets spilling down onto my chest.

She pressed up against me, kissing me urgently, desperately. Her nipples were like two small pebbles against my chest.

'Hurt me,' she said again.

'Juliette, I don't really . . .'

She raised her head and looked at me, the warmth of her skin on mine. I could feel her pale blue eyes deep inside me, way down in the savage parts of a man's soul where civilization has yet to penetrate. I felt myself harden, felt the warm, dull ache as everything but the need to fuck her faded back into the darkness.

Without warning she raked her fingernails across my chest, opening up four long, ragged scratches.

'*Jesus*,' I yelled, pushing her backward into the doorway, slamming her into the wooden frame.

I put my hand down to my chest. My fingers came away bloody.

Juliette moaned, and I looked up.

She was smiling. 'Hurt me,' she whispered.

And all of a sudden I *did* want to hurt her. I was furious at her, but I couldn't bring myself to say why. I lunged forward and grabbed her face with my right hand, squeezing her mouth between my thumb and forefinger. 'You want to be hurt, Juliette? You want me to hurt you?'

She looked at me, her face deformed as I squeezed her. She nodded. It was a very small movement, but she nodded. Her eyes said far more, there was no need for words.

And then the anger, and the lust, and the need to fuck her took me. I slapped her hard in the face and she gasped. She stumbled back out the door and I followed her into the bedroom. I put a hand out and snagged the front of her bra. With one vicious tug I ripped it from her and then pushed her back onto the bed.

I flew at her, pinning her arms over her head with one hand and mauling her breasts with the other. I sank my teeth into the soft creamy flesh just below the nipple. She screamed and I slapped her again.

It was like watching myself from a long way off. I

was there, but I wasn't there. Some other creature had control of my body.

When I could stand it no more I flipped her onto her stomach, tore her underwear to one side, and thrust myself deep into her, grabbing her hair and twisting it, dragging her face up off the bed. I shoved myself into her as hard as I could and she screamed again.

I wanted to hurt her, and hurt her, and hurt her.

When I came it felt like the end of the world. I cried out—not in pleasure, but in fear. It was so intense and angry it was like dying. It didn't feel like coming, it felt like she was sucking me out of myself.

It felt like she was eating me.

When it was over I rolled off her onto the carpet, panting. 'Oh, Christ.'

I felt sick to my stomach, the savagery of what I had just done appalled me. The sex had gone, and now there was only me. All I could do was lie there and moan. 'Oh God, oh God . . . '

'Sssshhh,' she whispered as she came to me.

I didn't dare look at her. 'Oh, Juliette, I'm so sorry. I don't know what happened. I didn't mean to . . . '

I couldn't even finish the words. Thick, hot tears squeezed out from underneath my eyes.

'It's all right, baby,' she said. 'I wanted it, I wanted you to do that to me. I *needed* it.'

I slowly raised myself from the floor and looked at her. She was naked and her skin was covered in angry red welts, scratches, bite marks.

'Oh, my God, look at what I did to you.'

She took my face in her hands, gently. 'I asked you to do that to me.'

'But, why . . . ?'

She smiled. 'It makes me feel safe.'

I didn't understand what she was saying. I do now—now it all makes perfect sense—but back then I was lost. 'Juliette, I . . .'

'Sssshhhh now,' she said and kissed me lightly on the lips. 'Enough talking.'

She led me into the bathroom and we showered together. No talking. Just heated soapy skin. We made love again, this time slowly and with great tenderness.

Later I lay in the dark and listened to her breathe as she slept.

There was a moment, lying there beside her, when I stumbled half-awake, half-asleep into a dream. I dreamed that it wasn't Juliette lying beside me, but some other thing entirely. Something with scales, and teeth like rows of needles sunk back into its ancient face. I woke from the half-dream in that terrifying way that we all lurch back into reality from the land of nightmares.

And when I reached out to touch the soft warm skin of her face, to reassure myself in the darkness that she was still the Juliette that I loved, I was only a little afraid.

28

In fifty-six days they will come for me. The warden will lead the way. Behind him will be the priest, and behind him five guards. They will stop at the door to my cell and the warden will inform me that it is time to move through to the execution suite. They will be professional and smooth, but they will be tense. The only people in the Garden who are easy with killing are the ones behind bars. I will be allowed to take only one book with me, nothing else.

Obviously the priest prefers it when the condemned man takes a Bible. I don't have a Bible, and even if I did I wouldn't take it with me. It would be somewhat hypocritical to turn to God at this late stage in the game.

The warden is a good man from what I can tell. He's married, or at least he was at some point because he has a wedding ring. His name is Dr Howard Merton, and I believe he has a PhD in criminology from Yale or Harvard or some such similar place. I've only ever had one conversation with him, when he came down to the admissions wing to see me the day I arrived.

'Hello, Mr Chance,' he said, extending a large hand. I took it and he shook my hand very slowly as he talked. 'I shake your hand to show you that I see you as a human being no matter what your crimes have been. Accordingly you will be treated with respect and dignity here.' He was a large man with the soft brown eyes of a bear. He wore a gray suit that was a few years out of date and a plain black tie. His shirt was neatly pressed and he reeked quiet authority.

'We are not here to judge you, Mr Chance—the court has already done that. Our job is to carry out the sentence that has been imposed as humanely as possible. If you treat my people with the same respect then we'll have no trouble. If you do not, then we *will* break you. I do not tolerate any form of trouble here, Mr Chance. Clear?'

I nodded. 'Yes, sir.'

He let go my hand, and after the warmth of his grip it felt suddenly cold.

'Good.' He turned and was gone.

I've seen two men go to the execution suite in the time I've been here. Both times the warden has led his small party down the block to the condemned man's cell. A hush falls over the Garden in the hours before they come. Everyone can feel it. Even the mad ones like my neighbor, Terry Beck, who spends most of his time shrieking and crying.

When the big door at the end of the block crashes open you can smell the fear thick in the air. Usually there are a few moments of silence before someone starts yelling.

And this is the thing I find the most disgusting about the whole execution process, when the other inmates start yelling messages of support to the condemned man like he's some kind of martyr.

'Be strong, brother.'

'Go hard.'

'We're all with you, man.'

'You're going to a better place.'

It makes me sick. The Garden is a place for killers. Every man on this block has killed to get here, and most have taken more than one. How many of their victims begged and pleaded? How many of these brave martyrs laughed as they shot, or hacked, or stabbed the life out of their victims? How many had a hard on?

And despite all this, when the warden and his group come to take one of these heartless murdering bastards away the others act like some kind of oppressed political group, chanting for freedom. All these killers, all these big men who felt so powerful when they were taking lives, buckle like cowards when it's their turn.

When they call out it's not from a genuine desire to support a falling comrade. They're just squealing in fear. They're squealing because, when it's their turn, they don't want to die alone.

73

It makes no difference. The warden and his party have rehearsed the scene many times. They open the dead man's cell and the guards flow in—not aggressively, just quiet and very strong. They're always the biggest guards who take men on the long walk.

There's no point even thinking about it, is the message their hulking silent presence announces.

The warden asks the dead man if he wants to take a book, and then they're out of the cell and moving, down the block, and through the pink door.

Those left behind keep calling out for a short while, but then the calls trail away. Everyone knows what's behind the pink door: a small cell, plain gray, with a single narrow cot and a little steel chair bolted to the floor. That's what they call the execution suite. That's where they keep you for the last hours before they take you through the final door.

Into the death chamber.

And nobody knows what's out past there.

29

I'm not afraid to die.

Not that I have much choice. In fifty-six days the warden and his little group will come for me. He will ask me if I want to take a book, to which I will reply yes. I'll take this notebook. I want you with me right up to the end. I want you to see it all.

Then they'll lead me down that last long walk, and if those cowards start to howl I'm going to tell them to shut the fuck up. When I take my walk I don't need the company of killers to serenade me out. I have enough poison to take with me as it is.

I've been trying to work out why I'm not afraid to die. I should be. Most people would feel at least some fear at the thought of being executed. I suppose you could say that would be normal. Yet with each day that it draws closer I feel a deepening sense of calm.

Part of it is that I'm tired—not physically tired, but *bone* tired. Weary to my very core. I sleep a lot in here. Mostly all I do is write and sleep. I can sleep through any kind of din, which is lucky, because death row at night is the noisiest place on earth. The spirits of the dead come visiting after lights out, and they tear away at the people of the Garden. The night is a constantly shifting landscape of moans and crying. In here the darkness brings no comfort or peace, only horror.

My dreams stopped the day James Goodlow handcuffed me and led me shackled from my house. None of the girls have been to see me since then. Not even pretty Carol Keenan, dead some eighteen months ago.

If any of them had a reason to come to me during the long dark hours it would be Carol. Her family will be at the execution; Gerald, my lawyer, has told me this. The only reason I keep going is for them, for Carol's family, and the others. The least I can give them is the satisfaction of seeing me die. I hope it brings them some sense of comfort, but I suspect there's no comfort to be found for any of us.

I do not fear death because, after all I've done, I have no right to fear death. That would be little more than self-pity, and I will not let myself have any of that.

30

Wendall Gates always knew I hadn't killed them.

'Takes one to know one aint,' he'd said, and he was right. Wendall had spent his life killing. He could smell his own kind from a mile away, and he knew I was faking it without me even needing to open my mouth.

If you'd told me five years ago that the last friend I would make on earth would be a convicted serial killer on death row, I'd have been a little disbelieving to say the least. Now, though, it seems to make a bizarre kind of sense. Almost anything can make sense if you want it to badly enough.

Wendall took an interest in me right from the start, almost as if I was some kind of pet project. His protection was a welcome consequence of his interest. He put the word out that I wasn't to be touched, which made my time on the row much easier. No one came at me looking for trouble, sexual or physical.

We took to playing Scrabble, something which in itself brought me some comfort. Juliette had always loved to play Scrabble.

It was at Wendall's instigation. 'Always pays a man to enrich his word power,' he'd said.

We play our matches in the yard. Wendall has his own set that he brings out during the exercise time, and we always sit in the far-left corner, away from the basketball hoop, where there is the least chance of being disturbed.

'So your wife liked Scrabble?' he'd asked me once when we were playing.

'Yeah, she loved it.'

'Did you two used to play?'

'Yup.' I trusted Wendall wasn't a cop by this stage, but I still didn't like talking about Juliette to anyone.

'You're lucky,' he said. 'I never had no one to play with most of my life.'

'Did you play as a kid?'

He glanced up at me, a twinkle in his eyes that I didn't quite understand. 'A little.'

'Do you have any contact with your family?'

'Not since I was a kid.'

'What happened?'

'Oh,' he said, scratching his nose in a thoughtful kind of way, 'things just didn't work out.'

'Did they separate?'

Wendall smiled, and there was something about it that was intensely disturbing. 'I guess you could call it that, yeah.'

I looked at him, waiting to see if he'd go on.

'Some other time, Simon.'

'Sure, no problem.'

'Charm.'

'What?'

'Charm,' said Wendall as he laid the letters out on the board. 'That's worth fourteen points with the triple letter score.'

I laughed. 'So it is.'

'So what else did the two of you do together?'

'The usual stuff. Walking, talking, movies.'

'Was the sex good?' His voice didn't miss a beat.

'I don't know if I feel comfortable talking about that with you, Wendall.'

This time he laughed. 'Jesus, Simon, take a look around you. You're on death row. Who the fuck feels comfortable about anything? Besides, dead men tell no tales, right?'

I thought for a moment. It couldn't do any real

harm to talk to him about that, and it made her seem closer to speak about her. 'The sex was *very* good.'

Wendall smiled, and his face looked almost fresh for a moment. 'Goddamn. I knew you two had to be doing the hot potato like a couple of rutting goats. It's always about sex.'

'What do you mean, it's always about sex?'

'All these guys in here, all the evil shit they've done—me included—it's all about sex.'

'I was talking about having sex with my wife, Wendall, I wasn't talking about killing people.'

'Oh, don't be such a fucking priss, Simon. You really expect me to believe that what happened to all those little girlies had nothing to do with you and your wife fucking?'

I looked at him, nervous at the sudden swing in the conversation.

His gaze was intense; he had crocodile eyes. 'Well?'

'It didn't.'

He just smiled. 'Your turn,' he said.

31

Wendall moved into the cell next to mine after they executed Terry Beck. I don't know if he organized for that to happen, or if it was just by chance. Either way, six months out from my own date with the warden's little walking party I got a new neighbor.

I was pretty happy that it was Wendall. Terry Beck hadn't exactly been the most stimulating company. He was a paedophile who'd abducted and killed a little girl in 1993. He wasn't the brightest of souls, and rumor has it that when the police caught him he still had her rotting body under his bed in his ratty apartment. Apparently the smell had alerted his neighbors. Having now had some experience of the stink of decomposing bodies, I'm not at all surprised the neighbors weren't happy.

Terry confessed pretty much straight away, and was sentenced to death in record time. He was here two years before I arrived, and from all accounts he'd spent almost the whole time sniveling.

I used to hear him at night after lights out, crying like a baby—which is disgusting enough in itself—but even worse was the fact that he used to jerk off all night as well. It can make for a long night when the person who sleeps four feet to the left of you snivels and moans all night, sniffing back the snot and slapping on the meat.

He would talk to himself as well, a kind of muffled whiny dirge that seemed to have no end.

'Not fair, gonna kill poor Terry for what ain't never his fault. Gonna kill him when he never meant no harm anyways. Wasn't his fault that the little bitch started to cry. If'n she hadn't never cried then he never would have hurt her none. No one cares 'bout that, though, no one cares that she's the one made him get all hotted up with her slutty little ways. No one cares 'bout that . . .'

And as he whined he beat out the time on his penis like a metronome.

Slap-slap-slap-slap-slap-

He was right about one thing, though—no one did care about poor old Terry Beck, least of all me. The night before they took him he was carrying on like a madman, calling out and slapping away like it was his last hope. Out of the misguided respect that characterizes the Garden, people let him go all night without an angry word. All of which is pretty hopelessly fucked up when you stop to think about what was running through Terry's mind.

When the warden and his party finally came for Terry the next day I was relieved. They took him for his last walk down the row and then out through the pink door. A few guys called out some stuff to him, but not many. Eight hours later he was killed as regular as clockwork.

And no one gave a damn.

Maybe that's as close to justice as you ever get with pathetic little wretches like Terry Beck.

The next morning Wendall shifted into Terry's empty cell.

'How the hell did you swing that?' I asked him through the bars. We could talk to each other, but all I could see was the faceless gray wall opposite us. That was okay though, it was easier to talk to Wendall when you couldn't see him. That way you could imagine him as being normal, which was all but impossible when you could actually see him.

Wendall chuckled. 'You just got to know which buttons to push, Simon.'

32

'Is the fibby coming back to see you?' Wendall asked me one morning.

'I think so.'

Wendall laughed, the sound winding its way slowly from his cell to mine. 'Looks like he's taken a shine to you, Simon.'

'Did they ever come and talk to you?'

'Once.'

80

'And?'

'And nothing.'

'You didn't want to talk to them?'

'They didn't ask the right questions.'

I thought for a moment. 'What kinds of questions should they have asked?'

'The right ones.'

Wendall could sometimes be a little evasive.

'So what did they ask you?'

'Oh, just the usual predictable crap. Why did I choose the victims I did, how did I plan it all, how did it make me feel?' He snorted. 'How did it make me *feel*? Jesus, what a bunch of stiffs.'

'Would you have told them anything if they'd asked the right questions?'

I heard Wendall's bed creak. 'I would have told them everything.'

'What do you mean, everything?'

Wendall snorted again. 'I would have given them it all—names, what I did, where the bodies are buried, everything.'

'So what should they have asked, then?'

'Tell you what, Simon, if you can figure that one out by yourself then I'll tell *you* everything.'

I laughed. 'What makes you think I give a damn, Wendall?'

'Haven't you ever wondered why I'm so interested in you and your pretty wife? You think it's just something to pass the time, Simon? You can't be that stupid.' I felt his cold mind reaching out to me through the wall and gripping my heart. 'You still haven't worked it out yet, have you, Simon? You and me got a shit load more in common than you think. We go way back, you and me, way back.'

'What do you mean?'

81

He laughed. 'I don't think so, Simon. You gotta ask the right questions if you want the right answers.'

'Wendall, please, what do you mean?'

There was no answer, just a creak of bed springs.

'Wendall?'

Nothing.

33

When I said before that no one cared when Terry Beck was executed, that wasn't quite true. There was one person who cared a great deal that he died, and now is as good a time as any to introduce her. Sondra Hilta cared about Terry Beck's death. She stood outside the prison announcing her concern to the world on a bullhorn.

'Two, four, six, eight. Terry Beck has got his date. Three, five, seven, ten. Send him back to hell again.'

She was always there for executions, and she always had some catchy little phrase worked out which she chanted from sun-up till the final moment.

'Two, four, six, eight. Terry Beck has got his date. Three, five, seven, ten. Send him back to hell again.'

Sondra doesn't have many friends in the Garden. In fact, a favorite topic of conversation in here revolves around what the inmates would like to do to her if they ever got the chance. God help her if there's ever some kind of mass escape. She'd be raped, tortured and butchered fifty times over.

In my cell there's a faint picture scratched into the wall over my hand basin of a woman tied naked to a tree. A broken bottle dripping with blood is impaled in her vagina, and several knives protrude from jagged wounds in her breasts. The inscription beneath the image reads: *Sondra finilly gets the fucking she deserves.*

This isn't an isolated piece of work; most cells have some graffiti or images dedicated to the infamous Sondra Hilta. In many ways she has become the focus of the resentment the inmates feel towards the world. She is the human face of the wider society that wants us dead, and as a result she is hated with an intensity that is almost palpable.

Her dedication is remarkable, if not a little disturbing. She hasn't missed an execution since they brought back the death penalty in the seventies, which means she's chanted her way through over two hundred executions. It doesn't matter what the weather is, Sondra will always show up. There are only two things you can depend on in rain, hail, or shine: the mail, and Sondra Hilta chanting down the hours till an execution.

'Two, four, six, eight. Terry Beck has got his date. Three, five, seven, ten. Send him back to hell again.'

Motivation is what intrigues me. What would possess a person to carry on the way that she does? I've tried to find out more about her since I arrived at the Garden. God knows you need something to while away the time; Sondra seemed as good a thing as any.

She looks quite attractive in the newspaper photographs I've seen. She's in her forties, with long blond hair and a delicate nose. It's the eyes that get me, though; there's something there that the photographs don't quite seem to capture. I think that's where you'll find her motivation, hidden away under those eyes.

I asked a guard about her once. Harry Wilkes is

one of the old-timers who's been here ever since they turned the Garden back into a killing machine in 1978. Harry was also a local—he'd been born in Stanton, which was the little town closest to where the prison was built. In Stanton everyone either works in the prison or is locked up in it.

'I don't know too much about her,' he said as we walked down the block for my monthly medical. For some reason the state requires that a man has to be sound of mind and body if he's going to be killed. It doesn't make a whole lot of sense to me, but then trivial things like reason drifted out of my life a long time ago. You'd be surprised what you can do without.

My hands were handcuffed behind my back, which was standard procedure whenever the guards had to take us anywhere.

'Did she have someone in her family who was killed or something?' I asked. It seemed the most obvious motivation.

'Yeah, she lost a daughter back in the late seventies, just after this place started killing people again. It was real sad.'

'Was she murdered?'

'No—well, not for definite anyway. She just didn't come home from school one day. She was only a dot as well, about nine or ten as far as I can recall.'

'Did they ever find out what happened to her?'

'Nope, never did. It was big news for a few months but then it gradually started to fade away. Sondra never did though, and when the authorities finally gave up looking for her little daughter Sondra started coming out here for the executions.'

We stopped at the door to the infirmary and waited for the doctor to finish with the guy ahead of me.

'Has she always chanted like that?'

'Not at first,' he said, leaning back on the bars and picking away at his fingernails. I could see that he felt something for this woman. 'She used to just stand there for the first few years, silent as a corpse, staring up at the prison. Once it was raining and I went to take her out an umbrella, poor thing was gonna catch her death.'

He paused a moment. 'So anyway, I took her out this umbrella, but she said no thank you. She said her little girl didn't have an umbrella that day and so she wouldn't have one either.' He swallowed, and his big bullfrog throat moved like a wave rolling over the ocean. 'Saddest damn thing I ever saw, I reckon.'

'When did she start the chanting?'

He shook his head as if clearing his thoughts. 'Oh, about six years ago, don't know why. She just turned up at one execution with a bullhorn and started hollering out her little sayings. Can't say I agree with what she does, but I can't honestly say I disagree with it either.'

Just as I was about to ask him another question the door of the infirmary opened and the moment passed. I was ushered in, poked, prodded, and ten minutes later duly pronounced fit to die. A different guard took me back, so I didn't get a chance to finish my conversation with Harry.

When I got back to my cell I went and had another look at the awful picture in the corner.

Sondra finilly gets the fucking she deserves.

Truth is, I think Sondra had already had more of a fucking than anyone ever deserved.

34

The fibby did come back to see me. A week after I'd had the conversation with Wendall about asking the right questions.

'Nice to see you, Agent Hanson.'

'Please, call me John.'

He was much friendlier this time. One thing I've learnt is never trust a friendly fibby. Friendliness isn't something that comes natural to them, they have to be trained to do it. Just like they get trained to fire a gun. Both things can be deadly in the hands of fibbies, in my experience, guns and friendliness.

'Okay, then, John it is.'

'There are a few things that I wanted to go over again with you, Simon.'

'Fire away.'

This time he didn't have any of his little tests with him; not even a file laid out on the table. It looked like we were just going to chew the fat a spell. I was worried, but I kept that to myself.

'It was about some of the details of how the girls were killed.'

I didn't speak.

'There were some inconsistencies in the file that I thought we could clear up.'

'What kind of inconsistencies?'

'Well, just some differences between your statements and the forensic evidence.'

'Like?'

'Well,' he said as he bent down to his briefcase and took out a file, 'take this, for instance.' He pushed a photograph over the desk at me. Lisa Simkin, seventeen, and the first body they exhumed in the basement.

As I looked down at the black and white photograph lying on the table, another more terrible image superimposed itself on my mind: her face in the ground, covered in dirt, her mouth opened in a frozen rictus scream, and dirt filling her like stuffing in a Thanksgiving turkey. She had started to rot, but not fast enough, and the stink was threatening to bring the world down upon us. So I had to dig her up again to do the job properly.

She watches me with white eyes as I scoop lime from the bag I've just bought from the hardware store. I try not to look at her, try not to breathe her. I sprinkle the lime down on top of her like snow. It settles on her hair. On her face. On her white, staring eyes.

'Simon?'

I shook my head and found myself back in the small gray interview room. Agent Hanson was looking at me again, intently. I was sweating and my hands were shaking. I knew he saw all that, but I pretended he hadn't.

Pretty Lisa Simkin is looking at me from the table as well. I do not return her gaze this time.

'I'm sorry, John,' I said, trying to sound relaxed, 'I was thinking about something else.'

Agent Hanson smiled coolly. 'Looked like you just saw a ghost, Simon.'

'You were about to ask me something, I believe?'

He paused for a moment, perhaps weighing up where to go next. 'You said in the interview with Detective Goodlow on the tenth of April that you killed Lisa before you buried her.'

'Yes, that's right.'

'And that's still what you're saying?'

'Yes.'

'Well now, that's where I'm confused.'

'How so, John?'

'Because Lisa was still alive when she was buried.'

I heard the words, but it was like I couldn't understand them. 'What did you say?'

'She was alive when she was buried.'

I could only look at him. I felt as if I'd just been shot in the stomach. 'You're . . . you're lying.'

He leaned forward in his chair and lowered his voice. 'Actually, Simon, the Medical Examiner back at Quantico says *you* were the one who was lying when you said you killed her before you buried her. All the wounds examined on Lisa were non-fatal.'

Just when I thought that I'd finally swum as far out into the black as I would have to go, the water suddenly got colder and deeper all over again.

I looked down at the photograph on the table, at her fresh smiling face and bright sparkling eyes, and I saw the other face beneath it. The one with the puffy black skin and milky white eyes. The one with the frozen rictus scream as if she'd suffocated in the cold clay floor of our basement. Which is exactly what did happen to her. She was pushed screaming under the earth, and she suffocated.

All alone, down under the dirt.

It was almost too much for me. 'Oh, Christ,' I mumbled, feeling the bile thick in my throat.

Agent Hanson leaned back in his chair and studied me. I knew I shouldn't be letting him see me like this, but I couldn't help it. The cruelty of it was almost too much to bear. All I could think about was that poor little girl, alone and afraid. Having to watch as the pit was dug, and then being pushed in. The feeling of lying in the earth as dirt was shoveled in on top of her. Knowing she was going to die in that hole. Knowing she would never see the people she loved again. The cold horror as she sank down into the earth.

'You didn't know, did you?'

I looked at him, feeling as if he'd just ripped my heart from my chest and laid it on the table between us. I couldn't speak.

'You didn't know she was buried alive,' continued Agent Hanson, his voice betraying his zeal. 'Which means you didn't kill her. Did you? You didn't kill her.'

I fought my way up to the surface again. I knew that I had to say something quickly to get back control of the situation.

'I don't like to talk about it, that's all.' My voice sounded flat, like a bad recording.

'You didn't kill that girl, Simon. That's why you look so shocked. You didn't know she'd been buried alive. It sickens you, doesn't it? To think about her dying in such a terrible way all alone down there.'

'It sickens me to think *about what I've done*,' I said, and this was as true as anything I ever told him.

'When are you going to give Juliette up, Simon? Do you want to take this with you to the grave?'

'I killed Lisa.'

'I don't think so, Simon,' he said as he stood, sliding the photograph into his briefcase.

'I did.'

He turned and knocked on the door.

'*I fucking killed her*,' I yelled at his back.

He looked at me when the guard opened the door. 'You can't protect Juliette, Simon.'

And then he was gone.

35

Home had been the trigger, the thing that opened the door for all the bad stuff to come in. I think that as long as we were travelling she was able to stay ahead of it, to keep it far enough behind so she could walk in the sun like the rest of us. But once we stopped, once we put our bags down in Bedford, it was only a matter of time until the blackness caught up with her.

I'd like to believe she was happy with me, but knowing what I know now of where she came from I don't see how that can be. Juliette spent her whole life either living in the black or running from it.

When we were moving it was easier for her, because while we were moving we didn't have as much shape, were just drifting through. We had about as much substance as a couple of pages of yesterday's news blowing down the street.

So, that of course raises the question of why she stopped? Why did she say what she said as we sat in Will's Diner that morning?

I believe that she knew what stopping in Bedford would mean for her, and for us. I think she knew how it would finish.

She must have.

So why stop?

In the end I think that maybe the answer was simple; I think she needed to do those things to keep herself alive. She was raised to breathe horror like air, it hadn't been of her choosing. So when she tried to make a new life with me in Bedford her old one slid inside it like a rapist's finger.

That's why she pushed that poor little girl screaming into the dirt under our house. The two of them were joined in that moment—Lisa choking as her head went down into the dark, and Juliette breathing because of it.

36

It was impossible to forget about the watch. I'd tried to tell myself otherwise, but the things that we tell ourselves and the things we believe are hardly ever the same.

'Is there something wrong?' she asked me at breakfast the next day. I'd hardly spoken a word all morning. I didn't know what to say—mostly because I still didn't really want to admit that I knew what was wrong.

'Nope.'

'You haven't said anything to me since we woke up.'

'I'm just tired.'

She looked at me then, across the cereal and orange juice that lay between us. It was a look so sudden and intense that I felt my breath catch in my chest.

'Would you tell me if there was something wrong?' she finally asked.

I tried to sound reassuring, and I don't know if that was for her or me. 'Of course I would.'

She held my gaze a moment longer, then shrugged and turned back to her breakfast.

I kissed her on the cheek before I left, and for the first time ever her skin felt cold on my lips.

37

I didn't even make it to lunchtime. I'd staggered through my first two classes with that little gold watch gnawing away at my mind. I tried to concentrate, but all I could see were the watches the girls in the class were wearing. I'd never noticed it before, but they all had them. My eyes were drawn to them like pins to a magnet.

At one point I found myself gazing intently at one of the girl's wrists as my thoughts trailed off. Her arms were folded across her chest and her watch stood out like a beacon. She moved her hand and I caught her eye as I looked up. She was looking at me with an embarrassed grin on her face, and I realized that she must have thought I was staring at her breasts. As I turned around, my face burning, I heard her whisper to her friend. They both giggled.

At the beginning of my third class I gave in.

'Okay, settle down.' When they had quietened I continued: 'Today I'm going to give you a study period. I need to go and take care of something important that's just come up, so you can spend the next twenty minutes doing your homework.'

There were a few sideways glances. This was pretty out of the ordinary.

'Uh, Mr Chance?' It was Nick Dewey, a nice but thick kid. He was good at football though, so he had as good a chance as any.

'Yes, Nick?'

'What if we don't have any homework?'

'Improvise, Mr Dewey, improvise.'

There were a few giggles, and then the kids got out their books and began to work. I was under no illusions—I knew the instant I was gone they'd be fooling around—but all I needed was twenty minutes to get down to the library, check out the previous yearbook and then get back. With any luck they would be controlled enough not to arouse any attention from the other teachers.

The library was on the other side of the school to my class and I went as quickly as I could without running. All I had to do was get there, find the picture I was after, and get back. No problem.

Except of course that there could be a problem, there could be a very big problem. The picture might show me something that was better left unseen.

The school librarian's name was Mrs Rice. I don't know at the time if she even had a first name—no one ever called her by it, and she certainly never encouraged its use. It was only at the trial, when they called her, that I discovered her first name was Evelyn.

A librarian called Evelyn, who would have guessed?

'Can I help you, Mr Chance?' she asked as I walked in. She was a terribly harsh looking woman. Plain and simple. Mrs Rice brooked no unrest in her library. I could tell from the lift of her eyebrows she was surprised to see me there. All the teachers in the school had classes pretty much back to back, so it was rare for anyone to come in by themselves during the day.

'Yes, Mrs Rice, you can,' I said, smiling and trying to sound nonchalant. 'I need the yearbook for last year.'

'Don't you usually have a class now, Mr Chance?' she said, pushing her brown spectacles back up her nose.

'Yes, I do, but there's something I need to check out for my next period so I left them studying quietly.' I was acutely aware I was in danger of babbling.

'And what would that be exactly, Mr Chance?'

I froze. I had no idea what I could use as an excuse because it had never occurred to me I'd need one. 'What would what be?' I stammered.

'This piece of information that you need to check?'

She was such a sour looking woman that I wanted to slap her, slap her and scream at her until she fell away from me begging for mercy. The picture was so vivid it jarred me.

'Spelling,' I said, with absolutely no thought as to what it meant.

'Spelling?'

'Yes, spelling. Now, where might I find the year-books?'

She looked at me a moment longer, the same look she gave me a year later in court, and then slid out from behind her desk.

'Follow me, please, Mr Chance.'

She led me over to the far wall of the library in the reference section. The yearbooks were in file boxes dating back to the early 1930s.

'Thank you, Mrs Rice,' I said as she passed me last year's copy.

'I expect so,' she muttered oddly, and then walked stiffly back to her desk.

I flicked through all the usual banal rubbish that fills up high school yearbooks until I found the orchestra section. My heart was thumping away and I was sweating. The first page showed a photograph of the entire school orchestra, and Milly was seated in the second row. Her face was little more than a blur though, and her hands were hidden. Cursing under my breath I turned the page.

And there she was. A full-page picture of Milly playing the cello at a school concert. She was wearing a black dress and her legs straddled the cello as she leaned in close to its curved wooden body. The bow was drawn back in her right hand, and her left was wrapped around the slender neck of the cello. Her eyes were closed and her mouth was open, just slightly, lending the picture an oddly erotic tone. She was beautiful.

But this wasn't what suddenly sucked the heat from my body out through my fingers and into the page. It was the watch she wore on her left hand, clearly visible in the photograph. Metallic and shiny, with a jet-black face.

'Oh, shit,' I whispered, only dimly aware of a disapproving hiss from the indefatigable Mrs Rice somewhere off on the periphery.

I knew it was the very same watch I'd thrown into the Bedford Municipal Dump less than twenty-four hours ago.

To M.B.

Milly Brown

38

I sat there, under the faint heat of Mrs Rice's glare, and tried to work out what it all meant. There was no more pretending the watch didn't belong to Milly Brown.

The missing Milly Brown.

And there was also no way of logically explaining how the watch came to be wedged down inside the tire well of our car. Which then begged the final and most bitter question: where was the car fifteen days ago when Milly disappeared? I already had a fair idea about the answer to that question, but I wanted to walk through it slowly to be sure.

Milly went missing sometime on the afternoon of Tuesday the twenty-fourth of February. She left her music teacher's house on Deep Spring Road at four o'clock in the afternoon and hadn't been seen since. It was only a fifteen-minute walk from her teacher's place to her home, but she never made it.

I mentally checked back through the days in my mind. I knew there'd been something significant about February for us, but I couldn't quite get it. Then I remembered what it was. Juliette had gone to Sauvarign—a town about two hours north of Bedford—to buy a rocking chair for the living room. She said she'd heard Sauvarign had a little antique store that sold cheap ones, and that's why she'd gone.

Of course, I only found that out after she got home later that night. She'd had the car during the day to do some grocery shopping, and was supposed to pick me up after school.

But she never turned up.

So after an hour I gave up waiting and took the bus. I remember sitting at home worrying about where she was. Thinking all the worst thoughts, as you do, until she finally arrived home just after nine that night.

'Where the hell have you been?' I demanded when she walked in the door.

'Out.' Her voice sounded odd, but I was too angry and relieved to care.

'You were supposed to pick me up after school, Juliette. What the hell happened?'

'Oh,' she said, 'that's right. I forgot. Sorry.'

'Sorry? Don't I get some kind of explanation about where you were?'

'Where I was?' She looked at me then, and her eyes

were so flat that I started to get scared all over again.

'Yeah, Juliette. Where were you? Christ, I thought maybe you'd had an accident or something. I was just about to call the cops.'

She winced when I said that, and I can't remember what I made of it at the time, but I have a better idea now. 'I went up to Sauvarign,' she said as she took off her coat and hung it up on the hook beside the door. Her boots were covered in mud and she took those off as well.

'Sauvarign?'

'I went to buy a rocking chair.'

'A chair?'

She sighed. An empty sound. 'Look, Simon, I need to take a shower.' Without waiting for a reply, she walked past me into the bathroom and closed the door. I heard the sound of the shower running. I was left standing there trying to figure out if I should still be angry or not. I recall that I didn't reach any firm conclusions on the matter at the time.

After she'd finished she came out to me, and she was different, somehow more alive. She was wearing only a towel and her wet hair dripped on me as she leaned over to kiss me.

'I'm sorry, baby,' she whispered. 'Please forgive me.'

'I was just worried, that's all.'

'I know.'

'I thought you could have been hurt or something.'

She undid her towel and dropped it in my lap. 'Love me,' she said.

That night she was insatiable—it was like nothing was enough for her, she wanted it over and over. I finally dropped into an exhausted sleep some time after three in the morning. I woke briefly once and she was sitting naked on the bed, looking down at me.

'Juliette,' I mumbled.

'Sshhh,' she whispered. 'Go back to sleep.'

'What's wrong? Can't sleep?' I was really only half awake, but I remembered what she said.

'No sleep for the wicked.'

Now I couldn't remember exactly what date that had been, but I knew it was a Tuesday, and I knew that it was about two weeks ago. There weren't that many dates to choose from. It had to have been the twenty-fourth. So one Tuesday late in February my wife took the car and disappeared for hours, and when she came back she brought with her a little gold watch that belonged to a girl who'd gone missing that very same day.

I decided I didn't want to think about this stuff anymore. I got up and put the yearbook back in its file on the shelf where I'd found it and turned to leave.

'Did you find what you were looking for, Mr Chance?' asked Mrs Rice as I walked past her.

I stopped and turned to her, and for just a moment she must have seen what was behind my eyes because her hardened surety seemed to falter a little.

'No, Mrs Rice, I found something else entirely.'

I smiled at her and went out through the brown wooden doors, but the smile carried nothing good in it.

39

I felt somewhat detached from the world as I walked back across the school. It was the last period for the morning and so the grounds were empty. The balance of the world shifted about me, almost like being in some bizarre other dimension where the people have gone but the world still remains, just somehow paler and a little flatter.

I had completely forgotten about my class, but was relieved to hear nothing but silence as I hurried down the corridor. It was short-lived. I entered the classroom to find Pervin' Mervyn sitting on my desk surveying the hushed students as they worked. His piggy little eyes rolled up to greet me.

'Ahhh, Mr Chance,' he said, his voice reeking of ill intent. 'So nice of you to join us.' There was a snicker from a student and his eyes swung round to silence it as quick as a frog taking a fly from the air.

'Could I perhaps have a word with you outside? If you have the time, that is?'

'Of course, Mr Mack.'

He followed me back out into the corridor.

'I would imagine that I don't need to remind you how fortunate you are to be teaching here, Mr Chance?'

'No, Mr Mack, you don't need to remind me of that.'

He smiled. 'Good. So perhaps you might be able to explain just why it was that your class was left unattended?'

'I had something I needed to check in the library.'

'I see.' He licked his lips, and the saliva made them glisten in the reflected sunlight of the corridor. 'And this was something that couldn't wait till the lunch break?'

'In hindsight that would have been the wiser choice.'

'Yes, I think so too. Can I assume this will not happen again then?'

I wanted to smash him in the face so badly it made

my arms hurt. 'Yes, Mr Mack, you can assume that.'

'Good.'

He smiled again and turned to go, but then hesitated. 'How is your lovely wife, Mr Chance?'

'She's fine, thank you.'

His eyes suddenly glittered as if he'd just licked them, his tongue moving too fast for human eyes to see. 'Give her my *fondest* regards, will you?'

'Of course.'

Mr Mack will never know how close he came to being beaten to a bloody red pulp in that moment.

40

When I got home that night she was sitting in the living room waiting for me. The only light was from a small lamp on the coffee table.

'Juliette, we need to talk,' I said. I had been preparing myself for this conversation all day.

'Sssshhh,' she said as she came to me.

'No,' I said, 'we need to talk.'

She kissed me then, slipping her tongue into my mouth. I could feel her body pressed up against mine in her thin cotton dress, her bare feet stroking my leg. Juliette has never felt the cold. I resisted briefly, and then I kissed her back.

It was so much easier just to kiss her.

'Come,' she said, and I went with her. Just like that.

'Where are we going?'

'There's something in the cellar I have to show you.'

I stopped dead. 'What?'

She turned. 'Do you love me, Simon?'

'You know I do, Juliette.'

'Then tell me.'

'I love you.'

'No matter what?'

I hesitated. 'What's in the cellar, Juliette?'

'No. Tell me first.'

'All right, no matter what.' My heart was thumping in my ears. I felt sick with fear. 'What's in the cellar, Juliette?'

'A girl.'

There was never any going back from that moment. It might have been possible before, but not now.

'Come on,' she said.

I followed her, and no walk that the warden can take me on could ever be as long as that one. I didn't really think about it at the time, but I was walking away from the world, away from the light. I went down into the darkness of our cellar with Juliette, and in a sense I never came back out.

It was weeks since I'd been down there. I hadn't liked it much in the first place and so, apart from when we'd first moved in and I'd stacked some empty boxes down there, I avoided it.

Juliette had been busy. She'd cleaned it up and bought a roll of cheap carpet to cover the floor. In the middle she'd put up a cot, and the girl was lying on that.

'Oh, dear God, Juliette,' I whispered as I saw her lying there. 'What have you done?'

And then the girl sat up.

'Hey,' she said, and I nearly screamed.

Juliette went and sat beside the girl on the cot, putting one arm around her and kissing her lightly on the cheek.

'Simon, meet Stacy,' she said and smiled at me.

'Hey,' said Stacy again. She was young, no more

than seventeen probably, with short black hair—pretty in a trashy kind of way. She wore a tiny green skirt and a tight white T-shirt. Even in the poor light of the single bulb I could see she had on too much make-up.

'What the hell's going on?' I asked Juliette.

'I got her for you.'

'What do you mean?'

'I want to watch you make love to her.'

I couldn't work out if I was relieved or horrified. 'What?'

'I want to watch you make love to her. I want to see what you look like when you do the things you do to me.'

Stacy smiled at me.

'Jesus, Juliette, she's just a kid.'

'Hey, mister,' Stacy protested, 'I'm twenty-one.'

'What's wrong, Simon?' Juliette put both arms around the girl. 'You don't like her? I think she's very sweet.' She slowly lifted the girl's T-shirt over her head. Stacy breathed in sharply as her breasts were suddenly exposed to the cold air of the cellar. She had a lovely body, and in the dim light her nipples were like two small pink smudges on her fair skin.

'It's not that,' I said, trying to summon up some resolve.

'Then what?' Juliette asked, gently stroking the girl's breasts.

'It's just that . . . ' There was nothing I could say. I *did* want to make love to the girl. She was beautiful. I knew it was wrong, but somehow that didn't seem to matter very much.

'Have her, Simon. I want you to have her.'

'Juliette . . . I can't . . . ' My words trailed off into nothing.

Juliette stood and took my hand. She kissed me

lightly on the cheek and led me over to the cot. Bending, she placed my hand on the girl's breast. Her skin was soft and warm, and her nipple felt hard as bone beneath my hand.

The girl closed her eyes and licked her lips. Everything slowed around me, thought fading away until there was only touch and sound.

'Make love to her,' Juliette whispered in my ear, 'for me.'

And so I did.

'Remember to put a condom on,' the girl breathed in the same ear later on, as I was about to enter her. I glanced up at Juliette before rolling the condom down. There was a look on her face that I couldn't fathom. It was like she was looking at us, but also looking past us.

And then the girl pulled me back onto her, into her, and I forgot everything.

Later on, after Juliette had given the girl her money and she'd gone, she asked me again if I loved her.

'Of course I do.'

'I know,' she said, 'I could see it as you made love to that girl. It showed in the way you touched her, the way you kissed her. Everything you did told me.'

I looked at her then to see if she meant what she said, and she did. There are so many things about her that will always be a mystery to me.

41

God sent one of his boys to see me today—Father Jack Morrison, spiritual leader of the Eden Hill Penitentiary. It turns out that Father Morrison visits all the condemned men as their date draws closer. He has the idea that redemption is good for the soul.

'Hello, Simon,' he said as he sat down on the chair in my cell. I'd been handcuffed and put in leg braces prior to his arrival.

'Hello, Father.'

'I apologize for the shackles, but it's policy here as you know,' he said. Father Jack wasn't a large man, but twenty years working the Garden had lent him a presence that demanded some respect. Sitting there in his dog collar and holding a Bible he looked vaguely ill at ease, as if the restraints of his office did not fit comfortably with him. The most striking thing about Father Jack, though, was his eyes. In the dim confines of my cell they looked almost completely black.

'That's all right, Father,' I said. 'I'd want the same if I had to sit in a cell with someone like me.'

He studied me with his great dark eyes. He'd been here many times before—not with me, but with a hundred other dead men—and I suspect he was trying to get the lay of me as quickly as he could. After twenty years in the redemption game I suppose he must be pretty good at it.

'I heard you've been given your date, Simon,' he finally said. 'October the fourth, isn't it?'

I nodded without saying anything. I've learnt, in recent times, that the cautious game is usually the best.

'How are you holding up?'

I smiled. 'I think I'll make it through to the fourth.'

'Has your lawyer been in contact with you lately?'

'No. He and I don't have a lot in common any more. He wants to save my life, and I just want to die.'

The priest nodded slowly. 'Have you repented for your sins, Simon?'

'No, Father.'

'I can help you.'

'Really?' I said. 'And how exactly would you do that?'

'Do you believe in God, Simon?'

'Aahh, Father,' I said as I shook my head, 'you've come to the wrong cell. I'm a godless man—didn't you read my file?'

'I don't read the files, Simon. I'm interested in your immortal soul, not your mortal sins. Man has judged you for those, it's God's judgement that should concern you now.'

'What can God do to me that hasn't already been done, Father?'

'He can save you, Simon. He can save your soul from the abyss.'

I looked at him calmly. 'I welcome the abyss, Father. I yearn for it.'

'I see,' he said, his voice faintly condescending.

'Oh really? And what do you see, Father?'

His dark eyes were like holes in his face. 'I see a man who is so racked with the guilt and pain of the terrible things he has done that he struggles to even breathe.'

Despite myself, I felt my chest tighten. 'I thought you said you don't read the files, Father.'

'I don't, I read men. You hurt greatly, Simon Chance. It covers you like a shroud.' His black eyes almost seemed to glow.

'I've done some very bad things, Father, things you can't even imagine.'

He smiled. 'Son, after twenty years in this place, you'd be surprised what I can imagine.'

'Are you married?' I asked him.

He shook his head, 'No, Simon, priests aren't allowed to marry.'

'I'm married.'

'Yes, I know.'

I grinned a cheerless grin. 'Of course you do. I sometimes forget that I'm a celebrity.'

'We're all God's children, Simon,' intoned Father Jack.

'Just some more so than others.'

'Everyone is equal in the eyes of the Lord.'

'Even those who rape and kill seventeen-year-old girls, Father? Does God love us too?'

'God loves all his children, Simon.'

I was growing tired of the banalities. It was like talking to a pamphlet. 'I think we're done, Father. I'm not interested in your redemption tricks, so why don't you just leave now?'

Father Jack exploded out of his chair. Throwing it backwards, he grabbed me by the neck and smashed me into the wall. My head filled with stars as I felt his hand tighten around my neck like a snake. *'Don't fuck with the Lord, son,'* he snarled, *'and don't fuck with me!'*

He dropped me back onto my bunk, and by the time I'd finished spluttering he'd resumed his seat again as if nothing had happened.

'What the hell was *that*?' I wheezed.

'I had a sense that you were fucking with me, Simon, and when you fuck with me you fuck with God.' He leaned in close, his eyes black holes. 'And *no one* in this place fucks with God, Simon, *no one*.'

He had my attention.

'I've been working here for twenty years, and in that time I've seen more men go to their deaths than I care to remember. I've seen them walking meekly down the block, and I've seen them dragged screaming. Now, I don't know what your lawyer has said, but you *are* going to die just like all the others. So cut the bravado shit.'

My neck still hurt, but I was starting to recover my composure again. 'What exactly do you want?'

'Same thing the Devil does, Simon—I want your immortal soul.'

'Meaning what exactly?'

'Meaning I want you to repent your sins before God and accept Him as your savior.'

'And if I'm not interested?'

He smiled. 'Then I'll beat you till you beg for forgiveness.'

I couldn't believe what I was hearing. 'Isn't there something in the priests' handbook about not beating people into conversion?'

Father Jack's smile never missed a beat. 'In here,' he said, 'there is no handbook.'

'You can't be serious?' was all I could say. To be honest I didn't really care if he did beat me—it was nothing more than I deserved—but the fact that he was saying it seemed utterly incomprehensible. 'You can't *hit* me?'

'Well, let's see,' he said, and went to the bars. '*Guard.*'

Andy Watson sauntered over. He was an arrogant man, one best not to cross. 'What's up, Padre?' he asked.

'Mr Watson, Mr Chance here thinks that I won't beat him.'

Andy smiled. 'Is that so?'

'It would appear to be, Mr Watson.'

Andy looked over at me. 'Don't fuck with this man, Chance, or he'll beat you till your asshole bleeds.'

'And wouldn't you be duty bound to report that, Mr Watson?' Father Jack asked.

He winked. 'Only if I saw it, Padre.'

'Thank you, Mr Watson,' said Father Jack.

'Welcome,' said Andy, and sauntered off again.

Father Jack came back and sat opposite me on the little metal chair. 'Seems like you're wrong on that count, Simon.'

42

It turns out Father Jack is one of God's *special* boys. He wasn't the usual kind of holy man, and he took the whole wrath of God thing extremely personally. He had his own reasons.

'That guy is a fucking nut,' muttered Wendall after Father Jack had gone.

I still couldn't believe what happened. 'He *attacked* me. Priests can't do that.'

'That goddamned son of a bitch can do about anything he wants in here.'

'He asked me if I knew where hell was.'

'He's a fucking nut.'

'What does that mean, do I know where hell is?'

'You ain't listening to me, Simon. The guy is a certified fucking nut.'

'Is he even a priest?'

'Oh, yeah, he's a priest all right. Ex-army. Went to Vietnam and everything. Problem is, only half of him came back.'

'He was in Vietnam?'

'So they say.'

'What the hell happened to him over there?'

'I heard lots of rumors—probably just the usual jailhouse horseshit though.'

'Like what?'

'Well, I heard he got captured by the gooks and they kept him in some sort of pit for a year. People all around him were dying, but Father Jack kept on going. The gooks left the bodies in the pit so they just kind of rotted around him. Apparently he didn't get fed much, but he still managed to survive a year down in that hole with those bodies stinking up and rotting away all round him. Makes you wonder, doesn't it?'

All I could think about were Father Jack's pit-black eyes. 'Makes you wonder what?'

Wendall chuckled. 'Makes you wonder what he ate all that time to keep himself alive.'

43

'Do you know where hell is, Simon?' Father Jack had asked once Andy Watson had disappeared back up the walk.

'No,' I said quietly.

He laughed. 'Good, Simon. I don't like bullshit—in fact, I find it offensive. Hell is not underground, Simon, it isn't some kind of fiery subterranean netherworld. Hell isn't under us. Hell is in us.'

'I won't beg your God for forgiveness, Father,' I said, 'so if you're going to beat me then you may as well start now.'

Father Jack's black eyes studied me for a long time in the dim light of my death row cell. Finally he spoke: 'I don't think so, Simon. I think you'd like to be beaten—I think it would satisfy your need for punishment. Perhaps it would be better for you to spend some time considering the nature of things.'

'And what exactly would you have me consider?'

'Well, for a start how about the nature of heaven and hell? How about the fine line that runs between God's Kingdom and the Devil's pit?'

'I've got just over seven weeks to live, Father, and I don't think I want to waste that time on theology.'

He smiled, and there was an emptiness in it that chilled me. 'You might think you've made your peace with the world, Simon, but I have a suspicion the world isn't finished with you yet.'

'That may be, Father, but I'm finished with the world.'

'Do you really think it's that simple? Do you really think you can just walk away from it?'

'I don't have any choice, Father. In seven weeks you'll come back here with the warden and you'll both take me down to the end of the hall. All the choosing has been and gone a long time ago.'

'You let a great evil loose in the world, Simon. If you think God will let you walk away from that then I'm afraid you have a lot to learn.'

'Any evil I brought into this world leaves with me.'

'And what about the evil that you're responsible for? What about that?'

I felt the ice cracking beneath my feet. 'I'll take all the evil I'm responsible for with me when I go.'

Father Jack dropped his voice, and with the background clatter of death row I could only just hear him. '"It is a fearful thing to fall into the hands of the living God." Hebrews, chapter ten, verse thirty-one.' He smiled. 'It's a fine line, Simon, between heaven and hell.'

Now it was my turn to feel angry. I was tidying up my mess as best I could. 'Are you fucking with me, Father?'

He leaned forward and put his hand on my shoulder. '*Don't worry, son,*' he whispered in my ear. '*When*

I start fucking with you, you'll know.'

Then he stood and called for the guard.

44

Why can't they all just leave me alone? I've said my piece. I've made my confessions, taken the blame, and accepted that I must die for it. I have a lawyer who seems to think that it's his job to get in between me and death, and I do the best I can to keep him to one side. I don't want to fight this thing, I want them to kill me. It's best for everyone that way.

So why can't they leave me alone?

It seems like everyone is pushing me. Everyone wants something more out of me. Confession isn't enough, they want a pound of flesh each to carve up and take away like a trophy.

Except, of course, I know it's more than that, what they really want is Juliette. They want her because she got away and that offends their sense of justice. The people who do the bad thing have to pay, but she's out there in the world, out there with everyone else.

I used to be a normal guy, that's the thing I don't understand—just a normal guy. Now my best friend is a serial killer, I am visited in my cell on death row by a cannibal priest who threatens to beat me if I don't repent my sins, and I'm being stalked by an agent from the FBI. I feel like a character in a book, which of course I am. I'm the hero in this book, the one I'm writing in this ratty little notepad as I count down the days to my execution—which, by the way, is now forty-seven.

I always wanted to write this kind of a story, just

not as an autobiography. Sometimes I wonder how things ever got so screwed up.

45

My parents have only been to see me once since I was arrested, and they've never been here on the row. I'm glad for that; this isn't the place for them. My mother sends me letters occasionally, and apart from the fact that the address on the front is for Eden Hill Penitentiary, you couldn't tell she was writing to her son on death row. She talks about the farm, and Dad, and my sister.

I don't know if they're planning to come for the execution, but I hope not. Next time Gerald comes in I need to ask him if I can refuse permission for them to attend. I don't want them to see me here. The son who left them in Nebraska five years ago isn't the same person sitting here. That young man disappeared somewhere in the great American wilderness, he wandered too far out to come back—which is a shame because I liked him.

My father hasn't been able to deal with all this. In the broader scheme of things I guess I can't really blame him. I could see it in his eyes when they visited me in prison during the trial. It was like he was looking at a stranger, a person who was as foreign to him as something from another planet. And of course by that time I was a stranger. I was no longer their son; I was a killer.

I was the monster.

'Are you getting enough to eat, dear?' my mother asked through the steel grill in the interview room.

'Yeah, Mom, I'm getting enough to eat.'

It was halfway through the trial, so the prosecution's case was just about to draw to a close. I had pleaded guilty at the outset, and the current hearing was to determine the sentence. My parents had sat through a fair amount of the forensic evidence, and today the first of the dead girls' parents had testified. Lisa Simkin's mother had sobbed her way through an hour. It was terrible to watch that poor woman up there on the stand. Lisa had been their only child. Now they only had each other, and the ghastly knowledge of how she had died.

Except, thanks to Agent Hanson's investigative zeal, I now know that she died even harder than was first imagined.

'This is such a cold place,' my mother said, looking around the visiting section of the prison and rubbing her hands together. 'Do you get cold at night, dear?' She seemed so out of place surrounded by concrete and bars. If you can imagine Marian Cunningham from *Happy Days* sitting in a German POW camp then you have some idea what it was like. She just didn't fit there. It was almost like the air itself drew back from her.

I smiled at her—attempting reassurance, but only half-heartedly. 'It's okay, Mom, we have plenty of blankets.'

My father sat beside her, but didn't speak. He was a large, gruff-looking man, with a thick white moustache that was a leftover from his wartime stint in the navy. He'd grown the moustache when he was nineteen, and the only thing that had changed over the years was that it had got progressively whiter. He had the wrinkled brown skin and callused hands of a man who has worked the land all his life.

'Your sister wanted me to tell you she was thinking

113

of you in her prayers,' said my mother. The mention of my sister put a painful weight on my chest. Sarah and I had always had a good relationship. She'd written to me a couple of times in Bedford, but I'd never quite got around to replying to her. Now it seemed I never would.

'Tell her I said thanks, would you?'

'Of course, dear,' my mother said. Her eyes misted over and she instinctively reached out for my hand. Her fingers hit the steel mesh and she self-consciously pulled her arm back. 'It's so cold,' she said.

'Stop *fussing*, Noelene,' muttered my father. 'Can't you see the boy's not cold?'

My mother turned to him as if she was going to say something, but then she seemed to lose whatever it was. Instead she looked down at the handkerchief in her lap that she was slowly screwing into a tight little ball.

'I'm okay, Mom. Really.'

She looked up at me and smiled quickly, but then her eyes filled with tears and she looked back down at her handkerchief.

'We're not staying anymore,' my father said to me.

'Okay.'

'It's too hard on your mother,' he said, 'and it's too hard on me. I can't watch the parents of those poor girls stand up there in court and talk about their pain. I can't do that.'

I nodded. I couldn't think of anything I could say to him.

'I know that's wrong,' he continued, 'but I'm just not strong enough to do it.'

'It's not wrong, Dad,' I said.

'*Don't you tell me what's wrong*,' he barked. My mother jumped and the guard looked over.

'I'm s-sorry,' I stuttered at him.

He looked down at his big farmer's hands. 'It *is* wrong. I have a share of all this, your mother and I both do, and it's weak of me that I can't sit here and take what's mine.'

'This is *not* your fault,' I said as I leaned forward on the small desk that lay between us. '*None* of this is your fault.'

He shook his head slowly, and there was a sadness in his eyes that almost stopped my heart. 'You don't understand, Simon,' he said, 'because you're not a parent. But when you make a child and send him out into the world, you carry a share of all that he does, for better or worse. And what we carry from now until the day we die is the knowledge that it was our son who did those terrible things to all those girls.'

There was so much I wanted to tell him, but I kept my mouth shut. I had no more choice in that than he did.

'I love you,' he said. 'You're my son, and nothing can ever undo that, but the things you did to those girls . . . ' He curled his hands into silent fists. 'If there was some way I could stop myself from loving you I would.'

'I'm . . . I'm so sorry,' was all I could manage.

'Don't waste your apologies on me, son,' he said, and his voice broke. A single tear rolled down his cheek. 'You'd best save those for God. Come *on*, Noelene.' His chair sounded like a scream on the linoleum floor as he stood.

'We love you, honey,' my mother said. Tears were running freely down her cheeks now.

'*Come on, Noelene,*' my father commanded. She looked at me one last time, all those years of hope and love crammed into that final moment.

My father didn't look back. It was not his style.

115

46

'What's wrong?' Wendall asked.

'Nothing.' It was night-time, and I'd been writing for an hour.

'Can't be nothing in a place like this. It always has to be something.'

I sighed. 'I was thinking about my family.'

Wendall chuckled. 'That'll do it.'

'I haven't seen my parents since the trial.'

There was a creak of bedsprings as Wendall sat up. 'You feeling a little homesick, Simon?'

'Don't screw with me, Wendall, I'm not in the mood.'

'I'm not, swear to God.'

'I don't know if your word carries much weight with God, Wendall.'

'Answer the question, Simon. You homesick?'

I paused, trying to figure out what his game was. Then I decided I was too tired to give a damn. 'Yeah, I guess I am.'

'What do you miss, Simon? Clean sheets? Your mom's apple pie? Watching your sister get undressed?'

'Forget it.'

'Okay, I'm sorry. It's a serious question, though— what do you miss?'

I thought for a moment. 'I guess I miss the smells the most.'

'Such as?'

'I miss the smell of the house when I woke up in the morning. Coffee and eggs. That's what my father has for breakfast every day. It was always the first thing that would tell me I was awake, even before I opened my eyes.' Wendall said nothing. 'And I miss

116

the smell of the farm.'

'You miss horseshit?'

I grinned. 'You're not from the country, are you, Wendall?'

He snorted. 'I did my time in the boonies, but I'm a city boy at heart.'

'The country doesn't smell of horseshit, Wendall, it smells clean. It smells of hay and living things.'

'You sound like an infomercial for an air-freshener.'

'It sure smells a whole lot better than this place.'

Wendall inhaled deeply. 'I love the smell of this place,' he said.

'It stinks in here, Wendall.'

'That's no stink, that's nectar. The rich aroma of sweat and fear. You just gotta love that.'

'You are one sick puppy, Wendall.'

'Apparently,' he said, and chuckled again.

'Do you ever miss your family?'

'I don't think about them much.'

'How come?'

'We pretty much went our separate ways a long time ago now.'

'You got any brothers or sisters?'

'A little sister.'

I put down my notebook and pen. This was further into Wendall's life than I'd ever been before. 'How much younger?'

'She's four years younger than me.'

'You know where she is now?'

'I got an idea.'

'Don't you want to see her?'

'Nope.'

I sat up on my bunk and leaned in close to the bars. 'How come, Wendall? Maybe she might want to see you.'

117

'I don't think she's gonna want to see me. Not after all that happened.'

I didn't want to push him too far, but I did want to know. 'So what happened?'

He laughed. 'All kinds of crazy shit, Simon, all kinds of crazy shit.'

'Do you know what she's doing now?'

'Oh, yeah,' he said. 'Turns out my little sister did all right for herself. Got married, got a little home in the suburbs—she bought the whole deal. Only shame is she lost the whole thing because of me.'

'You mean because of your convictions?'

Wendall laughed again. 'Nope, not because of that. She lost it all because of who I am.'

I stared at the wall between us, as if just the force of my curiosity would help me to see him. 'I don't understand.'

'It's okay, Simon. We got time.'

'I've got about forty-six days, Wendall.'

I heard his bunk creak, 'Like I said, we got time.'

I thought of trying to keep him talking, but in the end decided against it. 'Night, Wendall.'

'Night, Simon.'

And I went back to writing in my tatty little notebook.

47

Milly came for the first time the night after Juliette watched me with the prostitute in our cellar. It took me a long time to fall asleep, and when I finally did she was waiting.

I was sitting in the middle of a road in the darkness,

trees lining either side. I was aware of movement in the trees, but it was slow and liquid, not the movement of solid things. It was as if the darkness was a river flowing through the woods. At first it was soothing to watch, but gradually I began to feel more and more disturbed. I felt the coldness seeping into my bones.

I wanted to move off the road, but even if I could there was nowhere to go. Trees on one side, trees on the other, and road between the two. I tried to move, but my legs and arms were numb. I tried tilting my body over, so I could at least drag myself along the ground, but I was helpless.

I heard soft footsteps behind me, bare skin on the cold tar of the road. I longed to turn my head, to see what was creeping up on me from the blackness in the trees, but I could do nothing. My neck ached.

And then I felt her hand on my shoulder. I opened my mouth to scream, but there was nothing, no air to make it work.

You don't need to be afraid of me, she said. It was a young woman's voice.

I turned and there she was. I knew it would be her. Milly was standing at the edge of the trees looking at me, naked apart from a torn white shirt that hung off one shoulder. Her skin was so pale she almost seemed to glow in the blackness.

I need to show you, Simon.

'But . . . but you're lost.'

Milly's voice drifted over the cold road: *I was never lost, Simon. Come.* She turned and walked back into the woods. I tried to speak, but then I was in the forest with her, following her through the thick underbrush.

We walked for a time, and it could have been minutes or it could have been days. In my dreams time seems to follow different rules. At last we came out onto a small dirt road.

She turned to me, and we were face to face, almost touching. I could see a fine film of dirt covering her skin. It was crusted on her eyes, but she didn't blink.

There, she whispered, and I was dimly aware that she was pointing at something.

I turned to look and saw an old sign pointing down an even more overgrown road. The sign said 'Porter's No. 1'.

That's where you'll find the truth, she whispered.

I looked back at her, and this time her face was horribly deformed. The left side was missing, only a bloody pulverized mess remaining. *How far will you go, Simon? How far down that road?*

I tried to say something, but I didn't know how to make my mouth move. The words were there, bursting to get out, but my mouth simply refused to respond.

And then she was gone, and I was standing under the sign, looking down the shadowy road that was Porter's No. 1. I felt the current of the night pushing at me, flowing around me and down the little dark track. I knew I didn't want to go down there; I didn't know why, I just knew I didn't want to.

I started to struggle, to push back against the current. It was hard to breathe, and I felt my feet being dragged along the small track as the current picked up speed. I thrashed at the thick air, desperately trying to save myself, grabbing at a branch that came away wet and rotten in my hands. I looked down into the shadows, and saw a pale oval shape come into view, like a face coming up from the bottom of the sea. I closed my eyes and screamed as the darkness rushed into me.

48

In the movies people always wake from nightmares in a dramatic way. They invariably sit bolt upright in bed, covered in sweat, and panting. But you and I know it doesn't happen like that in real life. In real life there's a slow transition from dreaming to waking. A kind of consciousness limbo, where you're not quite asleep and not quite awake.

And that's the most frightening part of all, because your body is awake, and it reacts even though your mind's still not quite there yet. It's the slide between sleeping and waking that's the worst.

So it was for me. In that moment my body was in our bed, but my mind was still out there on Porter's No. 1, out there in the dark with that white face floating up at me.

'What's wrong?' Juliette asked from beside me, her voice still thick with sleep.

'Nothing,' I muttered, 'it was nothing,' and I think I was speaking to myself more than her. I glanced around the dim room not even knowing what I was looking for. Maybe it was Milly.

'Bad dream, baby?' Juliette mumbled.

'Yeah.' I shook my head to clear the dream away. 'Just a bad dream. Go back to sleep.'

'Uh-huh,' she said and rolled over.

I lay there for a while, completely awake, listening to the sounds of the house moving around me. I'd had a bad dream. That was all. Bad dreams happen, I told myself. It means nothing.

Except Milly's watch had somehow ended up wedged down the back of our car. Milly's watch looking like it had been wrenched from her wrist.

And a picture suddenly filled my mind. Our car, parked deep in the woods. The trunk is open. A pale arm is being dragged out the back in hitches and starts—a dead body is an obscenely heavy thing for just one person. As it slides out the back the watch-strap catches on the lip of the tire cover. The arm jerks once, then twice, as the killer tugs at the body to pull it free. The strap gives, wrenched apart just below where the band joins the body of the watch. The little gold watch slides down into the tire well and the body is pulled free of the car in a final, quick, uncontrolled dump.

And one more picture right on top of the last. Juliette taking off her muddy boots when she got back from her trip to Sauvarign. Boots that looked like she'd just walked a mile down an old muddy road.

Porter's No. 1.

I couldn't sleep; there was too much rattling around inside me. I slid quietly out of bed and left the room. It was cold, so I took my robe from the back of the bedroom door. The house was quiet and dark. At the end of the hallway I paused, almost like my being there was an accident. Then without really thinking I opened the cellar door and flipped on the light. I could see the green carpet Juliette had put down, and the cot. The stairs felt cold on my bare feet as I descended into the small dark space.

I stood for a moment, looking at the cot and think-ing about the girl. When I bent down and sniffed I could still smell her sex on it. I lay down on the cot, under the single bare light, and remembered what it had felt like to have her. She was so young and firm. Just lying there thinking of her made me hard again.

It was easier, you see? Thinking about fucking that girl while Juliette watched, thinking about how she smelt, how she felt as I slid inside her. It was easier than thinking about Milly.

So I jerked myself off, down there in our dark little cellar—clinging to the memory of the girl, and hiding from the things Milly had shown me in the dream.

And when it was over—when I'd grunted, and spat myself all over the thin mattress of the cot—Milly was waiting again. That's the thing with sex, when you're in it, you feel complete, but when it's gone, the emptiness is even more complete.

I lay there, panting, and staring up at the bulb. Empty.
How far will you go, Simon? How far down that road?

I saw myself as if I was standing watching. Lying on the cot, jerking off where I'd had sex with a girl who couldn't have been more than seventeen, a child no matter how you dressed her up. Someone's daughter. And I'd fucked this child while my wife watched me do it.

'What is *happening* to me?' I asked the darkness.

And if anything in that cellar heard me, it gave no answer.

49

I woke the next day in our bed and she was already gone, her side cold and empty. The car was gone as well. I ate breakfast by myself.

And I felt very alone.

After eating I caught the bus to school.

'Hey, Mr Chance,' chirped the driver when I got on. Her name was Anabel—at least that was what her little plastic name tag said, and she'd never bothered to contradict it.

'Hey, Anabel.'

'Wife got the car again today?'

'Yeah,' I said, fumbling the change into the dish. There was a vicious little clatter as the machine printed out the ticket.

'What does she do? During the day, I mean?'

I looked down at Anabel's smiling bus driver's face. I remember noticing the hair on her upper lip and thinking she needed to wax.

'I don't know what she does,' I finally said.

'Yup,' she replied, 'I'm the same with my husband. I got no idea what that bum does all day.' She laughed, the bus hissed, and we were away.

I got through another day at school by the skin of my teeth. I felt sick in the stomach and thin as paper. A couple of times I caught myself snapping at students. Mostly I just didn't notice anybody. Somehow I got through.

I saw the car in the drive as I walked up the street. She was home. I had decided there would be no more dancing around it; tonight we would talk about Milly's watch, and I would ask her about that day she said she drove up to Sauvarign.

'Juliette,' I called out at the front door. 'We need to talk.'

'Hey, honey,' she said as she appeared in the doorway to the living room. 'How was your day?'

'We need to talk, Juliette.'

She smiled and came down the hall. She looks like she glides when she walks. 'What can be so important that it can't wait for a kiss?'

'I need to talk to you about Milly Brown.'

'What about Milly?'

A movement behind Juliette caught my eye. It was Carol Keenan. Standing in our hallway looking at me.

'What about Milly, Mr Chance?' she asked, her face tense. 'Have they found her?'

All I could do was look at Carol, my mouth hanging open, as Juliette smiled at me.

'Yes, Simon,' Juliette said, 'what about Milly?'

50

She knew I knew—Juliette, I mean. That's the only sense I can make of it. She knew I knew. She wasn't afraid though, she knew me too well by then to be afraid. She knew me better than I ever will.

'Have they found Milly, Mr Chance?' Carol asked again.

'Uh . . .' I stammered.

'Come on,' said Juliette, 'spit it out, whatever it is.'

It was the way she said it, the tone of her voice; she knew I knew.

'Uh . . . no, I just wanted to tell you there's still been no word.'

'Really?' said Juliette and she touched my arm lightly. 'It sounded like you had something more on your mind.'

'No,' I said, looking at her, 'that's all.'

'Okay, then. Why don't you come into the living room?' she said as she turned and walked back down the hall. 'By the way, do you know Carol?' she said over her shoulder. 'She's one of the girls from school.'

'Yes,' I said. 'Hello, Carol.' My mouth felt dry.

'Hi, Mr Chance.' Carol smiled. 'I thought when you came in like that you must have heard something—about Milly, I mean.'

'No, sorry, Carol. My wife has been worried about

125

her just like everyone else.'

'Why don't you two come through?' Juliette called out from the living room.

There were two cups on the coffee table, both empty. Juliette and Carol had obviously been talking for a while.

'Carol is interested in some part-time work cleaning for us, Simon.'

'Really,' I said, looking at Juliette.

'I met Mrs Chance at the mall and she said that you'd been looking for someone to do a couple of hours cleaning a week.'

'It really was very fortunate,' said Juliette. 'We just got talking and it seems Carol's been looking for a job to make some extra money. One thing led to another, and here we are. Isn't that lucky?'

'Yes,' I said, 'very lucky. But I'm sure that Carol is much too busy to be cleaning house for us.'

'No, really,' Carol said. 'I'd really like to. I can use the extra money.'

'Yes, honey,' Juliette said. 'Carol's trying to raise funds to go on a Christian leadership camp in Hawaii next October. Isn't that nice?'

'Yes,' I said, feeling sick. 'That's great.'

She wouldn't be going to her camp in Hawaii. Come next October I'd be executed at the Garden for her murder. The camp would go on without her.

'So shall I show you around, Carol?' Juliette asked.

'Sure,' Carol said, getting to her feet.

I sat in the living room and listened to them moving around the house, talking and laughing. After a few minutes they came back in.

'Simon, would you mind giving Carol a ride home? I don't want her out walking the streets at this time of day, what with everything that's happened. Besides, the radio said it was going to rain tonight.'

'Oh no, said Carol, 'I'll be fine walking. I don't want to be a bother.'

'It's not a bother, sweetie,' said Juliette, touching Carol's cheek with her hand. 'Is it, Simon?'

I felt as if I were caught in a molasses pond. 'No, of course not.'

'So I'll see you at the end of the week then, Carol?'

'Sure thing, and thank you.'

Juliette smiled at her. 'Why, you're most welcome.' She walked us both to the door. 'Don't be long now.' she whispered as she kissed me on the cheek. 'I have a surprise for you in the cellar.'

Juliette's breath changes when she's aroused. It develops a deep musky aroma. Honey and sex.

I smelt it when she leaned in to kiss me.

51

'I hope you don't mind dropping me home, Mr Chance,' said Carol as we drove through the quiet streets of Bedford. There had been a noticeable emptying since Milly had disappeared. I guess that's probably a pretty primitive response. When the wolf takes one of the tribe we all draw closer to the fire.

'It's really no problem, Milly,' I said without thinking. Carol glanced at me sharply as I grunted. 'Sorry, Carol. I don't know why I said that.'

She smiled sympathetically. 'It's okay, Mr Chance. Everyone's worried about her.'

'Did you know her?'

'I do know her.'

'Yes, of course,' I said. 'I didn't mean to imply she

was . . . you know.'

'I know everyone thinks she's dead, but I just can't bring myself to think that yet.'

'Nobody wants to think that.'

'We aren't friends or anything. I mean, I know her, you kind of know everybody at school, but we aren't like close friends. She's a nice person though—at least she's always nice to me.'

There was a moment of silence as we drove along. 'You don't have to take this job, you know,' I said. 'My wife can sometimes be a little pushy.'

'No, it's okay, really. I need the money. Besides, Mrs Chance seems like a pretty nice person to me.'

'Yes, I suppose she is.'

'This is me just here,' she said, pointing to a tidy looking house on our right. I stopped the car and she opened the door. 'Thanks for the ride, Mr Chance.'

'You're welcome, Carol. I meant it about not having to take the job if you don't want to.'

She smiled. 'Really, it's fine. I'm grateful.'

'Well, okay then.' I wanted to tell her not to come back; I wanted to, but I didn't. I wish I had. I just didn't seem to know how to say it. I choose to believe that because the alternative is too horrible to contemplate.

She smiled a final time and was gone.

As I pulled away from the kerb the first spots of rain began to fall on the windshield.

52

It was dark by the time I got home. There were no lights on in the house, except for a single light from the open cellar door.

'Juliette.'

Nothing.

'Juliette.'

This time there was the sound of giggling from the cellar. Not Juliette, a young woman's voice.

'Juliette.'

I didn't want to go down there. Every time I did less of me came out. Except, of course, that wasn't the whole truth. There was another part of me that *did* want to sink down through the floor. This other part very much wanted to see what dark wonders Juliette had conjured up from the earth this time.

They were down there together, lying on the cot. Juliette and Stacy. The girl was wearing a white T-shirt and jeans, and Juliette was kissing her, a deeply passionate kiss. Juliette was silent but I could hear the girl moaning. Coming down the stairs I felt reality falling away from me like a discarded skin, something that was no longer of any functional use. I walked over to the cot and looked down at them.

Sex and death. I see it all so clearly now, but then I saw only what I wanted to see.

Juliette pulled herself away and looked up at me. 'Do you want her, Simon?'

The girl lay there panting. She opened her eyes and smiled. She was glazed and sluggish, obviously stoned. Somehow that made me want her even more. It was as if Juliette and I were alone in the world with this girl. She was ours.

Somewhere inside me, a long way down, there was another voice, very faint, trying desperately to make me understand something. 'Juliette,' I said numbly, 'we . . . we need to talk.'

She stood and put her arms around me. I could smell sex on her breath; hers, the girl's. She kissed me and I tasted them both. 'Do this thing for me,' she said, 'and I'll tell you everything you want to know.' She kissed me again. 'Everything.'

She took Stacy by the hand and led her over to a hook hanging from a low beam in the ceiling. She took some handcuffs from the pocket of her jeans and slid them onto the girl's wrists. When they were on she kissed her again, a long lingering kiss. Then she spoke to her softly. 'I want my husband to rape you. Is that all right?'

The girl smiled and nodded slowly.

'And I want you to fight him, to play as if it's real—okay, sweetie?' The girl nodded again. 'Good,' smiled Juliette. She lifted the girl's arms up and looped the chain of the handcuffs over the hook. Then she walked back to the cot and sat down.

I looked at her. 'I can't do this, Juliette.' I felt lost. The darkness had me in its grip again.

'Do this for me, Simon. Do it and I'll tell you everything.'

'I . . . I can't.'

'Please, mister,' the girl said, sounding like a bad porn actress. 'Please don't hurt me, I'm all alone.'

'Stop it,' I said to her.

'Please don't fuck me with that great big thing of yours.'

It was disgusting listening to her. '*Stop it*,' I snapped.

She squealed and thrust her chest out towards me. 'Oh *please* don't fuck me, mister.'

'*Shut up.*'

'Do it, Simon,' whispered Juliette. 'Hurt her.'

The girl moaned.

'*Shut up.*'

'Do it!'

130

'Oh pleeease, mister.'

'Shut the hell up!'

'Do it!'

The girl moaned again, and inside of me something gave way.

I strode across to her and slapped her hard across the face. She gasped. I grabbed her T-shirt and ripped it off her, then spun her round, grabbing her roughly and forcing her jeans down. She screamed as I pushed myself into her.

And, God help me, the more she screamed the harder I pushed. And pushed. And pushed.

53

When it was over I held onto the girl, panting. Stacy was still moaning. And just as before, once the sex was gone—without the hot press of lust—there was only truth, and the truth was an ugly thing. Standing there with my pants around my ankles, holding onto the girl, the truth was an ugly thing.

Juliette came up behind me and kissed me. 'Thank you,' she whispered in my ear as she pressed herself against me.

I pushed myself away from the girl and staggered back over to the stairs as I pulled up my trousers, then sat down heavily. My legs were shaking and I felt as if I'd been clubbed.

The girl groaned. 'He hurt me,' she mumbled.

'Shhhh,' said Juliette, and she reached up to undo the handcuffs. 'You were wonderful. You really are very talented.'

'But he hurt me,' the girl mumbled again. 'You said

it would just be playing.'

'I know,' said Juliette, helping the girl over to the cot. 'But I have something to make it stop hurting.'

The girl seemed to rouse herself at that. 'Can I have it now?'

Juliette smiled as she lay the girl down on the cot. 'Yes. Would you like me to do it?'

'Mmmmm,' moaned the girl. 'Please . . . '

Juliette took a small black leather bag from under the stairs. She unzipped it and laid out the contents on the girl's stomach.

'Cold,' muttered the girl.

'Don't worry.' Juliette lent down and kissed the girl's stomach. 'You'll be warm very soon.' She took out a rubber strap and tied it around the girl's upper arm. Then she shook the contents of a small plastic packet onto a spoon and heated it with a lighter. When the powder was liquefied she used a syringe to suck it up.

I watched it all with a sick fascination.

The girl moaned as Juliette pushed the plunger down and emptied it into her arm. She sighed once, and then was quiet.

Juliette packed up the little pouch, then looked over at me. 'She'll sleep for hours now.'

I followed her back upstairs to our bedroom. I felt tired and flat, as if all the human feeling had been squeezed from me.

'We need to talk,' I said as she undressed me.

'Tomorrow,' she said. 'Sleep now, and tomorrow we talk.'

I was too drained to argue.

54

I woke up later that night and the house was quiet and dark. Juliette wasn't there, and when I reached over to her side of the bed it was cold. I thought of Stacy, lying down in the darkness of the cellar, alone. And I was suddenly afraid.

Taking my robe from the back of the door, I crept down the hall to the cellar door. It was slightly open and moaning came from inside. It was an eerie sound in the darkness—human, but somehow inhuman at the same time, the sound of a soul being pulled from one place to another. I felt the hackles on the back of my neck bristling.

I wasn't sure I wanted to see what was making that noise, but I didn't seem to be able to stop myself either.

I edged up to the door and very slowly eased it open.

Juliette was with the girl on the cot. Stacy looked unconscious. She'd been stripped naked and the blankets were pulled back. Juliette moved over the girl's body like a lizard, licking her as if she were food. In the dim light Juliette looked like something from a horror movie, some kind of reptilian vampire, moaning and whispering to herself.

The door was caught by a draft and made a small creak. Juliette's head whipped round and she looked directly at me. I felt my breath catch in my throat. Her eyes seemed to almost glow in the dark cellar as she looked up at the door. I pulled myself further into the shadows of the hall, hoping she hadn't seen me.

She raised herself from the girl and peered up the stairs into the darkness. Her cheeks were streaked with tears, and I realized that what I'd first thought was a sexual moaning was in fact the sound of Juliette crying. She was perfectly still, probing the darkness as the moments stretched out. Then she turned back to the girl, and the moaning started again.

I watched her in horror, unable to stop myself. Although perhaps it would be more honest to say that I didn't want to stop myself.

A movement from the darkness behind Juliette caught my eye. I could just make out the shape of a person standing in the shadows, rocking from side to side. Juliette didn't seem to notice. When the person shuffled forward into the light and I saw who it was, I felt my heart squeezed almost to a stop.

Milly Brown stood gently swaying beside the cot. She ignored Juliette, instead she looked up at me. She was just as she had been in my dream, wearing her torn white shirt, and covered in filth like she'd been dragged from the earth.

How far? she mouthed at me silently.

I fell back from the door against the wall, no longer caring if Juliette heard me. It was too much. I fled back to the bedroom and, like a child, threw myself under the sheets as if that would somehow keep the monsters away, cowering there, shaking uncontrollably.

Then the door of the bedroom opened and I heard dragging footsteps come across the carpet and up to the very edge of the bed. A cold hand touched me on the shoulder, and I nearly screamed. It stayed there for a few moments, then was gone. I heard the bedroom door close.

To this day I don't know if that cold hand belonged to Juliette, or to Milly.

55

Juliette didn't return to bed that night. I found her the next morning sitting at the kitchen table drinking coffee. She smiled when I came in. She looked beautiful, and the dark spells of the night seemed to have passed.

'Stacy left an hour ago,' she said, and her eyes twinkled.

The image of Juliette lying on the girl last night came back to me. Lying on her and licking her like food. 'I didn't hear her go,' I said.

'I told her to leave quietly so she wouldn't wake you.'

'She looked like she was going to sleep for about two days last time I saw her. How come she got up so early?'

'I didn't want her here when you woke up.'

'Why?'

'Because,' she said as if it were obvious, 'she's not part of the day, she's only part of the night.'

'Was she all right when she left?'

'Why wouldn't she be?' There was something in Juliette's tone that was almost hurt.

'I don't know, I'm just asking if she was all right.'

Juliette looked at me. 'She was fine, Simon. I paid her and she left. End of story.'

I sat down at the kitchen table across from her. 'What's happening to us, Juliette?'

'What do you mean?'

I shook my head. 'No, don't do this to me. You said that if I . . . if I did that to the girl you'd talk to me.'

Juliette smiled. 'Did you like her?'

'I don't understand what's happening to us, Juliette.'

'There's nothing happening to us.'

'Last night I fucked that girl while you watched me. Worse than that, I hurt her, and you *liked* it.'

She tilted her head quizzically. 'Are you saying *you* didn't?'

'I don't like hurting people.'

'You did last night.'

'I did what you wanted, but I didn't enjoy it.'

She took a sip of her coffee. 'Liar.'

'I'm not lying.'

Juliette laughed. 'Oh, Simon, the only thing about a man that doesn't lie is his penis.'

'Why are you talking like this, Juliette? What's happened to you?'

'You wanted me to talk, so I'm talking.'

'What about the watch I found in the back of the car?'

She smiled. 'Ahhh, the watch.'

'What about it, Juliette? Where did it come from?'

'Why is it so important to you, Simon?'

I hit the table with my fist, hard enough to slop her coffee. '*Damn it, Juliette*,' I bellowed, 'just *tell* me!'

'Some things are better left alone, Simon, some things are better left where they fall.'

'Where did it come from? I have to know.'

She looked at me then, a long searching look. 'But *why*? What do you think I can tell you about that watch that could possibly make you feel better?'

I slowly shook my head. 'I don't know.'

'Do you think if I told you about that watch it would make a difference, Simon? Do you really think that anything we talk about here is going to change anything?'

'I . . . I don't know.'

She stood and came round behind me. 'Let it be,'

she said as she bent down to kiss me on the back of the neck. 'Somebody lost their watch, that's all there is to it.'

I could smell her, perfume and coffee.

'I just . . . ' But I couldn't seem to finish it. I didn't want to finish it.

'Let it be, Simon.' She kissed me again. 'I'm going to have a shower.'

I sat there in the kitchen with her kiss drying on my neck and the smell of her still in the air.

And I tried to let it be.

The only problem was, it wouldn't leave me be.

56

While she was in the shower I took the keys for the car and left the house. I drove down to the service station, telling myself I was just getting out of the house to clear my head. But when I walked in to Hatfield's Automotive to pay for the gas I'd just pumped I knew that the road maps were right next to the counter. I'd been buying my gas there for months. So I stood at the counter looking at the maps, and trying to pretend to myself that the whole thing was an accident.

'You right there, Mr Chance?' It was Billy Hatfield who asked the question, the twenty-something son of Brian Hatfield who owned the place. Billy had that born-here-gonna-die-here look written all over him. Just like his dad. Born-here-gonna-die-here was a Hatfield tradition.

'Uh, yeah,' I said.

'Just the gas?'

'Yeah. Well, actually . . . how much for one of these

maps here, Billy?'

'Let me just see,' he said, flipping through a stack of oily pages sitting by the cash register. 'Umm, that one right there is five ninety-five.'

I dithered for a moment, trying not to make a decision. But Billy was a busy man. 'So, you want one?' he asked.

I looked at him. 'What?'

'A map.'

'I guess so.' I gave Billy his money and went back to my car, then turned left out of the service station, heading for the country. I told myself I just needed to get away from the crowd for a bit, find some clear space in which to think. By now I was getting good at telling myself lies.

The prosecution made a big deal at the sentencing hearing out of me buying that map. They said I needed the map because I wanted to find the body again, and backed that up with testimony from an FBI expert who said that serial killers often go back to visit their dead victims. The prosecutor said this showed the callousness of my attitude to the girls, and the depth of the depravity of my crimes. I guess the jury bought that because here I am.

Herbert Forest lies ten miles due north of Bedford. Some people go out there and hike, but mostly people just ignore it. Acres of trees can be pretty boring to hike through—seen one tree, seen 'em all.

I pulled over to the side of the road as soon as the forest came into view. I knew why I'd come out here. Milly had asked me a question, and I'd come to answer it. I sat there for a few moments, just looking at the rolling green hills. What kind of secrets could a place like that hold?

All kinds of secrets, the forest seemed to whisper back.

I picked up the county map and turned to the index, flipping through until I found the P section. And of course there it was, right between Portell and Potter, shown on the map as a little dotted line that snaked off the main access road and down into a gully. It shouldn't have existed at all—dream roads don't flow into the real world. Turns out that sometimes real roads flow into dreams though.

Porter's No. 1.

The map key said that a dotted line indicated a minor road that was only passable with an off-road vehicle when it had been raining.

It took me a while to find it—the forestry roads weren't very well signposted—but after a few wrong turns I finally found the main access road that meandered through the forest to where I had to go. In any other circumstances it might have been a pleasant trip, winding down through the trees, but not today.

Milly had asked me how far I would go. I was about to find out.

I saw the signpost before I could read it. It didn't matter, I recognized the scene from my dream. I'd stood here with Milly and looked down into the darkness. In the dream it was the darkness itself that had pushed me down Porter's No. 1; I realized as I stepped out of the car that the only thing that could push me down there in daylight hours would be the strength of my own will.

For a moment I listened to the deep silence of the woods around me. It gave me some comfort to know that the silence would last long after I was gone. No matter what I found down at the bottom of Porter's No. 1. And no matter what found me.

From the map it looked like the road couldn't have been much longer than a couple of miles, although trudging down it with the mud sucking away at my boots it felt like a much longer walk. Sunlight filtered through the trees and fluttered across my face in small warm bursts. Strangely, I remembered all the good times as I walked, the times with Juliette when it had seemed the sun would never stop shining. I remembered her laugh, and the sounds as she made love to me. I remembered the hopes and dreams that had all seemed so real.

I felt such love for her as I trudged down that muddy little road. I knew where I was going—we all know what's waiting for me at the end of Porter's No. 1, you probably figured it out straight away—but I didn't let myself think about that. I wanted these last few moments of just walking in the woods and thinking of Juliette. Even now, sitting in this little cold cell and writing in my notebook, I can remember what that was like. It was the sweetest, saddest thing.

I saw her from a long way off, a flash of white at the end of the road. Her shirt glowed in the trees like a lighthouse warning passers-by of rocks and ruin. I became aware of her slowly. First just as a color. Then as a shape. Last of all as a smell. At some point I stopped thinking about walking. My legs carried me to her of their own accord.

Milly Brown lay face down in the mud, her arms and legs splayed out, and she was naked except for a torn white shirt. Her bone-white skin was stained here and there by large gray splotches. A broken tree branch stuck out from between her legs. She had been impaled on it. Even though there had been a lot of rain, it was obvious there had also been a lot of blood.

I dropped to my knees beside her. I should have felt something, looking down at poor dead Milly, but instead I felt nothing. Absolutely nothing. I was oddly disconnected from any kind of emotional reaction. I tried. I actually tried to make myself cry, but there was nothing. Kneeling in the mud beside that poor girl's body, deep in the silent woods, I felt nothing.

I sat like that for a long time, just looking at her. The stink of her was terrible, but even that seemed to be at a distance. I was aware of it, but not really touched by it.

Her body was covered in little marks and scratches, and blood and mud had matted her hair together in thick cords. I looked down at the branch between her legs. It had torn a great ragged hole in her and I could see small white things squirming in the raw flesh. Maggots were cleaning Milly up.

I thought of Patrick Brown, of that day I'd seen him standing staring at the milk in the grocery store. Patrick Brown who'd looked like a scream taken on human form. Milly had been lying here the whole time with the dirt in her face and the maggots inside her. Lying out here alone in the woods as her father and I stood staring.

I looked at her hands. There were long furrows carved into the ground by her fingers. And then I realized that she'd done that. Milly had clawed desperately at the ground as the branch was shoved inside her. She would have screamed and begged as she died. The pain and fear were beyond imagining.

Someone started to scream, far away. I turned in slow motion, trying to see where the sound came from. And then the scream caught up with me and it all became real.

And I felt.

In the mud and the blood, I felt it all.

The sun was going down when I finally came back to myself. The shadows had crept into the trees around me, and darkness wasn't far behind. I couldn't bring myself to look at Milly; it felt cowardly to leave her there, naked and alone in the darkness in a place that I was afraid to stay in myself.

'I'm sorry,' I whispered. 'Please believe me, I'm so sorry.'

I made myself look at her then, for what reason I don't know. Maybe forgiveness? Maybe I wanted this poor, dead, violated girl to forgive me for my weakness and my fear?

Milly was silent though. If it was forgiveness I was looking for there was none to be found.

There was one thing I did for her. I reached over and pulled the tree branch out from between her legs. There was a moment of resistance, and then it came free with a wet sucking sound. The stink was almost overpowering. I threw the branch aside and turned back to her. The hole the branch had left looked obscene. I couldn't stand the thought of her lying there open to the world like that, so I covered her with leaves.

'I'll tell them where you are,' I said to her. 'I won't leave you out here alone. I'll make sure you get home.'

I walked back up Porter's No. 1 feeling sick with grief—for poor Milly who'd died so terribly out here alone in the quiet trees, for her parents who would have to spend the rest of their lives being haunted by Milly's last moments, and for myself. Sick with grief at all that I'd lost when I finally went down to the end of Porter's No. 1.

How far, Milly had asked me, and I thought I'd answered her question. I thought I'd gone all the way down to the end of Porter's No. 1.

But I was as wrong about that as I've been wrong about so many things. The road I was on went a whole lot further than Porter's No. 1.

My visit with Milly in the forest was just a start.

58

I drove home in the darkness, not really thinking about where I was going. It didn't matter, I knew I'd eventually end up home again. The current only flowed one way now.

There were no lights on when I got home. The house was quiet and cold. I stripped off my muddy clothes and put them in the washing machine, then stood under the shower for a long time. Not thinking, just letting the water run over me.

'You should have let it be,' she said as I slipped into bed.

'I couldn't do that, Juliette.'

There was a long moment of silence as we both lay there.

'Where did you go?'

'I went to the forest.'

'And?'

'And I took a walk.'

She rolled over onto her side, facing me in the dark, her head resting on her arm. 'And what did you find?'

'I found a girl out in the woods.'

'Really? Was she pretty?'

I reached over and turned on the bedside light. It

hurt my eyes and I had to blink. Juliette kept looking at me, her pale blue eyes seeming perfectly adjusted to any light. She never had to blink.

'She might have been once,' I said, 'but not anymore. She was dead. Someone had shoved a tree branch so far inside her that she bled to death. I found her lying face down in the mud. She hadn't even been buried.'

Juliette just kept looking at me. She said nothing.

'Don't you have anything to say about that?'

'Like what?'

'Well, like who was it, just as a for instance.'

'I assumed you were talking about Milly.'

The whole conversation was bizarre. What we were talking about was bad enough, but the *how* was even worse.

'Why would you assume that, Juliette?'

'Who else would it be?'

'Did you go to Sauvarign three weeks ago, Juliette? There was mud all over your boots. As far as I know all the roads between here and Sauvarign are sealed.'

She tilted her head slightly. 'Are you sure you want to ask that question, Simon?'

Tears welled up in my eyes. 'To be honest, Juliette, I don't feel very sure about anything anymore. I used to be sure about some things, but now . . . now I don't feel sure about anything.'

'I asked you to leave it alone,' she said. 'Nothing good can come of this, Simon.'

I looked at her as the tears rolled down my cheeks. 'Oh, Juliette, I gave up on "good" days ago. Now I'd just settle for the truth.'

'Do you really want the truth?'

'Yes, Juliette, I really want the truth.'

She knelt beside me in the bed. She was naked, and

144

as she leaned in against me I could feel her warm, dry skin.

'I killed her,' she said.

Just like that.

I'd heard people talk about their heart breaking but I'd never really known what they meant. When Juliette told me she killed that girl, I actually felt my heart *tear*. Pain racked my body, great shooting bolts of pain that pushed me from the bed down onto the floor. I couldn't breathe, couldn't speak. Visions of Milly's bone-white skin flashed before me and the pain ravaged me again. It was immense. I curled up and screamed.

'Simon?' I heard her calling, but I was with Milly, with the dead girl in the forest. The dead girl who'd been raped with a tree branch.

'Simon? What's wrong?'

And then the tears found me, and all the pain poured out of me like a storm. I cried for a long, long time as she held me. Finally, when there was no more wet stuff left in me, I pulled myself back from the forest, back into our little house on the edge of town. We were both on the floor, Juliette sitting with my head cradled in her lap.

'Why?' I croaked.

She sighed. 'Why does anyone do anything?'

'Why did you kill her, Juliette? She was just a child.'

'Sometimes I . . . I feel lost.'

I slowly sat up and leaned back against the bed beside her. 'What do you mean, *lost*?'

'Being lost is the worst feeling, Simon.' Her voice sounded desperately empty in the small room.

'But why did you have to kill her, Juliette?'

'Because it's the only thing I know that makes it better. Because when they die I can breathe again.'

I heard the word and it squeezed me like a vice. '*They*? What do you mean *they*?' I turned to her and gripped her by the shoulders. 'What do you mean *they*? How many others have you killed?'

'I . . . I have to breathe, Simon. Can you understand that?'

'How many?'

'I have to sleep now,' she said, shaking herself free of my grip and then standing to get back into bed.

I reached up, grabbing her arm and pulling her around to face me. 'How many?'

'*I have to sleep*,' she screamed at me, droplets of spittle hitting me in the face. '*I have to fucking sleep*.'

I let her go as if she'd stung me. She jumped into bed and pulled the sheets over her head. 'I have to sleep,' I heard her whisper.

I looked at her shape beneath the blankets. I knew I should call the police. I knew that.

Instead I went and got a six-pack from the fridge, and sat with it in the living room, drinking in the dark. And after a while I went to sleep.

59

I woke up on the couch some time in the middle of the night. She was standing over me, looking down. I don't know how long she'd been there, but it frightened me to see her there in the dark.

'Juliette?'

'Shhhh.'

She lay down beside me. She was naked, and I could feel her skin against mine. The soft, warm thrust of her breasts against my chest. Her hands reaching for me. Her mouth. Her tongue.

'Love me,' she whispered.

I wanted to do the right thing, I've always wanted that, but I've had such a great deal of trouble figuring out exactly what the 'right thing' is. I kissed her back.

It was a desperate kind of love-making, as if we were trying to push back the dark with the strength of our coupling. I clung to her, and she to me.

And when we came, it felt like drowning.

60

Sitting here in jail, some forty-two days out from my execution date, it all feels a little unreal. Writing this down was supposed to be my way of telling the real story. But as I write, I wonder more and more how a story like this can possibly be real. I wonder how real people could do the things we did.

It must be real though; these walls are real, just like the steel bars that protect the world from me. The death chamber is real too. I haven't seen it but I can feel it, even from here.

The buckles that will strap me down onto the gurney are real.

All of it is.

61

This morning Gerald came in to tell me about the progress he's been making with my case. It didn't take long; everybody wants me dead. He looks a little thinner these days, and I worry that he's not sleeping as much as he should.

'You shouldn't fight this so hard, Gerald,' I said. 'You're starting to look very tired.'

'That's my job, Simon.'

'But I don't even want you to do this. I want it to happen.'

'The law says you have to have an attorney if they're going to kill you, and as long as I'm your attorney I'm going to fight to keep you alive.'

'Yeah, but why? Why do you even care, Gerald?'

He set down his pen and looked squarely at me, and for the first time I saw a glimpse of maturity in him that I'd missed up until then. 'Because killing is wrong, Simon. It was wrong for you to kill, but it's wrong for the state to kill you. You can't use one to justify the other.'

'How can you say that? How can you sit in this place with these people and say that?'

'I believe killing is wrong, Simon. That's why I took your case. I don't want my kids to grow up in a world where we say it's okay to kill people.' He pushed his spectacles back up onto his nose. 'And if the state kills you then that's exactly what we're saying—that you can kill people if you have a good enough reason. I don't think there's any reason that justifies taking the life of another human being.'

'What about your kids, Gerald? Would you kill for them?' I didn't want to be cruel, but I couldn't let that kind of naïveté go unpunished.

He sat there for a moment in silence. 'I'd kill to protect my children if I had to,' he finally said.

'No, no, any parent would do that. I mean, would you want to kill someone who'd killed your children?'

'No, I wouldn't.'

148

'I don't believe that.'

'You don't have to believe it, Simon. They're my beliefs, not yours.'

I don't know where it came from, but suddenly I felt the need to tear Gerald down from his moral high ground.

'And what if I'd killed your daughter, Gerald? What then?'

'I still wouldn't want to kill you, Simon. Now can we get back to the task?'

'This *is* the task, this is it right here.'

'No,' he said, 'the task is stopping the State from killing you.'

I laughed then, and I was surprised how mean it sounded. 'Now that's where you're wrong, Gerald. The real task is trying to decide if the State *should* kill me.'

'Please, Simon, can we just get back on track here?'

'Let's do that, then, let's get back on track. Have you seen the file on Milly Brown?'

'Yes, of course.'

'No, I mean have you really *seen* it?'

'What do you mean?'

'Have you let yourself really *see* it?'

'I've read the file, Simon.'

'Close your eyes.'

'What?' Gerald looked uneasy.

'It's okay, Gerald, I'm not going to do anything to you,' and that was both true and a lie in the same breath.

'What's the purpose of this?'

'I'm going to help you to see. Close your eyes.'

He looked at me as if he was going to say something, and then he closed his eyes.

'Good. Now picture a road leading down through

the forest, overgrown and muddy. Sunlight filters down through the trees in patches. It's quiet, peaceful.'

Gerald opened his eyes. 'We really need to do some work, Simon.'

'This *is* work, Gerald. Close your eyes, just for a few minutes, and then I'll do whatever you want. Deal?'

He looked at me and shook his head. Then he closed his eyes again.

'You can hear footsteps and voices. You see them approaching, a girl and her killer. The girl is naked except for a white shirt. She's been forced to strip before they started. The killer wanted her to know what was going to happen. She's crying and stumbling. The mud is soft, but it hides sharp stones that cut her feet. Soon they're bloody.

'The girl is pleading with her killer, all the usual things—not to hurt her, she won't tell, all that stuff. But the killer is unmoved by the girl's pleas, and occasionally pushes her to keep her moving.'

Gerald squirmed in his seat.

'And then they come to the end of the road. The girl turns to face her killer, knowing there's nowhere else to go. Her body shakes and she feels cold. She wishes for her mother. She wishes for her father's warm, protective arms. But there's no one here to protect her. She is alone in the worst kind of way, and she knows it.

'The killer tells her to kneel, facing away. She starts to sob now. The fear is almost overpowering. She doesn't want to die. She begs, but the killer simply repeats the command.

'So she kneels with her hands folded across her chest. She hears the sound of her killer's footsteps coming closer. She begins to pray, and here in this cold place she tries to think only of her mother's face.

'Then her vision explodes in a thousand stars as the hammer connects with her head. It fractures her skull and exposes her brain with a single blow. She collapses forward onto the ground. But she isn't dead yet—there's still a long, long way to go. Her vision is blurred, both from the blow and the blood. She's dimly aware of a cracking noise above her, the sound of someone breaking a branch from a tree. Then she feels her legs being pulled apart. She tries to speak, but her brain has been so damaged with the blow that she can only gurgle.

'And then the killer rams the branch up inside her. The pain is beyond imagining. She screams and screams. The branch is shoved in and out again and again. It tears her so far open that it ruptures her diaphragm, and punctures her lung.

'Can you see her, Gerald? Lying there clawing at the earth as the branch rips her open? Can you see her?'

'Stop it,' said Gerald, his voice tight.

'Look into her face as she dies there in the mud. See the agony as the killer rams that branch in and out of her. Imagine the horror of dying like that.' I dropped my voice just a notch, hardly recognizing it as my own. 'It's *your* daughter, Gerald. See your daughter lying there with that branch sticking out of her.'

Gerald's eyes flared open and he moaned, 'Oh, Jesus, *stop it*.'

'Lying there face down, her head smashed open, and dying in the worst kind of pain.'

'*Stop it.*' Gerald wailed as he pushed himself back from me, spilling the chair onto the floor with a sudden noisy clatter.

'What the fuck's all the noise?' someone further

151

down the block called out.

'See her, Gerald, your little girl, lying on the ground naked, her legs splayed out and that branch thrusting in and out of her as she claws at the mud with her fingernails.'

'*STOP IT!*'

'She's alive through all of it, screaming for her mother, screaming for her father.'

Gerald flung himself at the bars. '*GUARD!*'

'Watch her face as your little girl dies, Gerald. See the terror and the fear. Feel the horror of your little girl's death, feel the agony of being raped with a branch as thick as your arm.'

'*GUARD!*'

Then the guards were there, four of them. Andy Watson was first at the door. 'What the *fuck* is going on in here?' he demanded as he swung the door open.

Gerald collapsed out of the cell, sprawling onto the cold concrete of the walk. I stayed sitting quietly on my bunk.

'So what's the fucking story, Chance?' Andy demanded, his baton drawn and ready. The last one, Ralph Owens, was helping Gerald to his feet.

'Just talking with my lawyer, Mr Watson.'

'Like fuck you were,' Andy growled.

'The lawyer's okay, boss,' Owens called out from behind them.

Watson looked at me, and his eyes were hard, 'Don't fuck with me, Chance. You got six weeks left on earth, and it can be hard or it can be easy. Do you understand me?'

'Yes, sir.'

With a final warning glance, Watson backed out of my cell. He didn't take his eyes off me till the door was closed and locked.

Gerald had dusted himself off and was standing on the walk looking very pale.

'Still think you wouldn't kill me?' I called out to him.

Gerald shot me a glance that wasn't hatred but was something close. He walked up to the bars and stared me straight in the eye. His skin was almost gray, and a fine layer of sweat made him glisten.

'I do not want my children to grow up in your world,' he said, his voice shaking. 'And because of that I will *never* sanction killing a human being. Whatever atrocities you've committed are yours to bear, and yours alone. If it were up to me you would live to be an old man. That would be my punishment—you would *live*.'

As he walked away I thought to myself that maybe Gerald wasn't as naïve as I'd first imagined.

62

I was writing when Wendall's voice drifted in through the bars. 'That was pretty good.'

'What was?'

'That number you just did on the lawyer, that was pretty damn good.'

'I didn't do it for fun.'

Wendall chuckled. 'Oh, yeah, I could see that.'

'I'm serious.'

'Seems to me you spend a lot of time doing bad things and then saying you don't enjoy them.'

'Not everybody likes doing evil stuff, Wendall, as hard as that might be to believe.'

'You just don't get it, do you?' Wendall's bed creaked as he sat up. 'Everybody likes doing evil stuff, just not everybody has the courage.'

'I don't think so.'

'Well, look at the world if you don't believe me. There's evil shit goin' on all the goddamned time.'

'Just because evil things happen doesn't mean people are inherently evil.'

'Ah, bullshit, Simon. People love evil shit, it's just that most people only feel brave enough to do it in big groups.'

I put down my pen and stretched out on my bunk. 'You can't apply your own standards to the whole world, Wendall.'

'I don't. Most people are too chicken-shit to be like me, but they'd like to be.'

'Most people want to be a serial killer?'

'You better fuckin' believe it.'

Now I laughed. 'Well, I'm afraid I don't.'

'People love all this shit. Hell, I've even got a web site on the Internet devoted just to me. I'm telling you, people love this shit. When Hitler killed the Jews everybody said never again. But that shit happens all the time. Get a bunch of people together and pretty soon evil shit is gonna start to happen. It's axiomatic.' Wendall liked to slide in a few big words here and there.

'I don't believe that, Wendall. Bad people have been using that tired old justification since the beginning of time.'

'You of all people should believe it,' he said.

'How do you figure that?'

'Well, just take a fuckin' look around. You didn't get here for stealing milk. You got here because of all those girls.'

'Yes, but according to you I didn't actually do it.'

Wendall chuckled. 'Maybe you didn't do it, but you

sure as hell didn't stop it.'

He had this way of winding me into conversations that I'd had no intention of starting or pursuing. 'I . . . I wanted to stop it.'

'Bullshit.'

'I did.'

'Bullshit.'

'And how would you know?' I was starting to get angry because he was taking me out to a place that I didn't want to go.

'Simon, if you'd really wanted to stop it then it would have stopped.'

'Some things can't be stopped.'

'One phone call was all it would have taken. One little phone call.' I didn't reply. 'Maybe you should try and be a bit more honest about why you wanted it to keep going.'

And of course Wendall was right. I could have stopped it. I could have gone downstairs the night I found Milly's body in the woods, and made a single call that would have stopped it all.

But I didn't.

63

The fibby has been back—the indefatigable Agent Hanson. He with the briefcase and files. Agent Hanson worries me. Research isn't the only thing on his mind, that's obvious to me now. It was the pretext he used to get in to see me, but I think he's actually playing a much bigger game.

'Hello, Simon,' he said as he sat down opposite me in the interview room.

'Hello, John.' I thought I had a better handle on his game this time.

'How have you been?'

'Just fine, thanks, John.'

'Good.'

'So what brings you back to the Garden?'

Hanson studied me with his cool gray eyes. 'Curiosity.'

I smiled. 'How so?'

'I was curious about what really happened.'

'It's a little late in the game for that, isn't it?'

'Depends on how far gone the game is, I guess.'

I shrugged. 'I don't know about you, John, but six weeks out from my execution I'd have to say it's pretty much all over apart from the formalities.'

'I guess that depends on whether or not the game ends with you, doesn't it?'

'The game always ends when the player leaves the field, John.'

'Well, actually, Simon, I don't think the game ends until the *players* leave the field.'

'There's only one player in this game, John. I thought you FBI guys read the files?'

'You been thinking about Lisa Simkin much, Simon?'

I had, but I sure as hell wasn't going to tell him that. 'I think about a lot of things. I think about killing girls and I think about dying in six weeks time.'

He nodded slowly. 'It's just that the last time we spoke you looked a little thrown.'

'Is that right?'

'Yeah, it is. In fact, you looked pretty upset.'

'Must have been something I ate.'

'Well, now, it's interesting you should say that.'

'And why's that, John?'

'Well,' he said as he took another of his files from his nasty little briefcase of horrors, 'as you know I've taken a bit of an interest in this case. So I've been going back over the autopsy reports of the girls.'

'Really?' I tried to sound bored.

'Yeah. And the odd thing is that there's a lot of anomalies that needed a second look.'

'I'm real happy for you, John. I'm real pleased to know my tax dollars are being put to such good use.'

He smiled. 'So anyway, I went out to Bedford and spoke with the local Medical Examiner—a nice old guy, Dr Abrahams. You ever meet him?'

'He gave evidence at my trial,' I said, 'but we were never formally introduced.'

Agent Hanson stepped round the sarcasm without a backward glance. 'Like I was saying, he was a nice old guy, though I think he was a little out of his depth with this stuff. He did a pretty good job of establishing causes of death, but there was a whole bunch of other stuff that he missed.'

'Really.'

'Yeah, a whole bunch. So I had the bodies exhumed and flown up to Quantico.' He was watching me intently as he talked. 'Which reminds me, how come your lawyer never got an independent pathologist to have a look at the bodies? You could have torn old Doc Abrahams to pieces.'

'I didn't want him to.'

Agent Hanson studied me for a few moments. 'Because . . . ?'

'Because I didn't. It was pretty damn obvious to everyone that I was guilty. Why waste more time?'

'Maybe you could have got off with a lighter sentence.'

'Maybe I didn't give a shit.'

157

He shrugged. 'Anyway, I had the bodies flown up to Quantico and let our people have a look.'

'I bet the girls' families were real happy about that.'

'Well, when I explained to them what I was thinking they decided it was important enough to disturb their kids one last time.'

'And what could be so important that you needed to dig up the dead?'

Agent Hanson smiled one of his special FBI smiles. 'Justice.'

'Is that right?'

'Oh, yeah.' We sat there for a moment in silence. I knew what he wanted me to do. He was pretty good at the game, but I could still see the path he was laying down. I decided to let him lead me along for a while.

'And so what were you thinking?' I finally said.

'About what?'

'When you went to the girls' parents and told them what you were thinking, what was it?'

'Well, I told them that there were some things I wanted checked up again. I said I wanted to make sure that the people who killed their daughters were brought to justice.'

'People?'

He leaned forward in his chair and clasped his hands on the table. 'How's your wife, Simon?'

'She's fine. What do you mean, people?'

'She doesn't come in and visit you much, does she?'

'She finds it hard to think about what I've done. It disturbs her greatly.'

Agent Hanson smiled again. 'I'm sure she is greatly disturbed.'

'What do you mean, people?' I persisted.

'You might be able to fool inexperienced locals, but

you can't fool those guys of ours back in the lab. It's pretty obvious you didn't kill those girls, Simon.'

I had been expecting this. 'I wish you'd been around during my trial, John.'

'Oh, don't get me wrong,' he said. 'I'm not saying you're an innocent man, but I don't think you acted alone.'

'So you're going to try and implicate my wife in all this?'

He simply smiled at me.

'Well, you're a little late, John. She was found innocent and that means you can't come back at her.'

'I'm aware of the law. She can't be retried on the old offences, but she can be tried on new charges.'

'Such as?'

'How about first degree murder?'

'Except the only problem there is that I've already been found guilty of all seven homicides. You can't find her guilty of killing someone I've already been found guilty of killing.'

'All I need is for one of those girls to tell me something new, Simon. Just one girl, and then I can clear you and charge her in the same breath.'

'The dead don't tell tales, John.'

Agent Hanson looked at me with his cool gray FBI eyes. 'You really believe that, Simon? We can take a scrape of skin from the fingernails of a corpse that's been in the ground three years and pick the killer from a crowd of over a hundred million. You really think the dead don't speak?'

'I don't know anything about forensic science. All I know is I killed some kids and in six weeks the state is going to kill me. I don't have a problem with that. In fact I think it seems pretty damn fair. So my suggestion is that you go to hell, Agent Hanson.'

'Don't blame me, Simon—you were the one who told me.'

'And how do you figure that?'

'Last time I was in here when I told you Lisa Simkin had been buried alive. Your face gave me everything I needed to know. All the rest is just details.'

'I get upset when I think about this stuff, that's all. I don't like thinking about what I did.'

'I've been in this game a long time, Simon, and I've spent a lot of my life talking with men who've done things to innocent people that defy belief. I can tell when someone's lying to me. I can't stand up in court and explain how, but I can tell. You didn't know how Lisa died. I could see that in your face as soon as I told you.'

'Sorry to disappoint you, John, but I did kill her. I dug a hole, I pushed her in, then I filled it up one shovel at a time. I wanted to watch her as she sank into the dirt. I left her face till last.' I leaned forward and tried to sound as fucked up as I felt. 'I watched her eyes as she died, and I loved every minute of it.'

Agent Hanson stood up and picked up his briefcase. 'You're lying,' he said, and then turned and banged on the door.

'I killed that little slut, John. I buried her alive, and I jerked off on the dirt when I was done.'

Agent Hanson turned around then. 'Let me give you a hint, Simon—don't overplay your hand. Guilty men don't need to work so hard to convince people.'

'I did kill her, John.'

He smiled. 'You're lying.'

The guards opened the door, and he was gone.

64

Forty days. I just have to keep it together for forty more days. If I could, I'd take that long walk right now. I'd call in the warden and take that long walk down to the execution chamber right now. They wouldn't even need to use the straps; I'd lie there as quiet as could be while they put their little needle in. The warden would ask me if I had any last words and I'd say yes. He'd ask me what they were, and I'd tell him to hurry up and push the damn button.

65

As if things weren't bad enough, Father Jack was waiting for me back in my cell. It was turning into one of those 'devil and the deep blue sea' mornings.

'Hello, Simon.'

I sighed. 'Why is everyone in this place so fucking polite?'

He chuckled. 'Habit.'

'So have you come to work me over, Father?' I asked as I shuffled over to my bunk. After my little scene with Gerald they kept the leg braces and handcuffs on me whenever I was with anyone.

'No, Simon, just a friendly chat.'

'You'll have to forgive me for seeming a little hesitant, Father, but the last time we had a friendly chat you nearly crushed my throat.'

'Like I said'—he chuckled again—'habit.'

'What do you want with me, Father?'

'I want only your redemption, Simon.'

'And like I said last time, I'm not interested in your redemption games.'

It was there for a moment in his black eyes, a flash of rage that passed as quickly as it had come. Father Jack was just as dangerous as the fibby, but in a wilder, more unpredictable way. 'That may be, but have you thought about the people you'll be leaving behind?'

'You mean my family? I don't think there's anything I can do for them, Father.'

'I was thinking about the victims' families.'

'There's even less I can do for them.'

Father Jack nodded slowly. 'Do you ever think of them?'

'I think of them constantly, Father. They're the only thing that keeps me going.'

'Do you know if they'll be coming to the execution?'

I smiled. 'You make it sound like a party, Father.'

He looked at me with cold eyes. 'In a way, it is.'

I didn't know how to respond to that, to the coldness, so I didn't. 'I think they'll be there,' was all I said.

'You know that what you say at the end can make a great difference to them, don't you?'

'Yes, I've been thinking about that.'

'A man's last words are heavy, Simon, and they weigh just as heavily on those who hear them.'

I nodded.

'You're right that there's nothing you can say to ease their suffering, but you can at least not add to it.'

'How does it work?' I asked him. 'When do I get to speak?'

He studied me. 'Are you sure you want to talk about it now, Simon? There's plenty of time for all this later.' I knew he wasn't asking me out of kindness. Something moved Father Jack, but it wasn't kindness.

'I'd like to know, Father.'

'After the guards move you through into the chamber you'll be strapped onto the gurney. The doctor will insert a needle into your arm, and then she'll connect you up to the machine. At that point, she'll signal the warden that the execution is ready to proceed, and then he'll ask you if you have any last words.'

'Will the families be able to hear me?'

'Yes. There's an intercom that's turned on for that part of the procedure. You can say your piece, and then it'll be turned off again. After you've spoken the execution chamber will be cleared and the procedure will be completed.'

'I see.'

'You have a chance,' said Father Jack, leaning forward on the little chair, 'to spare them further suffering. You also have a chance to add to it, if you want.'

'You don't have to worry about me, Father—I won't be doing anything more to those poor people than has already been done.'

Father Jack nodded slowly. 'That's easy to say here, but when you're strapped down on that gurney with that needle sticking in your arm it's much harder to be noble.'

I laughed. It was a cheerless sound in my cold little cell. 'Nobility isn't important to me, Father. There's nothing noble about any of this.'

'I've sat with many men who've sworn they'd do the right thing, but when the end came they fell apart just as much as a man can.' The wild look was suddenly back in Father Jack's eyes, dancing around like flames. 'Death is nothing to fuck with, Simon. You can prepare yourself as much as you like, but when you feel that little needle burrowing into your arm, that's when you'll really know.'

I thought of Milly and how she'd died. I thought of the things that had burrowed into her body, both while she was dying and after.

'I don't expect I'm going to have too much trouble dying, Father.'

'You missed Harold Brooks' execution, didn't you?'

'The name doesn't ring any bells.'

Father Jack took out a candy bar and unwrapped it absently as he spoke. 'Harold Brooks was a double murderer. He killed a young honeymooning couple ten years ago. Shot the husband in the head, strangled the woman, and then burned their bodies in the car they'd been sitting in. He found God shortly after he came to the Garden. Harold spent those ten years reading his Bible and praying for forgiveness. He was adamant that, come his time, he'd do the right thing. I got to know him pretty well over those ten years. He was always wanting to see me and we spent many a long hour praying for the souls of his victims. He made a lot of friends here in the Garden, and he was a support to many during their last days.

'On the day of his execution he seemed calm and at peace with things. I sat with him for hours in the execution suite and talked. He said he'd made himself right with God, and that he was looking forward to standing in the presence of the Lord. I almost bought it. But as the hours ticked down I could see that maybe Harold wasn't as easy with things as he wanted everyone to believe. And it all started to unravel in the last thirty minutes. I could see it in his eyes.

'He was crying as we took him from the execution suite into the death chamber, and he wailed when he saw the gurney and started calling out to God for mercy. I think maybe Harold had thought if he just

164

prayed hard enough all those years then God would step in at the last moment with some kind of miracle.'

Father Jack took a bite of the candy bar. I'd never noticed before, but he had big teeth. Sharp looking teeth. I suddenly thought about what Wendall had said, about Father Jack in the pit, but then I shook it off.

'When they strapped him in and Harold finally realized that God was probably going to keep out of things he fell apart. The last ten years of devotion were swept away in a blink and he started gabbling like a wild man. The warden had to yell to make himself heard when he asked Harold if he had any last words. Harold quietened down then, and the look in his eyes was as pure dangerous as any man I've ever seen. He turned to the viewing gallery and looked straight at the mother of the girl he killed.'

Father Jack ran a hand through his hair, and I could see that this was still a painful thing for him to recall. 'I knew he was going to do something bad, but there was nothing I was allowed to do. A dying man can't be denied his last words. When Harold spoke his voice was as cracked and mean as any demon's has ever been. He looked straight at that poor woman as he told her how he'd raped her daughter and then burned her alive in the trunk of the car. He said that the daughter had screamed for her mother as she burned. He was still laughing when they pumped the poison into his veins.'

I sat back on my bunk and sighed. 'Nice story, Father—and your point would be what exactly?'

'My point, Simon, is that you don't fuck with God and you don't fuck with death. You might think you've got this whole thing wired, but when they take you through into the execution chamber and you feel those straps going over your chest it takes a different kind of strength than it does sitting here.'

'How about I write down what I'm going to say and you can have a look at it for me.' I was no more interested in Father Jack's opinion than I was in Andy Watson's, but if it would keep him off my back I was happy to do it.

Father Jack nodded. 'I think that would be a good idea, Simon. If you write it down then it's easier to stick to when the time comes.'

I smiled. 'My thinking exactly, Father.'

66

Every so often it all catches up with me. Most of the time I do a pretty good job of holding things together, but I guess you can only run for so long.

I only let myself cry at night, when it's dark. I need to maintain the demeanor of an evil man right up until the end. Because of that I've got pretty good at crying quietly. I lie in my bunk, facing the wall, and I cry until I'm empty. I'll never be empty of the terrible guilt I feel, but I do eventually feel emptied out of the ability to cry. Sometimes when I wake in the morning my pillow is literally soaking wet. It feels cold against my cheek, and for some reason I always think of blood.

They were so young, and they had families that loved and cared for them. I can hardly bear to think about the horror their families must now endure, but I make myself do it just the same. It's the least I can do.

The pain is indescribable. It tears at my soul with sharp claws that peel back my sanity layer after layer, ripping back the skin until the flesh lies bloody. In those moments it feels like I'm going to die—that the sheer immensity of it will kill me—but of course I never do.

I'm not telling you this in some kind of pathetic attempt at gaining sympathy. I deserve this pain. It's mine, bought and paid for. If anything, I'd take on more. I'd take on all the pain that those poor girls' parents must feel. I'd gather it up and swallow it down into my body whole if I could.

But of course I can't. The families sleep with their pain each night, and I sleep with mine.

I sometimes wonder, as I lie awake and stare at the roof of my cell, if they're awake at the same time. None of us able to sleep, none of us quite able to grasp the reality of the terrible things that have happened.

If I could, if I only could.

That's the dead man's prayer here in the Garden of Eden.

If I could, if I only could.

67

Gerald came back again. I'd wondered if he'd abandoned me after the job I'd done on him. I guess I was hoping he had. Gerald is too zealous for my liking.

'I have some good news, Simon,' he said.

We were sitting in my cell again, though this time I was handcuffed and shackled. He didn't look nervous, which surprised me. In fact he looked grimly happy.

'What's that, Gerald?' It had been a rough night, and I wasn't particularly interested in going another round about how he was going to keep me alive.

'I spoke to an FBI agent yesterday, a John Hanson.'

'Yeah, I know him.'

'Well, it seems he has some information that might get us a stay.'

Suddenly Gerald had my attention. 'What do you mean?'

'I mean Agent Hanson has turned up some new forensic information which might enable us to get a stay.'

'Like what?'

'He didn't say, but he said he'd keep me posted.'

I tried to keep myself calm. 'I don't want a stay, Gerald.'

'I know you don't want a stay, but it may not be your choice.' Now I could see that Gerald was pissed. 'Like I said at the beginning, if you don't at least try to fight I'll bring in a psychiatrist and have you declared mentally unfit to be executed.'

'I'm sane, Gerald. I just want to die.'

'Well, I'm not prepared to let that happen.'

'Why *not*?'

'I've been down that road with you once, Simon. I'm not doing it again.'

Now I was starting to get really frightened. I couldn't keep going much longer—I had to die at the beginning of October. 'All right, then, bring in your shrink.'

Gerald looked at me for a long time, saying nothing.

'*What?*' I finally exploded.

'Why are you in such a godawful hurry to die, Simon? What are you afraid people are going to find out?'

'I'm not afraid of anything,' I said, battling to retain some level of composure. 'I just want it to be over.'

'No, that's not it. There's something else going on. And that's why you want to die—you don't want anyone finding out whatever it is that's got you so scared.'

'I want to die, Gerald. Now bring in your fucking shrink.'

He nodded. 'Okay, Simon, if that's what you want.'

'It is.'

'But remember, if the psychiatrist says you're mentally ill they won't execute you. Are you sure you're up for that?'

'Just bring him in.'

'Okay,' Gerald said as he shrugged his shoulders. 'Let's toss the coin and see what comes up.'

I sat quietly on my bunk after he'd gone. I knew the guards wouldn't come down to take off my shackles for at least an hour. It was their unofficial punishment for my having caused a stink with Gerald the other day.

It didn't bother me. I had a lot to think about.

68

The day after I found Milly in the forest I went back to school. Business as usual. What else could I do? I told Juliette to stay at home, not to worry, and that I'd figure something out. Like I said before—I'm a man, and men need to fix things.

So I kissed my wife goodbye and walked down the road to catch the bus. It was a strange feeling, like everyone could tell, like they all knew where I'd been and what I'd seen. I felt like I was leaking Milly Brown from the pores of my skin. It was only a matter of time before someone would smell her on me.

'Hey, Mr Chance,' Anabel said as I got on the bus.

'Hey, Anabel.'

She frowned. 'You don't look so good. You been sleeping okay?'

'Not really,' I replied. 'I had a bad night.'

Anabel shook her head and took my change. 'Seems like there's too many of those going around in this town at the moment.'

I thanked her for my ticket and went and sat up the back. The sun was streaming in through the windows and it should have been warm, but it wasn't. I think that sometime during the hours I'd sat with Milly in the forest I'd caught a special kind of chill, a *bone* chill that went all the way down to the very heart of me.

Mervyn Mack was waiting for me when I got to school. 'A word, Mr Chance,' he said.

'Of course,' I replied as I followed him into a small meeting room off the staffroom. I knew what it would be about—he'd want to tear strips off me for being absent yesterday. 'Before you start, Mr Mack, let me say that I'm very sorry about yesterday, but there was a family emergency.'

'Was there?' said Mr Mack, his tone heavy with sarcasm. 'Nothing wrong with your lovely wife I hope?'

There was something in the way he spoke about Juliette that made me want to punch him every time— it felt as if he was licking her with his words. I know that sounds strange, but that's the best I can do to describe it.

'No, she's fine, thank you. It was something else.'

'I see.' He smiled and I could see a piece of food stuck between his two front teeth. Something black.

'Some family business out in Herbert Forest, was it?'

I felt the blood draining from my face. 'I beg your pardon?'

'Something urgent that took you out to Herbert Forest?' He looked so goddamned smug as he said it.

'I don't know what you mean,' I said. I had no idea how Mr Mack knew I'd been out in the forest. I could only assume that I'd been seen, which set off a train of thoughts I wasn't at all prepared for.

'It's just that someone I know saw you out there yesterday, and so I assumed that must be somehow involved with the family emergency you were speaking of.'

'No, I was just . . . driving.' I knew I sounded like an idiot, but I was panicking.

'Is that so?'

'Yeah, I had to pick up a friend up out that way.'

'I thought you said it was a family emergency?'

'He's like a family member.'

'Is that so?'

'Anyway,' I said as I tried to get out of the conversation, 'I'm sorry and it won't happen again.'

'That's quite all right, Mr Chance, these things happen. All you need to do is ask if you need time for those kinds of things.'

He was being too reasonable, which worried me. 'Thank you, Mr Mack.'

'You're welcome, Mr Chance. Now I'll let you get back to your day. No doubt you have lessons to prepare.'

'Yes, of course.'

I sat in the staffroom, drinking coffee and worrying. I had no idea who'd seen me, or exactly where they'd seen me. I also had no idea what Pervin' Mervyn would do with that particular little piece of information when Milly's body was found.

I had no doubt that the police would find her. I'd already decided that I was going to tell them.

69

I had too much going on in my mind to think about delivering any kind of coherent lesson, so I set most of my classes written work to do for the day. Pictures of Milly kept flashing into my mind, making it hard to concentrate on teaching.

There were some serious questions I had to think through, not the least of which was what the hell I was going to do about Juliette. She'd killed that girl in the most vile of ways and then left her body lying in the forest. I still had little idea why, and no idea whether she'd do it again. Which of course was the really big question—was Juliette dangerous, and would she do it again?

And there was another question out beyond that one, an even harder one: if Juliette was dangerous what the hell was I going to do about it?

Then I thought of Milly lying naked in the forest. I thought of the sound the branch had made as I pulled it from her body. I was no shrink, but deep down I knew that a person who could do that to a girl was more than dangerous. A person who could do that was unlikely to be able to stop themselves from doing it again.

Which really only left the issue of what the hell was I going to do?

'Mr Chance?' I looked up and Theresa was standing there.

'Yes, Theresa?' She had long blonde hair, just like Milly, and in my mind I heard the wet sucking sound of a stick being pulled from dead flesh. I shivered.

'Are you okay?' Theresa asked.

'Yes,' I said, wiping my forehead absently with my hand. 'I think I'm coming down with a cold or something.'

'Maybe I should come back another time?' she said.

'No, I'm okay. How can I help you, Theresa?'

She reached into her bag and pulled out a neatly stapled sheaf of pages. 'It's just I made those corrections we talked about and I wondered if you'd mind having another look at my story?'

'I'd be happy to,' I said as I took the story from her. *Shrapnel Tears* it said in bold on the cover page, and underneath that 'A Short Story by Theresa Wright'.

I didn't ever read that story again, at least not the copy Theresa gave me. The next time I saw it was in the *Time* magazine article that I read in my little death row cell.

Theresa smiled at me. 'I really appreciate this, Mr Chance.'

'It's a pleasure to do it, Theresa, you really are very talented. I expect you'll do great things with your writing.'

She blushed. 'I just want to get a few stories published.'

'With your talent, you're bound to publish a great many stories.'

I was wrong about that. She would only ever publish the one story, albeit in *Time* magazine, and she wouldn't get to do a great deal more with her life either. In fact, Theresa would be dead less than three weeks after that conversation, raped and stabbed almost beyond recognition on the little cot in our cellar.

'I hope so,' she replied on that long-ago morning. Hope wouldn't be enough to save her though; in a sense I suppose she was already dead.

'I'm sure of it,' I said, and at the time I was.

'Can I tell you something?' she asked.

'Sure, Theresa.'

'Since you read that story for me and said all the nice things you did I've actually started to believe that it might be possible.'

'What might be possible?' I asked her.

'The big dreams, the ones of fame and fortune, all that hokey stuff.'

I smiled. 'There's nothing hokey about big dreams, not a thing.'

'That's what I think,' she said. She smiled and left, vanishing out the door and into the busy hum of the hallway traffic.

I didn't see her again until that very last time, and by then all the light had gone from her eyes. By then there was only horror and death.

70

In the middle of all this Juliette disappeared for four days. I got home from school and she was gone. She'd taken the car and left. At first I thought she must be getting some groceries, but as time wore on it became obvious she'd been gone too long for it to be anything as mundane as eggs and milk.

I was worried, as you'd expect—about what could have happened to her, but also what she could do. Even though I couldn't admit it to myself at the time, I was worried she'd be out there killing again.

I didn't go to bed that night. Instead I sat in the kitchen and got quietly drunk. I didn't drink a lot as a general rule, but lately alcohol felt like the only kind of lubricant that could get me through. Without it my brain tended to seize up, almost as if the weight of my thoughts put the whole system under too much strain.

Sitting there in the small hours of the night I thought about walking away. Simply picking myself up, walking away, and starting over somewhere else. I could leave the house in the clothes I was wearing, catch a bus, and be miles away by dawn. I could forget everything I'd seen, forget Juliette—forget myself even. I could start afresh somewhere else and leave all the fear behind me.

And there was a moment—sitting in the dark, empty house—when I almost did. I felt the glue that fastened me to my life peeling back from my skin, almost as if the world had tilted on its axis and gravity itself was sucking me away. I have often wondered where I'd be now if I had let go that night. Maybe I could have just watched it on television like everyone else.

But then the moment passed and the world tilted back again.

Hello, Simon.

I looked up from the label I'd been peeling from my bottle of beer. It was Milly. She stood in the dark kitchen with just her torn white shirt. I couldn't see her very clearly in the gloom, but I could easily imagine the details that the darkness hid.

'Hey, Milly,' I slurred, 'pull up a chair.' If I hadn't been so drunk I suppose I might have been scared.

I heard her cold feet whispering against the linoleum floor of the kitchen as she came closer. I smelt earth and the stink of decay. Then she was sitting facing me.

How far are you willing to go, Simon?

I smiled, lifting my beer bottle to toast her. 'Now that's the thirty thousand dollar question, isn't it?' I drained the rest of the bottle and slammed it on the table. 'How far *am* I willing to go?'

She looked at me in the darkness, her eyes a deeper black than the night itself. *It's a long road, Simon.*

'That it is, Milly,' I said, and reached for another beer. 'I think perhaps it's too long for the likes of me.'

You know what needs to be done.

'Well, now, that's the thing,' I said, 'because I don't think I *do* know. I've been trying to work it out, but I just can't seem to get it figured.'

You know, she said, her voice sounding oddly empty.

'I don't know anything,' I said. I was starting to feel sick. Too little sleep, too much beer, and too much talking with dead girls in the small hours of the night.

Suddenly Milly leaned forward and grabbed my wrist. Her skin was cold as ice and hard as stone. *It's not too late yet*, she hissed. *It's not too late to turn back.*

I tried to pull away from her grip, but couldn't. 'Let me go,' I whined. I'd like to say it was something different—something more heroic—but it was just a whine.

It's not too late yet, she hissed again, and I could smell her breath now, the chill stink of the grave. *It's not too late to turn back.*

I wrenched myself away from her frozen grasp, throwing myself backward in my chair and spilling onto the ground. I scrambled to my feet, panting, but she was gone. There were no dead girls in my kitchen, there was only me, and a few empty bottles of beer.

71

I woke up the next morning having slept the night on the kitchen floor. My neck ached almost as much as my head. The house was empty and quiet, and it was also very cold. I struggled to my feet, moaning as the movement set off a new pounding behind my eyes.

I stepped over the empty bottles on the kitchen floor and staggered down to the bathroom. I glanced in the bedroom as I passed but Juliette wasn't there. I hadn't really expected her to be.

I'm bad with hangovers at the best of times, and hopeless at the worst. I guess that's the reason I could never be an alcoholic—I just can't cope with the after-effects. I rummaged around in the medicine cabinet until I found the aspirin. There was only one left in the bottle. I knew that wouldn't be enough to kill the pain, but it was a start.

Then I stripped off and stood under the shower for a long time as the hot water drummed over me. I felt nauseous and my head hurt like someone was scraping fingernails down the inside of my skull. The longer I stood there the worse the nausea became, but the thought of moving was just too much to bear.

It was only the sudden and powerful need to vomit that got me going.

I scrambled from the shower over to the toilet, spraying water all over the floor. I collapsed to my knees and heaved as everything inside of me came out in a hot, acrid rush. Whenever I vomit I always feel like my head is going to explode. It never does, but it always feels that way.

Hunched naked and dripping over the toilet bowl, I felt about as miserable as I'd ever felt in my life.

Looking down into the purple goo in the toilet wasn't helping things, so I lifted my head.

And that's when I saw the finger marks on my arm. Thick black bruises that encircled my wrist like a child's hand painting. I could make out the perfect imprint of four fingers and a thumb.

I screamed and fell backwards from the toilet, my wet butt hitting the cold tiles with a loud slap. I held my wrist up under the stark fluorescent light. The outline of the hand was unmistakable.

The outline of Milly's hand.

'Oh fuck, oh fuck, oh fuck . . . ' I muttered as I struggled to my feet. I turned on the hand basin faucet and squirted liquid soap onto my wrist. Lathering it up under the hot water, I tried desperately to scrub the marks away. But they wouldn't shift. Soap was no match for the angry black bruises.

I stopped scrubbing and sat down on the toilet. The stink of vomit drifted up between my legs but I didn't care. I sat like that for a long time.

72

You see, the problem is that I don't believe in ghosts. I could believe in dreams, and I could even believe that Milly—or at least my unconscious representation of Milly—could visit me in a dream, but I couldn't believe she'd visit me in real life.

Milly was dead. I had seen that for myself, and dead girls don't grab you by the wrist hard enough to leave bruises.

I've always been a rational man, and I believe in rational things. Milly grabbing me in the night was not a rational thing. I didn't believe it. Not then. Not now.

So after the initial horror of seeing the handprint on my wrist had faded a little, I was able to think along more rational lines. The reality was that in my drunken, guilt-ridden, fearful state I must have grabbed myself. I'd been alone in the house so that was the only possible explanation. In some kind of alcohol-induced delusion I'd grabbed myself and squeezed hard enough to leave the bruises.

I know some of the people reading this book won't believe this. Some of you will think it never happened and that I invented the whole scene for a little drama in the story.

I didn't, but fair enough.

I also know there'll be some of you who'll believe that it really was Milly who left that bruise. You'll believe that somehow her restless spirit visited me in the dead of night and squeezed herself into me like light on a film negative.

I choose not to believe that. I don't believe in ghosts or restless spirits. Dead is dead. When I saw Milly's body in the woods it was painfully obvious that whatever had been *her* was gone; all that was left was the clean-up work. Romantic notions of spirits and visitations are the stuff of hippies and horror novels.

So believe that Milly grabbed me if you like; just know that it's not my belief. Like I said, I'm a rational man.

73

Sometimes you can tell something's wrong as soon as you enter into a room. That's what it was like when I walked into the staffroom at school—people were gathered in small clumps talking in hushed tones. Mostly it was their eyes though, a look that told me.

'Have you heard the terrible news?' asked Mrs Gamble as I walked over to get a cup of coffee. Mrs Gamble was the school secretary and she never had an ill word for anyone. Most days she was almost painfully cheerful, but today she looked anything but.

'What, Mrs Gamble?'

'Oh, it's terrible,' she said. 'Just terrible.'

'What? What's happened?'

Mrs Gamble looked up at me with teary eyes. 'Another girl has disappeared, Mr Chance. Lisa Simkin didn't arrive at school yesterday, but no one knew anything was wrong until her parents called the police last night when she didn't come home.'

I closed my eyes as I felt dread rushing through me.

'Mr Chance? Are you all right?'

I felt Mrs Gamble's hand on my arm, but I couldn't speak. All I could think about was the fact that Juliette had been gone all night. 'I'll be all right, Mrs Gamble. It's just . . . it's very bad news.'

Mrs Gamble dabbed at her eyes with a little white handkerchief that she pulled from her sleeve. 'It's so horrible, isn't it? First Milly, and now Lisa.'

'Yes, it is,' I said. My mind was churning. I'd known about Milly, and I'd done nothing. Now Juliette was missing and Lisa Simkin hadn't come home.

'Simon?'

I turned and saw Bill Chapman, the school principal, standing with a tall black man.

'Yes, Bill.'

'This is Detective James Goodlow,' he said, gesturing towards the imposing figure. 'He's investigating Lisa's disappearance and he wants to speak to all the staff. Do you have a few moments?'

'Yes, of course,' I said as I held out my hand. 'Hello, Detective.'

James Goodlow's hand swallowed mine whole, the hand that Milly Brown had grabbed in my dream. 'I appreciate your assistance, sir. Can we sit over here?' he said, pointing to a couple of chairs in the corner. We sat down and he took out a small notebook. 'At the moment we're treating this as a missing person case. We have no particular reason to believe that Lisa Simkin has come to any harm, but I'm sure you can appreciate the urgency of the situation. Particularly given that she's the second local girl to go missing.'

'Of course,' I said. 'How can I help?'

'Did you know Lisa?'

'No, not really. She was just another student. She wasn't in any of my classes.'

'But you have seen her about the school?'

'Yes, just in passing though.'

'I see,' he said scribbling notes down in his little notebook. 'Are you aware of any personal difficulties she may have been having? Any problems with boyfriends, that kind of thing?'

'As I said, I really didn't know her at all. Apart from seeing her around the school I know very little about her.' Goodlow nodded as he wrote. 'You may want to ask Mr Mack about her though,' I said. 'I believe she's in his English class.'

'Unfortunately Mr Mack is off sick today, but we'll probably visit him at home later in the morning.'

'Do you think she's been abducted, Detective?'

Goodlow's eyes studied me. 'Obviously we're concerned, given that Milly Brown is still missing as well. Did you know her?'

'Milly Brown?'

'Yes.'

'No. I'm fairly new to the school so I don't know many students outside my own classes.'

He nodded. 'How long have you been here?'

'Only about four months.'

'Really? So what brought you to Bedford?' His tone was light, almost conversational. His eyes were anything but—they glittered like knives.

'Oh, nothing in particular,' I replied, trying to sound equally conversational. 'We'd been drifting around a while, seeing the country, and we just decided we liked the place.'

'We?'

Shit. 'My wife and I.'

'Is your wife a teacher as well?'

'No.' I smiled. 'She loves kids, though.' I regretted it as soon as it was out of my mouth. It sounded a little try-hard.

'Do you have kids?'

'No.'

'So the two of you live alone, then?'

'Uh huh.' I decided it would be safer to try and say as little as possible.

'You like it here in Bedford?'

'It's very pleasant.' I looked down at my hands and saw with horror that my shirtsleeve had ridden up high enough to reveal the outer edge of the hand-shaped bruise on my wrist. I quickly pulled it down again.

'Pleased to hear that,' said Goodlow.

'Is there anything else I can help you with, Detective? I don't wish to be rude, but I have a class to prepare for.'

Goodlow stood and held out his hand, 'No, that should be all for now, Mr Chance.'

'Only too happy to help,' I said as I shook his hand

in return. 'I just hope you find her.'

'So do I, Mr Chance.'

I stayed in the staffroom for another twenty minutes or so, making it look like I was reading my lesson plan. In truth I was sitting there with my mind going a hundred miles an hour. Once I saw Goodlow sit down with one of the other teachers I gathered my books and headed for the door. I wanted to leave while he was distracted.

But as I passed him he looked up and smiled. I smiled back. A social reflex. Then Goodlow turned back to the teacher he was interviewing, and I was out the door and into the fresh clean air of the morning.

74

I remember talking with Goodlow in the holding cells under the courthouse as we were waiting for the jury to bring the verdict back after the sentencing hearing. I didn't expect it would take them long. I was right. They were out for only thirty minutes, and I suspect most of that time was spent waiting long enough to make it look like they'd deliberated properly. In truth, I believe they'd decided to kill me by the end of the first morning of the trial.

I don't blame them. I would have felt the same way if I'd had to listen to what they'd had to listen to.

'When did you first start to suspect me?' I asked Goodlow as we sat there.

'Pretty much that very first time I met you after Lisa Simkin disappeared.'

I smiled. 'I thought as much.'

'It was just too much of a coincidence, you saying

you'd only been in town for a few months.'

'It's always the stranger, isn't it?'

'Not always, but it was this time.'

'Was it just that? The timing? Or was it something about me?' I have to admit to being pretty curious about the way Goodlow's mind works. He's an interesting guy—and besides, we had to fill in the time while we waited for the jury to come back in.

'There was something,' he said as he took out a cigarette. 'You mind?' I shook my head and he lit up. 'After a while you get to know when people are hiding something.'

'And I looked like I was hiding something?'

'Yeah, I guess you did.'

'How?'

'Well,' he said, exhaling smoke, 'you were a little too helpful.'

I laughed. 'So helping the police isn't a good idea, then?'

'People aren't that helpful in real life. Most people are busy. They gotta get somewhere, or do something, so they'll talk to you, but they resent it a little bit at the same time. The only people who want to talk to cops for any length of time are either crazy or guilty.'

'So which do you think I was?'

'Now or then?'

'Now *and* then.'

He inhaled again. 'Then I thought you were maybe holding back on something.'

'And now?'

'Now I think you're both.'

'Guilty *and* crazy?'

'Yeah, guilty and crazy.'

As bizarre as it sounds, I was actually more hurt by him calling me crazy than guilty. 'You really think

I'm crazy?'

'I hope like hell you are.'

'And why's that?'

Goodlow turned his head and looked at me. His gaze is one of the most intense I've ever encountered. He could even teach the fibby a thing or two. 'Because, Simon, it's too frightening to think you were sane when you did those things. If you were, then I don't know what hope there is for the world.'

I thought for a moment. 'I see what you mean,' I finally said. 'The only thing is, I don't feel crazy. I feel pretty much the same as I have my whole life.'

'I guess that means you've always been crazy then.'

I smiled. 'I guess it does.'

The court-appointed psychiatrists had found me legally sane, but I knew what Goodlow was saying. Who would want to believe that normal people could do this shit? The world is full of normal people, so that's a road you just don't want to go down.

'What do you think the jury is going to come back with?' I asked him.

'I think they're going to come back with the death penalty.'

'Me too.' I looked at him. 'Would you be happy with that?'

He took another long draw on his cigarette. 'Yes, I would, Simon.'

'Me too.'

Goodlow looked at me for a long moment and I thought he was going to say something. But he never did. Fifteen minutes later the jury came back in.

75

The house was still empty when I got back that night.
The day had churned me up, and walking home from
the bus stop I'd got churned up even more.

Milly Brown was dead.

Lisa Simkin was missing.

I'd known about Milly and I'd done nothing. Now
another girl was gone. Maybe Milly finally had some
company out there in the woods.

To be honest, I think I was a little relieved that
Juliette wasn't home. I wasn't sure I could face her. I
didn't want to have to ask her about Lisa—I was too
scared of what she would say.

I took a pizza from the refrigerator and watched it
slowly heat in the oven, not thinking much about anything. I was tired of thinking. I tried to eat the pizza,
but only got halfway through one piece; it tasted like
sick on a slice of cardboard. I got a beer instead.

Lisa was all over the local evening news, with pho-
tos of her house and the school. The picture of Lisa
herself showed her leaning against a tree wearing a
black top with little flowers on it. She was smiling,
and even in the slightly grainy photograph she looked
pretty. The media were quick to draw comparisons
between Milly and Lisa's blonde-haired good looks.
They were hungry for patterns. Patterns made for better stories. Patterns made for more fear.

I turned the television off. I didn't really need to
see any more.

As the light slowly faded I had another beer. Courage is a fickle thing, and in its absence alcohol makes
a fine substitute. I knew I had to call the police and
tell them about Milly, but I was frightened. I guess I

was frightened about all kinds of things, but mainly I was frightened because every step I took made the whole thing more real.

It's not too late to turn back, Milly whispered in my mind.

And I wanted to believe that, I really did, but I think it had always been too late to turn back. Right from the moment Juliette sat down beside me in that bar in New York City. I don't think there was ever any turning back after that. Now there was just going on, all the way, right to the end.

I rang for a cab and got my coat. I didn't want to call the police from home in case they traced it, so to be on the safe side I decided to make the call from a payphone in the middle of town.

'Where to, chief?' asked the cab driver. The photo ID on the dashboard said his name was Dan.

'Gallery Bookshop,' I replied. It was the biggest bookstore in town and there was a payphone right across the road.

'Did you hear another girl went missing?' Dan asked as we pulled away from the kerb.

'Yes,' I said, trying to sound disinterested. I didn't really feel up to a cab driver conversation. That could be wearying at the best of times.

'I bet she's dead,' he said. 'Missing girls always end up dead.' I didn't reply. 'I hope they catch this bastard soon,' Dan continued. 'Sick son of a bitch should be goddam hung. All these commie liberals going on about how cruel the death penalty is—shit, best thing in the world with these kinds of people is to put 'em down like dogs. Some people give up the right to be alive, you know what I mean?'

I could see him looking in the mirror, but I ignored him.

'Anyway,' he said, 'they should find this bastard and then they should kill him like he's killed these two girls. An eye for an eye, right?'

Dan talked the whole way. It didn't seem to bother him much that I wasn't responding. I guess I could have been dead and Dan would have still kept going. He had a wedding ring on his finger, and I remember thinking that I pitied Mrs Dan. Imagine living with that.

I paid him, and waited until he drove off before I went across the road to the payphone. There were only a handful of people on the streets, either on their way to a restaurant or on their way home. Just the usual traffic of any main street after dark.

I stood with my hand on the receiver for a long time, still wavering about what to do. I knew that if I told the police about Milly it would inevitably bring them closer to our door. There was also a chance that they might catch Juliette out there with Lisa. That was perfectly possible. Maybe I wanted that. I don't really know. Whatever the case, I picked up the receiver and put my cold little dime in the slot.

76

Click.

'Bedford Police.'

'I have some information about Milly Brown.'

'Yes, sir. Would you like to speak to one of the detectives?'

'Yes, thank you.'

'Please hold, sir.'

Click.

'Burke, Operations.'

'I have some information about Milly Brown.'

'What's the nature of your information, sir?'

'I know where her body is.'

A pause. 'Can I have your name, sir?'

'No, I just want to tell you where she is.'

'It would really help if I could get your name, sir. Any information you can give us is confidential.'

'I said no names.'

'Okay then, sure. Where is she?'

'In Herbert Forest, at the end of a road called Porter's No. 1. She's lying under a tree and she looks like she's been dead for a while.'

'How do you know it's Milly Brown?'

'I . . . I just do.'

'How did you find her, sir?'

'I . . . uh . . . I'm a hunter. I found her when I was hunting.'

'It would really help us if you could come in and make a statement, sir.'

'No, I just wanted you to know where she was. Her family will be wanting her back.'

'That's true, and you've been a big help to them. Do you know anything about any of the other missing girls? Do you know anything about Lisa Simkin?'

'No.'

'We really want to find her.'

'I don't know anything about that.'

'Do you have a number so I can call you?'

'No. Goodbye.'

'Wait, I just need to ask you one more thing.'

'Goodbye.'

'Wait—'

Click.

77

I went to a bar and ordered a beer. Out there in the night they were scrambling to get to Milly. They would find her, and tonight she'd sleep back in the arms of the world. It would be a hard night for her parents. They would finally have their question answered.

I could imagine the scene. A knock at the door. They open it and there's a cop standing there. It'll most probably be someone they know from the team, a senior detective. Probably it'll be Goodlow. They'll know straight away—if not when they hear the knock at their door, certainly when they see Goodlow's face. Sometimes faces say all that needs to be said.

I'm very sorry, Mr and Mrs Brown, but I'm afraid she is.

There'll be wailing, and tears, and pain in abundance. All the horror that's been circling over them for the last few weeks will finally have a foothold in their hearts. There will be no stopping it now. There will be no mercy.

'Can I get you another one?' It was the bartender. He was in his mid-forties and looked like he could only exist behind a bar, as if he'd simply blink out like a blown bulb if he ever attempted to leave.

'That would be good,' I said.

'You looked like you were thinking about something pretty important.'

'I guess I was.'

The place was quiet. Apart from him and me there was only a couple sitting down in the back corner.

'You never can tell,' he said as he wiped the bar absently with a yellow cloth.

'Never can tell what?'

'Never can tell what folks have on their mind when

they come into a place like this.'

'Really?'

'Oh, yeah. You can always tell when a person's thinking about something, you just can never tell what it is. You can make guesses, but you can never tell for sure.'

I smiled into my beer. 'And what would be your guess about me?'

'Well,' he said, scratching his chin with a long pale finger, 'you're here by yourself on a weeknight, so I'd say it's probably troubles from home.'

'I guess you must get a lot of that in here?'

'Oh yeah, I get my share. Sometimes I think that working in a bar isn't much different from being a shrink. Except maybe people are more honest with me than they are with their shrink.'

I laughed. 'You're probably right.'

'What do you do for a living?'

'I'm a teacher.'

His face suddenly became serious. 'Out at the college?'

'Yup.'

'I heard another girl's gone missing.'

'Apparently.'

'I heard it was Lisa Simkin—is that true?'

I took another sip of my beer. 'Yup.'

'Damn, that's too bad. She's a real pretty little thing too. I know her dad, comes in here all the time. Nice guy.'

I was getting a little loaded by that time. Except it was a different kind of loaded. My body felt drunk but my mind felt as cold as it ever was. I held up my glass. 'Well, here's to him then.'

The bartender looked at me. 'There's no call to be like that. He *is* a nice guy and so is his kid.'

'I'm sorry,' I said, putting down my glass. 'I didn't mean any offence. I'm just . . . I'm tired.'

The bartender shook his head. 'That's okay,' he said. 'I guess everybody round here is getting a little wound up. We never had anything like this happen in Bedford before. This has always been a safe place to raise kids.'

'Maybe it isn't anymore.'

'I think you're right there. Seems like the devil has come to Bedford these days.'

I remember thinking to myself that I wished it was the devil. I wished it was Satan himself. Anything was better than the truth.

78

I stumbled out of the bar when it closed around midnight. The street was pretty deserted by then and I needed to find a cab home.

Home to my empty house.

Except that wasn't quite true, I thought to myself as I held my bruised wrist up to the dull glare of the streetlight. Milly was there. And maybe Lisa was there by now too.

'Hey.'

I turned around and saw Stacy looking at me in her permanently glazed sexual way. She had a tiny red dress on and a matching red beret. Standing under the streetlamp with her short jet-black hair she looked like an urban terrorist whore.

'Didn't mean to frighten you,' she said.

'I . . . you didn't frighten me.'

'It looked like I did.'

'Well, you didn't.'

'Okay.'

We stood like that for a moment. I didn't know what to say to her.

'I haven't seen your wife for a while,' she said as she leaned back on the lamppost and tucked her leg up underneath her. I could see a flash of white cotton under the short slut-red dress. I knew she wanted me to see. She was playing me for just another horny male fool—which, I guess, wasn't that far from the truth. I let my eyes do their thing.

'She's away, on business.'

'Oh.'

It was the strangest feeling, standing there at night on the deserted street. It felt like we were the only two people in the world. Off in the distance somewhere I heard a car horn.

'So what are you doing?' she asked, and the other question—the question underneath that one—stared at us both.

'I'm going home.'

'Alone?'

'Yes, alone.'

She pushed herself away from the lamppost and slowly walked over to me. Then she took my hand, pushed it up under her dress, and started to slowly rub herself against me. It was like a scene from a bad German porno movie.

But I didn't move my hand away.

'Can I come home with you?' she whispered.

'I . . . I don't want to do this,' I said, trying to sound like I meant it.

She moaned and leaned forward to lick my neck. Even in the cold night air I could feel the heat of her body. 'I'll make you feel good.'

What could be wrong with feeling good for a little while? And I wouldn't be doing anything that I hadn't already done—right?

'Come if you want,' I said.

She looked up at me, and in the light her face was that of a child—painted and lipsticked, but still that of a child. 'A hundred bucks for an hour,' she said. 'Okay?'

I didn't say anything. All I could do was look at her.

'A hundred bucks, okay?'

A child playing dress-ups. A child who would fuck me for a hundred bucks.

'Okay, then,' she said, her voice taking on a slightly desperate edge. 'Fifty bucks and you can do anything, okay?'

I nodded—not because of the money, but because I couldn't stand to listen to her sell herself away so cheaply. If I'd had to listen to much more I don't think I would have been able to fuck her. And I did want to fuck her.

It turned out she wasn't a child who'd fuck me for a hundred bucks after all; she'd do it for fifty.

79

'This place smells funny,' said Stacy as she descended into the cellar. There was a faint odor in the air, but I was too drunk and horny to give much of a damn. And I knew that we had to do it down there—Stacy belonged to the cellar world.

The strange feeling from the street was more intense down in the dark. There was no one, only the two of us. She was alone with me in the belly of the earth, and I could do with her as I wanted.

'Sit,' I said, pointing to the cot as I sat across from her on a wooden box.

She sat down on the cot and started to unbutton her dress.

'No,' I said. 'Wait.'

She looked over at me. 'What do you want to do?'

'I just want to look at you.'

She smiled and I thought how pathetic she was, this seventeen-year-old girl sitting down here in the dark with me. Selling herself to strangers for money. Letting whoever could pay a few bucks do whatever they wanted to her.

'What?' she asked, smiling. 'You want me to watch me do myself?' She brought one hand up and started to rub her breast. It was the bad German porno look again.

'Don't do that.'

She let her hand fall back into her lap again. 'What then?'

'I want to talk.'

'What about?'

'About you.'

She frowned. 'I don't talk about myself with clients.'

'Is that what I am, a client?'

'Yeah.'

I smiled, and was surprised at how *evil* the smile felt. I felt like I'd taken a face down off the wall and was trying it on for size. This one was from the rack of secret faces Juliette and I kept down here in the dark.

How far? Milly had asked me, and sitting there with Stacy I suddenly felt drunk enough to find out.

'So why don't you talk about yourself, Stacy?'

'Just because.'

'That's not an answer, Stacy—that's like spitting when you've been paid to swallow.'

'You're not paying me to talk.'

I took out two fifty-dollar bills and laid them on the ground. 'I'm not paying you to spit.'

She looked at me, and I could see something in her eyes that I couldn't quite name. 'I don't like talking about myself because the fucking isn't anything to do with me.'

I smiled again, and this time the fit seemed a little better. I guess if you wear anything long enough it'll eventually start to feel like it's yours. 'It's *all* to do with you, Stacy. Without you there's nothing.'

'That's not how it feels to me.'

'And how *does* it feel to you?'

'It feels like nothing to me. It's just rubbing.'

I laughed. 'Rubbing? Is that all? Just a little friction?'

She looked hurt. 'You're making fun of me,' she said. 'That's not very nice.'

'I'll tell you what's not very nice, Stacy—fucking men for money isn't very nice. Opening your legs for anyone with a dollar bill isn't very nice.'

'I gotta live,' she said. She was trying to sound hard, but I could see tears in her eyes.

Way in the back of me the Simon who'd grown up on a farm in Nebraska was shouting something, shouting some kind of warning. But out front the Simon with the evil smile was enjoying the game. And Stacy was keeping her promise, she *was* making me feel good. 'You call this *living*?' I said. 'Sitting down here talking dirty with me? Knowing that sooner or later I'm going to come over there and push myself inside you? That's not living, Stacy, that's dying in bits and pieces.'

'Why are you doing this?' she asked, and this time

196

I could easily hear the hurt.

'Take off your clothes,' I said. She looked up at me, and I could see how much she hated me. And underneath that I could see how much she hated herself.

'You don't *have* to,' I said. 'I'm not going to force you. It's your choice, Stacy.' I reached out and touched the fifty-dollar bills with the toe of my shoe. I felt the cruelty flowing through me like warm clotted cream.

She got up and slowly slipped off her dress. Then she simply stood there shivering in her underwear.

'All of it,' I said. When she was naked I told her to sit down again. 'Now, you were saying that this was a living?'

She folded her hands across her chest and I could see she was cold.

'No, Stacy, keep your hands at your side.'

'Can't we just do it?' she said.

'We *are* doing it. You said that for fifty bucks I could fuck you however I wanted.'

A single tear rolled down her cheek. 'Please . . . don't be . . . ' she sniffed, 'don't be mean to me. You don't have to be mean.' She sounded like such a child then, like a little girl lost in the dark. It was far too late for that though—I was too drunk and too fucked up to care anymore.

'What's the worst thing that anyone's ever done to you?'

'What do you mean?' she asked, her voice shaking.

'You heard me, what's the worst thing?'

She sniffled, a small sad sound. 'A lot of guys don't pay,' she finally said. 'They do it and then they refuse to pay.'

I shook my head. 'No, no, Stacy, not that. I mean the *worst*. And don't lie to me . . . because I'll know.'

She sighed and closed her eyes. 'There was this

197

guy,' she said finally.

'Yes . . . ?'

'He used to take me to his house when his family was out.'

'Keep going, Stacy.' I could see fat tears sliding down her cheeks.

'He used to make me undress and lie down in his bath, and then . . . ' Her voice trailed off into small sobs. She put her face in her hands and cried. 'I used to feel so . . . so fucking *dirty*.'

'You are,' I said as I stood and went over to her. 'You *are* dirty, Stacy.' I grabbed her by the hair and twisted her head up till she was looking at me. Her eyes were puffy and red and her make-up had run down her face in thick, black watery lines. 'What did he do, Stacy?'

'He used to piss on me and call me horrible names. He just stood there and pissed on me and called me all kinds of horrible things. It was like I was a thing, like I was this awful, disgusting thing that wasn't good for anything more than pissing on.' She started crying again.

I looked down into her broken face, I saw her desperate, hopeless pain, and it just made me want to fuck her even more.

She said something else, but I can't recall what it was.

I fell on her.

80

Some time before dawn I woke up alone in the cellar. My head hurt, I was cold, and I could smell her sex on me like cheap cologne. The things I'd done to her during the night flickered through my mind like an old grainy movie, and I moaned despite myself.

A line had been crossed, and this time I hadn't been pushed—this time I'd jumped of my own free will.

The cot tilted when I moved and I instinctively grabbed for the side. For a moment it felt like the whole thing was going over, but then the legs clonked down onto the ground again. I looked over the side and noticed for the first time that the green carpet Juliette had put over the dirt floor was no longer flat. It was all bumpy, as if someone had churned up the ground underneath. I guess I hadn't noticed it before, what with all the alcohol and nastiness to distract me.

I stood up and pulled the cot off to the side of the cellar. Reaching down, I grabbed the side of the carpet and flicked it back, gasping involuntarily as it flew up past my face. The unpleasant smell I'd noticed before came up from under the carpet like a wave. I dropped the carpet and coughed. It was a thick, acrid smell, like old vinegar.

The ground had obviously been recently dug up. The weight of the carpet had done something to flatten it again, but it still looked more rough than smooth. The legs of the cot had worn four dimples into the ground, and in one of them I could see a small white object protruding from the dark earth. It was about an inch long and half an inch wide.

I bent down so I could see it better, and the movement made my head pound. There were fine lines running across it, and at one end I could see a faint flash of red. I touched it and was surprised to find it oddly soft. I leaned in closer and started to brush the dirt from around the small red area at the end. It took me a few moments to register what I was looking at, and when I did understand I felt my insides collapse. I moaned and threw myself backward across the floor until my hip slammed painfully into the stairs. I couldn't speak, couldn't breathe even. The horror of the moment consumed me fully.

I could only look over at the little object I had excavated from the earth: at the single finger, its nail painted bright red, pointing at me from the earth.

I heard a creak behind me, and I looked up and saw Stacy standing in the open door at the top of the stairs. She was wearing only her underwear and had a glass of water in her hands. Her face was streaked with mascara and old tears.

'What's wrong?' she asked, and I could hear the hurt still thick in her voice.

I looked back over at the finger sticking out of the dirt, pointing at me. From behind me I heard Stacy coming down the stairs. 'I was just getting a drink,' she said. 'Can you give me my money so I can go home now?'

81

Let me bring you back into the Garden for a minute or two. I won't keep you long, but it's important. Wendall got his date today—three weeks after me, October twenty-fifth.

'Fuck this shit,' he muttered after they brought him back from seeing his lawyer.

'What's up?'

'Bastards want to kill me.'

'Did you get your date, Wendall?' I sat up on my bed and leaned back against the cold bars.

'That stupid prick lawyer of mine just told me. End of next month.'

'That's too bad, Wendall. What'd he say about appeals?'

'He went on about some shit about the fifth circuit or the seventh circuit, or some fucking thing. It's all bullshit anyway, nobody's ever gonna let me out of here.'

'Are you scared?'

Wendall laughed. 'I'm not scared—dying doesn't bother me. It's just the loss of opportunity that bothers me.'

'How do you mean?'

'I wasn't done killing yet, Simon. I still feel like I got a lot of death left in me. I wanted to get out so I could go on one last trip.'

'Trip?'

'Yeah, man,' he said, and I heard him light up a cigarette. 'Take to the tar, cruise up and down the highways and byways of this great country of ours.'

'Is that what you used to do?'

'I'm a travellin' man, Sam, a hunter. Staying in one place has never been my style. Hell, I've killed pretty much all over the place.'

'How many people *have* you killed, Wendall?'

I heard a faint crackle as he sucked on his cigarette. 'A few.'

Somehow I found him most frightening when he said the least. 'Does it ever bother you?'

'Why would it?'

'Because they were people, Wendall. Someone's daughter, someone's sister.'

He laughed. 'Guilt is for the weak. The only things that ever bother me are the ones who got away. I think about them a lot.'

'Like who, for example?'

He coughed. 'There was this one little piece in some small town just outside of Atlanta. She can't have been much more than fourteen. Her name was Ruby. I got her talking real easy, and then just as I was about to take her these two state troopers drove up. It broke my heart to have to leave her there. I swung back round that way a few times over the next couple of days, but I never saw her again. Ended up taking this ugly bitch who died pretty much straight away.'

'Jesus, Wendall, you really are one sick mother.'

'That may be, Simon, but they're gonna fry your ass before they get to me. How many days you got left now?'

'Twenty-nine.'

'So I guess you get to warm it up for me, huh?'

'I guess so.'

'You decided what you're gonna have for your last meal yet?'

'Not yet.'

'I got it all figured out. I want some big old lobster in hot butter sauce, something real expensive. Make the bastards pay right up until the end, that's what I say.'

'You figured out what you're going to say to God?' I asked him.

Wendall fair brayed with laughter. 'Hell, Simon, I don't figure on getting close enough to God to actually say anything. I figure He ain't gonna have much to say to a person like me. How about you?'

'I don't believe in God.'

'Well, that's convenient.'

'It's not convenient, it's the truth.'

He chuckled. 'In here, when someone says something's the truth, that usually just means it's convenient.'

202

'It's true, I gave up on God a long time back.'

'My old man used to be a preacher,' Wendall said.

'Really?'

'Oh, yeah, one of those travelling holy rollers that used to move round the country collecting souls for God.' He laughed. 'I guess that's where I get it from. I'm just a regular chip off the old block.'

'Must be true what they say about preachers' kids then.'

'What do you mean?' he asked.

'Don't they say it's the preachers' kids who're always the wild ones?'

'My old man was a real bastard,' he said quietly.

'Why? What did he do?'

'What did he do? What did he *not* do is more like it.'

'Are you going to tell me you're the product of childhood abuse, Wendall? I expected a little more from you.'

He laughed, and it was a genuinely evil sound. 'No, Simon, I am who I am because of dedication and hard work.' There were many times during my conversations with Wendall when I was glad for the layers of concrete and steel between us. 'I don't blame my father for my life,' he continued. 'I thank him for it.'

'Because?'

'Because he introduced me to the notion of good and evil. Sitting listening to him talking to all those hick farmer holy rollers about heaven and hell was what got me thinking. And watching him after the sermons with their daughters and wives got me thinking even more.'

'Thinking about what?'

'About how fucking weak people are, and how easy it is to use them for whatever you want.'

'That's the big message that you took away from childhood?'

'Yup.'

'That's a really heart-warming story, Wendall.'

He laughed. 'Yeah, I guess it is.'

82

In these last few days of my life Wendall has become an almost constant source of dark wonders. He's becoming more open as the days tick slowly on. I have the sense that Wendall and I are on a ride together, and I'm not entirely sure I can see where it's heading.

'You know why they use the injection now?' he asked me one night.

'What?' I mumbled. It was after lights out and I'd been almost asleep when his voice drifted in from the dark.

'I said, do you know why they use the injection now?'

'Wendall, I'm trying to sleep.'

'There's plenty of time for that shit later, Simon. You got a needle waiting down the end of the corridor and you don't have time for a story? This is a good one, you'll like it.'

I sighed. 'Okay, Wendall, why do they use the injection now?'

His bed creaked and I heard a faint metallic clink as he leaned back against the bars of his cell. 'I heard this from Larry Harper. They did him late last year, before you got here, but he'd been in the Garden for fifteen years so he knew a lot about the place by then.'

'So . . . ?'

'Hold your fuckin' horses, Simon. You gotta let me put the story in context.'

'Context?'

'Yeah, man, fuckin' context.'

'Okay, sorry, put it in context.'

'So anyway, Larry told me this right before they did him. He was scared as shit by the end and I guess he just wanted to talk. I was pretty bored so I listened to him. Besides, you never know what's gonna be useful.'

'You've got a heart of gold, Wendall.'

'Are you gonna crack wise-ass all the time, or are you gonna let me finish?'

'Okay, okay, sorry.' I was awake now, and I *was* kind of interested.

'They used to use gas back in the old days, but then in the seventies they had that case that shut the death penalty down for a couple of years. You know about that one, Simon?'

All death row inmates know about that case. Wendall was talking about the US Supreme Court decision Furman v. Nebraska in 1972. Basically a bunch of judges ruled that the death penalty was in violation of the Eighth Amendment in that it constituted 'cruel and unusual punishment'. More than six hundred death row inmates across the country sentenced between 1967 and 1972 had their sentences commuted to life as a result of that decision. I guess back then all those cons must have thought it was Christmas. It didn't last long though. The different states just changed their laws to get around it. Revenge is too strong a thing to hold back for long. Utah kicked things off again on January seventeenth, 1977, when they executed Gary Gilmore by firing squad. Since then just about everybody's got back on the killing machine.

'Yeah,' I said. 'I know about that one.'

'Well, this is the good bit, because for the four years between when they stopped and when they started again, no one paid the gas chamber too much attention. What was the point, right? For all anyone knew it was just gonna rot.' He laughed. 'Which is exactly what it did. It just sat there getting dusty, and rotting.'

'Is there a point to this little history lesson, Wendall?'

'I'm serious, man—keep jerking me around and I don't finish the fucking story.' Wendall sounded genuinely peeved now.

'I'm just asking, Wendall.'

'Yeah, well, how about you just shut the fuck up and listen?'

'Sure.'

'So anyway, when the State changed the law so they could crank things up again in 1978 they thought they'd just take up where they left off. The first scheduled execution was this black man called George Clutterbuck.'

'What'd he done?'

'Fuck knows, killed some kids or something—that's not important. But what is important is that back then there were all kinds of budget problems or some shit and so they cut corners to save money. They got a guy in to check the gas chamber to make sure all the seals and shit was still okay.' Wendall chuckled. 'The only thing was that the guy they got in was some local hick who was basically just a plumber. He'd never even seen a gas chamber before so he didn't have a blue clue what the fuck he was doing. So this guy checks it out and says he thinks everything's shipshape and ready to go. A week later they bring old nigger Clutterbuck in and strap him in the chair. The warden asks him if he has any last words and Clutterbuck just says he hopes God has mercy on them all.' Wendall chuckled again in the darkness. 'Then the warden backs out of the chamber and they lock it up tight. Apparently they had a big crowd there for the execution, given it was the first one in nearly six years. There was some of the victim's family there plus a whole swag of officials. The Governor himself turned out for Clutterbuck's execution.

'So the executioner pulls the lever and his little bag of joy drops into the acid. Old nigger Clutterbuck made the usual mistake and tried to hold his breath—if you do that you just end up going into real bad convulsions—so old Clutterbuck is kickin' and buckin' in the chair and whining like a little girl. All that must have been hard enough on the witnesses, but then one of the guards out front starts to notice a funny smell.'

'Is this a true story, Wendall?' I asked.

'No shit, Simon. The fuckin' seals in the chamber had perished enough to let the gas out, and the stupid fuckin' plumber never bothered to check them properly. So this guard starts to smell this funny smell, like almonds, and before he can do anything about it he starts to feel faint and falls over. About that point everyone else started to smell it as well, and then all hell broke loose. They went for the door in a rush. Only problem is, the door opens inwards so the crush of people meant they couldn't open it. What a fuckin' thing that must have been.' Wendall laughed. 'All those people yelling and hollering like a bunch of sissies. It took three of the guards to push the door open from the other side, and by the time they finally did four people had died—the first guard who fell over, the governor's secretary, a reporter, and one of the victim's family. All the rest ended up in hospital.'

I sighed. 'What a nightmare.'

'First time I heard about it I nearly pissed my pants laughing,' said Wendall. 'They all go along to watch old Clutterbuck die, and then the gas reaches out through the glass and tries to take them as well.'

'So I guess somebody decided a lethal injection was safer.'

'Yeah, I guess so.'

'Nice story, Wendall.'

He laughed again. 'I thought you'd like it.'

I lay there in the dark for a while with Wendall's pictures running through my head. 'Why'd you feel the need to tell me about that, Wendall?'

He was quiet for a long time, and I was just thinking he hadn't heard me when he spoke to me very quietly.

'Think of it as an appetizer, Simon. Something to get your juices flowing.'

'What do you mean?'

He chuckled softly. 'Have you figured out the question yet, Simon?'

'No, I haven't. Truth is, Wendall, I'm not even sure I care anymore.'

'Oh, don't worry,' he said, 'you'll care.' And then he went silent.

Like I said, I think Wendall and I are on some kind of dark ride together. I have no doubt he's going to reveal all in his own good time. He doesn't seem the type to start something and then not finish it.

I must admit, though, I kind of hope they kill me before we get to wherever Wendall is taking me. I suspect that wherever it is, it won't be anywhere good.

83

One month out from my execution and the death machine is starting to get well and truly warmed up. There are rules in the Garden for how you kill people, and once the execution order is received the whole thing starts clicking smoothly into place. You can say what you like about the Garden, but in here they're real good at killing people.

Two pre-execution reports are prepared within the last month. The first is prepared three weeks out, the second one week out. Both reports include input from the warden, the guards and Father Jack. Sometimes they also include information from a psychiatrist if there's a concern that the inmate might be a little shaky in the head. That report must make for pretty interesting reading.

Yesterday when Father Jack came to see me I asked him what he was going to say about me.

'I don't know, Simon,' he said as he sat across from me in my cell on the well-worn steel chair.

'Well, what do you usually say?'

'I usually make a few comments about the inmate's spiritual and emotional well-being.'

I laughed. 'And just what the hell does that mean, Father?'

'I guess it means I tell them if you're right with God or not.'

'You really think anybody in this place ever gets right with God?'

He thought for a moment. 'I do, yes.'

'That doesn't seem right to me, Father.'

'And why is that, Simon?'

'It seems to me that people in here shouldn't get

209

the chance to make it right with God.'

'God forgives our sins, Simon.'

'Well, that's just not right.'

Father Jack stared at me with his dark eyes. 'Maybe God is more forgiving than you are.'

'I think some things are beyond forgiving.'

'And the things you did, Simon—are they beyond forgiving?'

I shook my head slowly. 'The things I've done are beyond everything. Beyond forgiving, beyond your God, beyond everything.'

'And just exactly what did you do, Simon?' The question was as quiet and sharp as a pinprick.

'You've read the file, Father.'

'I'm not asking what the file says, I'm asking what *you* say.'

'I say what the file says.'

'Well, then, I guess I'm asking you what you did.'

I sat there for a few moments, thinking. Part of me did want to tell him—it was such a heavy load to bear, and I had a feeling Father Jack would be one of the few people in the world who really could understand.

Father Jack, who spent a year in a pit full of corpses and somehow came out alive.

But I'd come too far to put down my burden now. I was trapped by my own actions. If I stopped now it would all have been for nothing, and I simply couldn't bear the thought of that.

'Why can't people just let me be, Father? I've taken responsibility for what's mine, so why can't people let me be?'

'Have you?' he asked quietly.

'Have I what?'

'Have you taken responsibility for what's yours?'

I shook my head. 'I'm sitting here, aren't I? I'm

waiting out these last few weeks and then I'm going to walk down the corridor with you and the warden without any fuss. I'm going to let you kill me without any trouble because that's what I deserve. What else can I do?'

'You can tell me what you did.'

Now I was starting to get pissed. 'Why don't you read the *goddamn file*?'

He was out of the chair and on me in a flash. I tried to bring my hands up to protect myself but the shackles held me back. Father Jack pinned me against the bunk with his hand at my throat and his knees on my chest. *'Don't you dare blaspheme in my presence, you little cock sucker,'* he hissed into my face. *'I know a hundred different ways to hurt you that'll never show, so watch your fucking mouth!'*

I gasped as he lifted the weight from my throat and sat back in his chair as if nothing had happened.

'You want to know why people won't leave you alone, Simon? he asked, his voice even again.

I nodded, and struggled back up into a sitting position on the bunk.

'Because you're the only one who can stop it. You've convinced yourself that going quietly to your death is a noble thing that somehow makes up for your part in it all, but that's a lie. The truth is you're too scared to do the right thing, and that sickens me.'

'What is the right thing?' I wheezed.

'Give her up,' he said as calmly as if he were asking me to pass the salt. 'You have to give her up.'

'I can't do that, Father.'

'Well then,' he said, going to the bars to wave for a guard, 'may God have mercy on your soul, Simon, because more young women will die. I know it. You know it.' He looked at me one last time as the guard

211

opened the cell door. 'Hell isn't a place, Simon—hell is what we do.'

I wanted to say something else to him, but he was gone before I could think of any reply.

84

Father Jack is right, of course, hell *is* what we do. I've thought about that a lot since he said it. It would be easy for me to blame others for the hell that my life has become, but that wouldn't be honest. I'm to blame for the state of my life.

And of course there's the other thing he said, the thing about more girls dying, though I try not to think about that because I don't want to go there just yet. I still have a month left to decide what to do.

The easiest thing would be to just do nothing. To let them kill me and then to roll away from the world without a second thought. I never asked for all this, it simply found me. It's not my fault that it all went so bad.

And if it wasn't for the image carved into my mind of Theresa's face looking up at me as she died, I could almost believe that.

85

We'll get back to Stacy in the basement in a moment, I promise, but first let me tell you about Gerald's shrink. His name was Dr Case, and he was a real piece of work.

'Hello, Mr Chance,' he said politely as he walked

into the interview room. 'Pleased to meet you.'

'Really?' I said. 'Whatever for?'

He looked uncertain how to respond as an awkward silence played itself out. I have to admit I was kind of enjoying myself. I knew I could convince him I was sane enough to be killed.

'Please,' he said finally, 'sit down.'

'Why, thank you.'

When we were both seated he opened his briefcase and pulled out a file with my name written in careful black printing on the top. 'Do you know why I'm here, Mr Chance?'

'You're here to assess my current state of mind, I believe.'

'That's correct. And do you know what the purpose of my assessment is?'

'Yes,' I smiled. 'It's to see if I'm sane enough to die.'

He coughed a little. It was a nervous thing. 'That's correct, Mr Chance. I have been engaged by your lawyer to assess your current mental status for the purposes of determining if you are fit to be executed.'

'I think you're going to find that I'm fit as a fiddle,' I said.

'Indeed. Well, as you can imagine there are a number of questions I'm going to need to ask you.'

'Fire away.'

He started in with the usual round of questions, all the standard stuff. Was I sleeping well? Yes. Was I eating? Yes. How was my mood? Fine. Did I hear voices? No. It only got interesting when he began asking me questions about paranoia.

'Do you ever feel like people are persecuting you?'

'Constantly,' I said, and I could almost see his shrink antennae bristling.

'Who do you feel is persecuting you?'

213

'This guy.'

'Which guy?'

'The one who speaks to me from the television.'

'I see. And how often does he speak to you?'

'Most nights.'

'What does he say?'

'He says he wants to kill me.'

'And what is his name, this guy?'

'Tommy.'

'And Tommy says he wants to kill you?'

'Yes.'

'Why do you think he wants to kill you?'

'Because he has to.'

'He has to?'

'Yes.'

'Why does he have to?'

'Because they're making him.'

'They?'

'Yup.'

'Who are "they"?'

'All them,' I said, pointing at the walls around me.

Dr Case looked around at the empty walls. 'And who exactly are "they"?'

I leaned forward on the table and looked him squarely in the eye. 'The voters,' I whispered.

'The "voters"?'

'That's right, the voters.'

Dr Case stopped writing. 'Are you talking about Governor Thomas Walls, Mr Chance?'

I smiled. 'Sure, Dr Case, who the hell did you think I was talking about?'

'And when you say he talks to you from the television, you mean you've been listening to the evening news broadcasts where he's been talking about the pending executions?'

'That's right, Dr Case. That bastard wants to kill me.'

He smiled, and it was the saddest excuse for a smile I think I've ever seen. 'Very good, Mr Chance.'

'Look, Dr Case, why don't we just cut through all the shit and get right down to it?'

'Fine,' said Dr Case, 'let's do that.'

'You want to know if I'm crazy or not, right?'

'I suppose you could put it that way.'

'So ask me.'

'All right, are you crazy, Mr Chance?'

'Nope.'

'So why do you want to die?'

'Because I feel bad about what I've done and I think it's fair for the State to execute me.'

'And what *exactly* do you feel bad about?'

'That's a stupid question, even for a shrink. How about the fact that I raped and murdered a girl? That good enough?'

'What I'm interested in, Mr Chance, is the nature of your stated remorse. Do you feel guilty for having killed those girls per se, or are you in fact just expressing some kind of obsessive emotional reaction to a situation that you have no real cognitive understanding of?'

'Where do you people learn to talk such shit?'

'Just answer the question please.'

'Ask me a sensible question and I'll be only too happy to answer it.'

I could see Dr Case was starting to get angry, which suited the hell out of me. 'Sane people don't want to die, Mr Chance.'

'That just shows how little you understand, Dr Case. Did you read my file?'

'No, I like to form my own judgement.'

'Christ, how can you form a judgement about the

state of my mind if you don't even know what I've done?'

'That's what I'm trained to do.'

'Well, consider this: I killed Theresa Wright by stabbing her over thirty times. I stabbed her in the breasts, the vagina, and the face. All this happened after I'd raped her. I held Theresa's body in my arms and watched her eyes as she died, and then I stabbed my own wife in the chest. What do you think about that?'

A fine sheen of sweat coated his forehead. 'I think you would have to be at least partially insane to do something like that to another person.'

'Wrong again, Dr Case. You'd have to be completely fucking insane to do something like that and then still want to live.'

'Sane people don't do things like that to other people, Mr Chance.'

'Crap. Sane people do that shit all the time, it's just the insane ones who feel good about it. I did an evil thing that I now greatly regret. I want to die. I deserve it. That's all there is, Dr Case, end of story.'

He looked like he was going to say something else, but in the end he must have rethought it. 'I'll be making my report available to your lawyer in a couple of days,' he said as he gathered his things.

'No rush,' I said, leaning back in my chair.

I think Dr Case was more pleased to leave me than he had been to meet me.

86

Gerald came in the next day to see me. For some unexplained reason they made us meet in the interview room. I don't like the place much. It stinks of hope gone sour.

'So what'd the shrink say?' I asked him.

'He said you were sane.'

'Now there's a surprise.'

'Don't look so smug, Simon, we're not done yet.'

'Oh, and how's that?'

'I'm meeting with Agent Hanson tomorrow to talk about the new forensic information he's come up with.'

I sighed. 'I don't want you meeting with him.'

'He may have information that could swing things our way, Simon.'

'No, Gerald, he may have some information that would swing things *your* way. My way is down the bottom of this corridor. I'll say it one more time, I don't want you to meet with him.'

'Well, that's just too bad, Simon, because I'm going to.'

'If you do I'll sack you.'

Gerald smiled. 'That's a pretty empty threat now, Simon. If you sack me this close to your execution I'll use that as immediate grounds to get a stay based on the fact that you have inadequate representation.'

'What a crock—they won't grant a stay based on that because they know everyone'll start sacking their lawyers.'

'That's probably true, Simon, but do you really want to take that risk? Believe me, if you sack me then I'll make getting a stay my personal crusade to the extent that what I'm doing now will look like goofing off.'

I wiped a weary hand across my eyes. 'Why the hell can't you just let it be, Gerald?'

'Because my instincts tell me there's something going on here that needs to be stopped'—he leaned forward over the small table—'and my instincts are never wrong.'

'Fine,' I said. 'Go see the fibby if you want, but I want to know everything he says and I want your word that you'll talk to me before you do anything else.'

'You have my word.'

I looked at him. 'Good.'

It wasn't good, but it was probably the best I was going to get.

87

And now, let me take you back down into the cellar—with me, and Stacy, and that little finger poking up from the earth.

I have never experienced a feeling of such complete and total paralysis as I did that morning. The horror was so overwhelming it had disconnected everything. Stacy was coming down the stairs behind me, and I was frozen solid.

'Can I have my money now?' she asked.

I heard her footsteps coming closer, and I scrambled desperately in the depths of my brain, flailing for the little switch inside my head that would let me move again.

'What did you do?' she said as she reached the bottom. 'This place *really* stinks now.'

And somehow, don't ask me how, that was enough to get me moving. I staggered to my feet and turned to face her.

She stopped, obviously frightened. 'What?'

'Nothing . . . I . . . if you go upstairs I'll bring you your money.' I was acutely conscious of the fact that I was completely naked. And I could sense the finger pointing at my back.

'I need to get my dress,' she said, nodding at the bundle beside the cot.

'Your dress?'

'Yeah, my dress.'

I stood staring at her with no idea what to do.

'Please,' she said. 'I just want to get my dress and my money, and go.' She looked around, wrinkling her nose. 'This place stinks.'

'I . . . of course,' I said, backing away from her. I figured that the finger was about three paces backwards, and if I kept my body between it and Stacy she wouldn't see it. I was right about the distance. On the third step I felt my heel come down on something sharp and hard. There was a small gristly snap as I put my full weight on it.

I had to fight the urge to vomit.

Stacy just stood there looking at me.

'What?' I finally asked her.

'I don't understand you.'

'What do you mean?'

'Well, at first I thought you were a nice man—I mean, you and your wife have some pretty strange tastes, but I thought you seemed a nice person. You were nice to me the first time.'

I couldn't think of what to say to her. The finger pushed up against my foot.

'And then you did what you did last night. How can you enjoy that?' she asked, her eyes beginning to mist up again. 'How can you enjoy treating a person like that?'

Standing there, with my foot on the little finger, I felt as if the world was sliding into craziness. 'I . . . I'm sorry.'

She shook her head slowly. 'Yeah, I bet.'

I just wanted her to go, to get her dress and her money and go. 'My wallet is in my pants,' I said, pointing to my clothes. 'Take whatever's in there.'

She slipped her dress over her head and then reached down and took my wallet from my pants. 'There's a hundred and twenty bucks in here,' she said, looking over at me.

'Fine, take it.'

'Thanks, I guess.'

A thought suddenly inserted itself into my head, a nasty little thought that nearly made me scream: I wondered what I'd do if I felt the finger wiggle under my heel.

'Just take it and *go*,' I snapped. I didn't want to be harsh, especially after what I'd done last night, but if I didn't take my foot off that finger soon I *was* going to scream.

'Okay, okay,' she said. 'I'm going.'

She brushed past me and started up the stairs, then stopped halfway and turned to look at me. 'You didn't have to be mean,' she said.

The absurdity of it all was too much; I started to giggle. She looked at me with her mascara-stained face and I could see the tears were back in her eyes again. 'You're a real *bastard*,' she spat at me.

I couldn't have stopped myself if I'd wanted to— the laughter poured out of me as if she'd slit me open with a knife. I fell to the ground, only dimly aware of the sound of her footsteps as she fled the cellar and ran from the house. I laughed until my belly ached and my cheeks were wet with tears. It was all too absurd. Too macabre. I laughed until I realized I was screaming, and then I ran upstairs to the toilet and vomited till there was nothing left.

88

It was a long time before I could face going back down into the cellar. A long time and a lot of beer. I called the school and said I was sick, and then sat down at the kitchen table and got myself quietly drunk. I'm not thankful for many things, but I do thank God for alcohol. Without it I would never have been able to get this far. I would certainly never have been able to go back down those stairs.

So I got as drunk as I could with what I had in the house, and then I went back down into the dark. I'd hoped that the finger would be gone, that somehow the earth would have just sucked it down into the depths and there'd be nothing more for me to do.

But it was still there.

I knelt down on the cellar floor, the earth chilly against my legs. Reaching out, I slowly stroked the finger. The skin was waxy and cold. Then, because there was nothing else I could have done, I began to brush away the dirt.

I remembered watching documentaries on television of bearded archaeologists digging up old bones. I remembered watching them gingerly peel back the earth as they uncovered monsters that had been dead for millions of years. I tried to make myself feel like that, like a scientist objectively digging up fossils.

And for a while that worked.

Slowly I uncovered the finger, and then worked my way back down to the hand. Stripped free of dirt, it lay there like a study in horror. The nails were broken and bloody, and the hand covered in cuts and scratches. It looked like a fleshy white spider, ravaged by sharp beaks for sport and then cast aside when all the fun had been pecked from it.

I have no idea how long all this took. Time seemed to have little meaning down there. I just kept pulling the dirt aside with my hands, singing absently to myself as I worked: *'Finger bone connected to the . . . hand bone, the hand bone connected to the . . . wrist bone . . . '*

The arm now lay completely exposed, and I'd cleared enough dirt from her side to make out the pale swell of a breast. I followed the line of her shoulder up to her neck, then with exaggerated care cleared the dirt from her face. I can't remember if I was singing or crying as I did it.

Eventually she lay before me, half in and half out of the ground. She looked very different to the pictures on the television. Her face was covered in dirt and marks, her eyes partially open and milky white. The blood had settled in her body, leaving ugly black bruises.

I could still tell it was her, though.

'Hello, Lisa,' I whispered as I brushed the dirt from her cheek.

She didn't reply. She was well past that.

I kept going until she was completely uncovered. There was a moment—when I was digging around her legs—that I nearly lost it. She had a carving knife in her. I think I screamed, or I moaned, or maybe I just kept singing quietly. I don't know. But sometime before dark I lifted her free of the earth and laid her out on the cellar floor.

89

I sat with her in the cellar for a long time. Not thinking. Not feeling. Eventually thoughts started to seep back into my mind, ideas and images that pulled at me. Staring at her battered and decomposing body, I felt the choice as clearly as if I were standing in front of two doors: insanity on the left, rational horror on the right.

I wanted the escape of insanity. Sitting down there, just the two of us alone in the darkness, I actually yearned for it. But madness was no longer an option. I'd made my choice a week ago when I'd walked down to the end of Porter's No. 1 and found what I'd found, and then done nothing.

Milly was Juliette's alone, but Lisa belonged to the two of us.

I suddenly remembered Goodlow's question in the staffroom two days ago: *Do you have kids?*

I giggled in the darkness. 'Two girls,' I said aloud. 'One lives in the forest and one lives in the ground.'

The sound of my voice in the quiet of the cellar was jarring, and I suddenly felt the closeness of the outside world. I made myself stand and go upstairs. After washing the dirt from my hands, I took my coat and left the house.

It was the smell that I was worried about, the stink of decay. Anyone coming in would notice it straight away. There was a hardware store three blocks from our house. I would need some supplies if I was going to contain the situation.

What an absurd picture it must have been: *Shortly after finding a dead girl in his cellar, Simon Chance sets out to contain the situation. He strides down the street*

confidently, his wallet in his back pocket and a shopping
list in his head.

I guess I thought if I could just push her back down into the ground, then everything would be okay. I was pretty inexperienced then—I didn't know that some things can't be held down.

Rot floats.

So I went to the hardware store to pick up the little bits and pieces I thought I'd need. I've since found out that the guy at the store has suffered terribly as a result of his brush with me. I read about him in one of the many magazine articles that came out around the time of the trial. Apparently he can't deal with the fact that he was the one who sold me the shovel and the bag of lime.

I feel bad about that. He was just doing his job. There's no reason for him to take on any blame. Still, I guess that's just what good people do.

'Hey, there,' he said, looking up from his paper as I walked in through the glass self-opening doors. I can't really remember too much of what he looked like now. He had black-rimmed glasses, I remember that, but nothing else about him really stood out. Mr Average selling hammers and nails.

'I need a shovel and a bag of lime,' I said without returning the pleasantry. I was running on empty at that point, and didn't have anything left for social lubricant.

He looked taken aback. I guess I must have been a little out of it, all things considered. He was quoted in the magazine article as saying my eyes looked like I'd 'walked straight out of hell'. It's possible, I guess, but I think it's more likely that he's romped things up a bit now he has the benefit of hindsight.

'Alrighty,' he said, gesturing to the far wall covered

in tools. 'We got shovels for all kinds of jobs. What exactly were you fixing to do?'

I stopped. 'What was I fixing to do?'

'Yup.'

I didn't quite know how to respond. 'With the shovel?'

'Yup.' The hardware guy looked at me, a hardware-guy smile stretched over his face. It was the kind of a smile you stuck on with duct tape. It'd wear well all day, and at night you could peel it off and soak it in water. 'Are you digging a trench or moving some fill?' he asked.

'Moving some fill,' I said, which was about as close to the truth as I thought I could get.

'Alrighty then,' he said, and turned back to his rack of tools. 'You'll be needing something like this.' He took down a long-handled shovel and passed it to me. 'This one's the Stanley 2000, we sell a lot of these. Good value and hard-wearing. We actually sell a lot of these little babies to tradesmen as well as the DIYs.'

I had no idea what a DIY was, but I took the shovel anyway. 'This is fine.'

'We got more if you want to look?'

'No, this is fine.'

'Alrighty. Now what else were you needing? Lime wasn't it?'

'Yes.'

'Alrighty, we got some bags over here.'

I followed him over to a pile of plastic sacks. 'How much were you after?'

I thought of Lisa lying naked and dead in our cellar. In the picture in my mind she seemed to stretch out forever. 'Quite a bit.'

'Alrighty,' he said, pulling some sacks down off the pile. 'We got ten, twenty, and thirty-pound bags.'

'Let me have one of the twenty-pound bags.'

'Alrighty,' he said, and stretched the smile out a little more. He picked up the bag and went back over to the counter. 'Alrighty, that'll be sixty-five dollars.'

I knew if he said alrighty one more time I'd have no choice but to pound on him with my new shovel, and once I got going there'd be no stopping till he was so far from alrighty he'd never come back.

It was a close-run thing in the end. He ran my credit card through the machine while I stood there gripping the wooden handle of my brand new Stanley 2000, my virgin shovel. He whistled tunelessly, and the sound made me think of air escaping from a corpse. I signed the receipt and bolted from the store before he could say anything else.

90

My plan was simple. I'd go back to the house, dig a much deeper hole in the cellar floor, and rebury her. Simple. The lime would go in the hole as well—I had this dim recollection that the Nazis had spread lime on corpses during the war to help them decompose quicker. I didn't know if that was actually true, and to be honest I still don't. The science of decomposition isn't something I've ever felt the urge to study.

Things didn't go the way I'd planned. In fact, things started going bad pretty much as soon as I began digging, because the more earth I moved the worse the smell got. I told myself that was because Lisa must have been leaking into the dirt underneath her, but in the back of my mind I knew that couldn't really be so—she'd only been in the ground two days at most.

It was when I got down about a foot below the depth that Lisa had been buried that things started to come completely undone.

You know the sound a shovel makes in soil? Kind of like a dry cough? Well, about a foot deeper in the ground I dug the shovel blade in again and it hit something solid. And this time it didn't make a dry coughing sound; this time it was more like a wet thud.

I froze.

Something flooded through me that was a cross between electricity and ice. My body knew what the shovel had found long before my brain did. I froze for what felt like a lifetime—holding the shovel in a white-knuckled grip and trying not to move it. The truth is I was desperately afraid of moving it.

Eventually, though, it became worse not knowing. I pulled and it came away easily, as if it were sliding out of a big bag of grease. I slowly raised the head of the shovel up to the single pale bulb that hung above me. Even with my hands shaking in the weak light I could see there was more than just dirt clinging to the steel. It glistened in the light of that little bulb.

Things get blurry for me after that. I know that sounds like a cop-out, but I can honestly only remember bits and pieces of what followed. I remember digging, and flashes of color in the dirt. I remember uncovering a tangle of pale limbs, and I remember the first face.

I think I remember the first face because it was the one I split open with the shovel. The blade had hit her just below the bridge of her nose, and it looked like someone had been at her head with a can opener. That's what I see in my nightmares—an obscene gash splitting her rotting face in two.

I remember those things, but the rest of it's a haze.

It was only much later that I found out there were three bodies beneath Lisa, the runaways who'd gone missing over the previous few months.

James Goodlow was the one who told me about them. There was Sarah Parker aged fifteen, Jessy Steinbeck aged sixteen, and Mary Holmes who was also sixteen. These three girls have been the hardest for me to connect with—I didn't know them before they died, you see? I don't have a concept of them as people, just as a dim memory of tangled white limbs.

And that terrible can-opener face.

I don't know why I can't remember much about that night of digging. I guess I must have gotten pretty drunk, judging from the empty bottles I found when I woke up the next morning, and maybe because it was all so terrible my brain decided to block most of it out.

The problem is that I can still *imagine* it. I can see what it must have been like even now as I write this. That's the problem when horror happens so close to home—it's all too easy to fill in the blanks. I can see the hole in the cellar floor, and the tangle of limbs. I can even imagine the smell. It must have been appalling because the other three had been down there for months.

I do remember sprinkling the lime on top of Lisa. The other three were beneath her. I remember the white powder drifting down onto her face, covering her in a fine layer like icing sugar on a cake. And her milky white half-open eyes looked up at me.

I do remember that.

And then the next thing I remember is waking up on the couch in the living room the following morning, covered in filth, stinking of sweat and death, and my head pounding like a demon. It was morning and sunlight streamed in the windows.

I staggered over to the windows and pulled the curtains shut. The sunlight hurt my eyes—and besides, there was no more room for sunlight in my life.

91

Are you starting to understand now? Can you see? You'd probably had to have spent the night digging with me in the cellar to fully understand, but I guess you can get some notion of how things got to be this fucked up.

I found a dead girl in the dirt under my house, and what did I do? Did I call the police? Did I call her family and tell them where they could find their daughter? Did I help her to get home?

No.

I went down to the local hardware store, I bought a shovel, and I pushed her back down again. I pushed her back down into the earth and when I found some more I pushed them under as well.

Except rot floats—that's what fucked the whole thing up. I didn't know it at the time, but I know it now.

Rot floats.

92

Darkness. The faint sounds of a man crying farther down the line. The sharp clink of metal on metal. Midnight conversations with Wendall in the Garden of Eden.

'Hey, Simon?'

'What?'

'You figured it out yet?'

'What?'

He chuckled softly. 'Me.'

'Can't we do this later, Wendall?' I was tired.

'Nope.'

I sighed. 'Well, I don't want to talk right now.'

'That's a shame, because I was gonna tell you something important.'

'What?'

'It was me.'

'It was you what?'

'I killed her kid.'

Wendall always had a way of getting my attention. 'Whose kid?'

He chuckled again. 'Sure you don't want to do this later, Simon?'

'No, I changed my mind.'

'How come?'

'Because I want to know.'

'Why?' I could almost hear the smile.

'Because.'

'What a bullshit answer.'

I sat up on my cot and leaned back against the cold bars. 'I want to know because I'm interested—okay?'

There was a long moment of silence as he considered my answer. 'Okay,' he finally said, 'that'll do for now.'

'So whose kid did you kill, Wendall?'

'Sondra's.'

It took me a moment to understand what he was saying. 'You mean Sondra Hilta, the woman who chants out at the executions?'

'The self-same one.'

'But her kid disappeared in 1978! You must have only been about twelve years old back then.'

'Eleven, actually.'

'Holy shit, Wendall, you can't be serious.'

'As serious as a sermon on Easter Friday.'

'You killed her little girl when you were only eleven years old?'

'Yup.'

'What in God's name for?'

He chuckled again. 'I didn't kill her in God's name, but close.'

'What do you mean?'

'I killed her in my father's name.'

'How could an eleven-year-old kill another kid?'

'I didn't kill her myself, exactly—I made my sister kill her.'

'Your *little* sister?'

'Yup.'

'But . . . *how*?'

'She was friends with my little sister—the two of them used to play together.'

'I don't believe you, Wendall. How do you make a little girl kill her friend? Kids just don't do that stuff.'

His bed creaked and his voice sounded suddenly cold in the darkness. 'Are you sure about that, Simon?'

And I guess I wasn't. I hadn't been sure of anything much for a very long time. 'Tell me, then,' I said.

There was the brief hiss of a match lighting. I heard him inhale deeply and breathe out slowly, and I caught a faint whiff of cigarette smoke through the bars.

And then he started to talk.

93

'We rolled into Milburn one afternoon in the summer of 1978. It was hot that day, and we were tired. We'd been driving a long time. My old man was pretty thick with God, and when he rolled into town it was like the advanced party for the Almighty Himself—as if the Good Lord sent my old man out ahead of Him to sort out the flock into the saved and the hell-bound.'

'Was he a Baptist?' I asked.

'You know, Simon, I never really knew exactly what he was.'

'Had he been ordained?'

'Who the fuck knows?' he said, sounding angry. 'Are you gonna let me tell the story or are we just gonna fuck with details?'

'Sorry, Wendall.'

'So anyway,' he continued, 'we'd never stayed long in one place—usually it was just long enough to take money from people's pockets and their daughters' virtue from between their legs.' Wendall chuckled his snake-in-the-grass chuckle. 'My old man had a thing for young skank. He didn't exactly like kids, but he did like them young. So whenever we rolled into some new place he'd start looking for girls he could introduce to God's loving ways.

'I used to watch him. The first time I crept under the truck when he was working on this little bitch who couldn't have been more than fourteen. In about fifteen minutes he had her praying and crying like she was gonna die if God didn't hear her. He had her naked and begging him to do her in twenty-five, and by thirty her little cherry had been popped and he was zipping up his fly again. That man was a fucking *master*.

'He started off telling me we were only going to stay in Milburn for one night, but the pickings were so good we ended up staying a week. It was the longest we'd stayed anywhere for a long time, and my little sis loved the chance to mix in with other kids just like she was normal. It was so goddamned funny—she'd be outside playing tea parties with some of the local kids and he'd be inside fucking their older sisters. I'd crawl under the truck and listen to them praying and moaning as he popped them, and she'd be playing with their little sisters right alongside.

'It all would have been okay if I hadn't sneezed. I was under there early one afternoon listening to him fucking some trailer-trash skank when it happened. I knew straight away he'd have heard me—he could hear a penny drop a mile away. All of a sudden the moaning stopped and there was a clumping of footsteps across the floor of the truck. The door slammed open and I saw his big pale hairy legs come storming out. I was scared stupid, just like a goddamn rabbit caught in the headlights. Then I saw his face as he bobbed down and I knew it was all over. Next thing I know he's got one of his big old hands knuckle deep in my hair and he's dragging me kicking and screaming out into the sunlight.

'I'm not scared of many things, but back then I was sure as hell scared of my old man. He'd beaten me unconscious more times than I could count, so I knew he was gonna do something *real* bad this time. He dragged me into the truck and threw me down so hard that my head slammed into the floor and bloodied my nose.

'"*Stand up*," he screamed at me, and I did, even though my knees were shaking and my nose was bleeding like a goddamned hose. He was screeching like a crazy man, "What in hell were you doing down

233

there, you dirty little pervert? Were you spying on me?"

'I tried to deny it, but he fucking knew. The girl was cowering on the bed, looking at us both. She was naked and she had a sheet pulled up around her. He grabbed it and pulled it away from her in one tug. "Is this what you've come to see?" he hissed at me. "Have you come to see *her*?"

'I was crying by then, pathetic little tears like a girl. He smacked me round the back of the head, and I can't say I blame him for that. Crybabies need a goddam slapping.

'"*Is it*?"

'I nodded my head like the fucking wimp I was and he laughed at me.

'"You see, Mary Louise?" he said to the girl. "This is what I was warning you about. Boys are bad, and they all want to squeeze their dirty little things inside you. Do you see that now?" She nodded her head. "All boys are the same, bad through and through. So full of sin they have to squeeze it out any chance they get." He turned back to me, and his eyes were blazing like fucking searchlights—at least that's how they looked when I was only eleven. "Pull down your pants," he said. And I was such a little pussy that the only thing I could do was whimper. "Do it," he said, and I did. "Now," he said to the girl, "you see that nasty little thing? You see his little boy-maggot?" She nodded. "That's the evil heart of him—that's what he wants to stick in you so he can fill you up with his sin. Do you see?"

'Standing with my pants down around my knees I felt like a goddamned freak. I could see how revolted she was by me, that goddamned piece of skank. She was the one being fucked and she looked at me like *I* was the freak.

234

'"Put it in her," my father said to me. I looked at him as if he'd just asked me to shit in her mouth. Still I couldn't say anything. Pussy.·

'The girl looked horrified too. "I don't want him to . . . " she started to say, but my father snapped at her, "Be quiet, child," and she did. Just like that. "Lie down." And she just lay back down like she was a robot.

'My old man was a fucking master—whatever else you say about him, you can't deny that. "Get on her," he said to me, and I couldn't move. All I had to do was fuck the little skank but I was such a pussy I couldn't even move. He hit me again. "*Get on her.*"

'So I did. I climbed up on top of her, with my nose dripping blood all over her and my dick as limp as a dead worm.' Wendall chuckled in his cell, and the sound chilled me. 'She closed her eyes and made this face the whole way through, like it was just the most disgusting thing she'd ever had to do. *Bitch.* And every time I tried to stick my limp little dick in her she'd wrinkle up her nose and make this noise—kind of like a grunt, except very quiet. I never got it in her, I just ended up rubbing against her till he let me stop.

'"Get off her, you fag pervert," he finally said. I clambered back down onto the floor and pulled up my pants. "That was just about the most pathetic thing I've ever seen," he said. "Now watch how a man of God does it."

'He undid his fly and pulled his big old thing out. Then he got between the girl's legs and knelt like he was praying. He closed his eyes and started to mumble. I couldn't hear what he was saying, but it sounded like there was a bunch of Hail Marys and Holy Ghosts in there. Then he finished praying, picked the girl up and shoved her down on top of him. He must have

235

hurt her because she started screaming and struggling like she had a baseball bat in her. There was blood too, I remember that. And all the time my old man was laughing and carrying on like he was on a direct line with God.'

'Jesus, Wendall,' I said, 'that sounds horrible. What'd you do?'

There was a pause and smoke drifted out from his cell into the corridor. 'I ran,' he finally said. 'I just picked myself up and I ran.'

'Where'd you go?'

'I went down to the river, and that's where I found them.'

'Your sister.'

'That's right, Simon,' he said, beginning to sound irritated again. 'Now are you going to shut up, or don't you want to hear how this ends?'

'Sorry.' I kept forgetting how he hated to be interrupted when he was on a roll.

'Anyway,' he continued, 'I don't know how I ended up down there. And I didn't know they were gonna be there, so I couldn't have planned it. I guess I just did the running and it was fate that did the steering. They were playing house in the rocks beside the river when I burst out of the bushes. I was going too fast to stop and I knocked the both of them over before I finally clattered to a halt on the stones. My sister must have seen the look on my face because she knew enough not to say anything, but Sondra's little bitch sealed her own fate—she looked at me and giggled. She was dead from there on in.

'"What the *fuck* are you laughing at?" I yelled as I scrambled to my feet and walked over to her. "*What the fuck are you laughing at*?" They were both scared then. I'd stopped running, but I was panting like a dog and my head was buzzing with so much angry shit it felt like a fucking beehive.

'"She wasn't laughing at you—were you, Margaret?" said my sister, as she started to stand.

'"Shut the fuck up," I told her, punching her in the forehead. She dropped moaning to the ground. "Now, what the fuck were you laughing at, bitch?" Margaret didn't know what to say, I could see that. Her little skank mouth didn't seem to feel the need to be so smart anymore.

'"I wasn't laughing," was all she said. I saw tears in her eyes and I remember feeling strong for the first time in my life. Hell, looking down at that piece of skank sniveling in fear, I felt like God fucking Almighty. "Lie down!" I yelled at her, and she did. You could have knocked me down with a goddam feather. I'd told her what to do and she did it. Just like my old man. And suddenly I knew what I had to do. I sat on top of her, pinning her arms to the ground with my knees. She was crying real good now, crying and begging me to let her go. Fucking skank bitch.

'"*Leave her alone, Wendall*," my sister whined from behind me, and I could hear how goddamned scared she was. I felt drunk with it all.

'Then I reached down and picked up a rock. It was kind of pyramid shaped, with a sharp point at one end. When Margaret saw me raise that rock over my head she started to scream. She didn't scream for long though. She stopped pretty much straight after the first blow. I still remember how it felt as I brought that rock down into her head. It was kind of a soft-meaty-crunch.'

He sighed. 'I rolled off her and I felt more alive than I'd ever felt before. My little sister was crying, and Margaret was making this wet gurgling noise.

237

That's when I had this great idea.'

'What?'

'I picked up the rock and went over to my sister. I gave it to her and told her to finish Margaret off.'

'Jesus,' I whispered, imagining the raw horror of that scene: the children, the tea party by the stream, the blood.

'Oh, yeah,' he chuckled, 'it was a fucking master stroke. She refused to at first, but I just went and got a stick and tortured Margaret until finally my poor sis had no choice but to do it.'

'So your sister killed her?'

'What was left of her after I'd finished. I made her pound on that little girl till she was ground meat. Couldn't even tell it was a person at the end, except for the clothes.'

I felt sick. 'What did you do then?'

'We washed ourselves up in the river and went home. That night there was a big storm and the river flooded. She must have been washed way off downstream somewhere. And the next day we left Milburn.'

'And that's it?'

'Yup.'

'And no one ever knew?'

Wendall laughed. 'Not till now. Cool story, huh?'

I looked over at the drawing of Sondra Hilta above the wash basin in my cell—the crude figure of a woman tied to a tree, a broken bottle dripping cartoon blood sticking out from between her cartoon legs: *Sondra finilly gets the fucking she deserves.*

'Yeah, Wendall,' I said, 'that's a real cool story.'

94

Two days after I'd reburied the girls in our cellar Goodlow came calling. There was still no sign of Juliette and I hadn't been back to school yet—I knew the town would be ablaze with the news that Milly's body had been found. Call me a coward, but I couldn't have faced that.

So instead I sat at home and drank beer. I hadn't washed or shaved for three days, and when I opened the door and saw him I must have looked about as much like a killer as a person could.

'Hello, Simon.' He was smiling, as if he hadn't noticed how I looked. But I knew better. Right from the first moment I met him I knew that this was a man who noticed *everything*.

I cleared my throat. 'Detective Goodlow.'

'You haven't been at school for a few days,' he said.

'I've been a little ill.'

'I see,' he nodded. 'Is this a bad time?'

'Not at all, please come in.' He followed me through into the kitchen. I didn't take him into the living room—it was littered with empty bottles, and was also closer to the cellar. 'How can I help?' I asked as I sat down in one of the kitchen chairs.

Goodlow sat directly opposite me. 'Did you know that we found Milly Brown's body?'

'No, I haven't been out much in the last couple of days.'

'Really?'

'Uh huh.'

'Is your wife home?'

'No. She went to visit with her family for a few days.'

'I see. You mind?' he asked, taking out a cigarette.

'No, go ahead.' Ordinarily I would have, but I thought the smoke might help cover up any smell that was still in the house. I'd left all the doors and windows open for three days so I was pretty sure the smell was gone, but I wasn't absolutely certain of it.

'All this stuff is a bitch,' he said as he took out a book of matches and tore one free. He had big hands, but he worked his fingers like tweezers. 'We're not used to this kind of thing here. Mostly my job is pretty quiet, which is how I like it.'

'Have you always lived in Bedford?' I asked, trying to sound relaxed and conversational.

'No. I moved here from Chicago eight years ago.'

'So what convinced you to give up the bright lights?'

He inhaled deeply, making the end of his cigarette glow bright orange. 'Too many years working homicide, I guess. One day I just decided I'd seen enough dead people to last me a lifetime.'

'And now here you are.'

He nodded slowly. 'And now here we are.'

There was a moment of silence as the words lay between us on the table. 'How can I help you, Detective?' I finally asked.

'You ever been out to Herbert Forest?'

'No,' I said, and regretted it as soon as it was out of my mouth. Mr Mack knew I'd been out there earlier that very week. I felt the sudden suck of quicksand all around me. One mistake now and the ground would have me.

'Really?' he said, smiling. 'Just about everybody in town has been out there at one time or another.'

I had to make a decision at that point about either going back, or keeping going forward. In the end I decided that innocent people probably never went

240

back to correct things. 'No, I've never been out there—
the great outdoors isn't really my thing.'

He laughed. 'I know what you mean.' And then
the laughter was gone and he was all quiet and careful again. 'So you've never been out there?'

'Nope, never.'

He took out a little black notebook and wrote a few
words. It was the same little black book he later pulled
out and read from at the trial. 'We found Milly in
Herbert Forest.'

'I see.'

'She was at the end of a small road called Porter's
No. 1.' It was strange hearing him say the name aloud.
Until then the only person I'd heard speak of Porter's
No. 1 was Milly.

'Never heard of it,' I said, trying to sound like it
was nothing to me. 'How did you find her?'

'An anonymous caller.'

I smiled. 'I thought tip-offs only happened on television.'

'Can you tell me where you were on the afternoon
of the twenty-fourth of February, Simon?'

'Am I a suspect, Detective?

'I guess no more and no less than anyone else is.'

'That seems fair,' I said. 'I was at school in a staff
meeting. Anyone there can vouch for me.'

'Can you tell me how long the meeting went for?'

'It started right after school and went through until just after five.'

'And what did you do after the meeting?'

'I marked a couple of papers in my classroom and
then came home.'

'Anyone see you in your classroom?'

'Not that I know of.'

'How'd you get home? Did you drive?'

'No, I took the bus.'

He scribbled down some more notes.

'Can I get you some coffee, Detective?'

He looked up. 'Can you keep a secret, Simon?'

His question threw me. 'What do you mean?'

'Can you keep a secret?' The way he said it was bizarre, like a kid whispering something in class behind the teacher's back.

'I . . . I guess.'

'She was tortured.'

I swallowed. 'Who?'

'Lisa Simkin.'

He was good. He was *very* good. Just as I thought he was about to invite me into the deep end, I discovered we were already far out at sea.

'Lisa Simkin?'

He nodded. 'Tortured real bad.'

'I didn't know you'd found her.'

'We haven't . . . not yet.'

'Then how . . . ?'

'I saw what he did to Milly Brown.' I didn't want him to tell me, but I knew he would. Goodlow had come to do some trawling—he wanted to drag his net along the bottom for a bit and see what came up. So he told me. He talked for half an hour about the autopsy, telling me what the coroner said about how she'd died. He also told me how long it had taken her to die. By the time he was finished I felt empty and sick.

'That's awful,' was all I could say.

He shook his head. 'In all the years I was working homicides I never saw anything even close to what this guy did to Milly.'

My hands were clasped in front of me on the table, and I didn't want to move them because I was afraid they'd be shaking too much. 'So how do you know that Lisa's been taken by the same person?'

Goodlow took out another cigarette. 'Because this kind of guy doesn't stop. He didn't start with Milly, either—she was just another link in a very long chain.'

'You think there are more?' Disjointed pictures of tangled white limbs half covered with dirt filled my mind. I saw the girl's rotting face, cut almost in half by a shovel.

He blew smoke across the table at me as if he was dusting my thoughts for fingerprints. 'You can bet on it, Simon. This man is a monster, a killer born and bred. He *needs* to kill. It's like a hunger with him, a hunger he feels driven to feed. He isn't going to stop until we catch him.'

'And you think the same person has taken Lisa Simkin?' I asked again, feeling the world fading around us.

'I know it.'

'How?'

'Like I said, Simon, he has to feed.'

'So she's dead, then?'

He nodded.

'And she was tortured like Milly?'

'I'd like to say I didn't think that, but I can't.'

We sat there for a long moment, staring at each other across the void of cigarette smoke and secrets. 'What are you going to do?' I finally asked.

Goodlow smiled. 'I'm going to stop him.'

I swallowed. 'And how are you going to do that?'

'He'll come to me.'

'What do you mean?'

'He'll come to me,' Goodlow said as he leaned forward and lowered his voice ever so slightly. 'One way or another, he'll come to me.'

I can't remember much else; he left shortly after that. But I do remember that last bit very clearly: *He'll come to me. One way or another, he'll come to me.*

95

On Monday the twenty-third of March, four days after I'd found Lisa, I went back to school for the last time. It was a clear sunny day, the air was crisp and clean, and I walked to the bus stop with a ghost. This time it wasn't Milly, or any of the other dead girls, but the ghost of possibilities that walked down the road with me.

I felt it beside me as soon as I left the house, as if it had been waiting outside for me all this time—unable to enter, but unwilling to leave. It was the ghost of the life that I could have had, and it walked beside me silently, not saying anything, just keeping pace. I felt a deep sadness come over me as I looked at him: a young man, clean-shaven and clean-living. A young man with a wife and a job, and a mildly successful writing career on the side. I saw a house, a dog, and eventually kids. A boy and a girl. I saw someone who lived a good life and worked hard for the people he loved.

But it was just a ghost, a dead reflection of someone who'd passed away long ago. There was no life in it, only the tragedy and heartbreak of possibilities lost. So I left it standing on the side of the road at the bus stop, and I didn't look back as the bus drove away. I never saw it again.

I think if I'd known that it was going to be my last day of teaching I would have tried harder. It would've been nice to have finished on a slightly more coherent note instead of the total mess that it ended up being.

'What should we do, Mr Chance?'

I looked up and saw the whole class staring at me. I hadn't told them what to do. 'Oh . . . uh . . . turn to . . . uh . . . '

'Are you okay, Mr Chance?' It was Michelle Rawlings. She was a nice kid, bright enough. She'd do well.

'Yes, thank you, Michelle. I'm still feeling a little unwell.' Someone snickered, but I ignored it.

'You want me to get you a glass of water or something?' Michelle asked. Someone from the back of the class made a loud kissing noise and Michelle blushed bright red. 'Shut up, dorks,' she snapped as she turned to face the boys in the back row.

'All right,' I said, 'that's enough. Now everyone turn to chapter five of the text and start reading.'

There was a moment of silence, and then Michelle spoke again. 'Which text, Mr Chance?'

A picture suddenly filled my head: a spade slicing into Michelle's face just above the bridge of her nose, splitting the skin and bone, opening her up like a tin can. I flinched and let out a small yelp as I covered my eyes.

'Mr Chance?'

It was a few moments before I could look back at them, and when I did I could still see that terrible image burnt into the darkness when I blinked.

'I need to go out for a moment,' I said, stumbling to the door. I didn't look back—I couldn't stand to see Michelle's face with that other terrible one superimposed on top of it. I went down the hall to the teacher's bathroom and splashed cold water on my face. That helped.

'Is everything all right?' I turned and saw Pervin'

Mervyn smiling at me. He always seemed to be smiling lately.

'Everything's fine.'

'You don't look fine.'

'Everything's fine,' I repeated.

'Really?'

'Really.'

'I hope your lovely wife is looking after you, Mr Chance,' he said, and licked his piggy lips. On any other day I might have got through that conversation, but this wasn't any other day. It took everything I had just to keep going; I had nothing left for Pervin' Mervyn's games.

'What exactly do you mean, Mervyn?' My voice was flat and low, and fool that he was he didn't recognize the danger he was in.

His grin never faltered, not even when I called him by his first name. 'I just hope that she's looking after you . . . adequately.'

I took a small step towards him. 'And why is that, Mervyn?'

'A man has . . . *needs*. You know what I mean?' He licked his lips again, and that was what tipped the balance—the little pink tongue sliding over his lips like a well-trained slug.

I heard a wet slap as my fist connected with his face, and felt a crunch. He went down like I'd shot him, and his great belly wobbled when his butt thudded into the ground. Jets of blood appeared on the front of his white shirt like magic. His nose had undergone some fundamental changes.

'You bastard,' he whined, holding one hand up to his broken and bloodied nose. 'You hit me, you fucking *bastard*.'

Somewhere inside me the brakes came off. I'd been

carrying everything around for days and I longed to put it all down. More than that, I longed to *smash* it all down.

I lunged at him.

'*Nooo* . . . ' he protested, but it was too late for all that. My knees hit him in the chest and he grunted as I knocked him backward onto the floor.

I raised my fist and he tried to cover his face with his hands. In that moment I knew I was going to kill him. I could see it as clearly as I could see the blood on his face.

'*I bet I know what you were doing in the forest,*' he squealed, '*that day you were away . . .* '

And I stopped, just like that, with my fist hovering over his face like a hammer.

'*I bet I know . . . I bet I know why you were out there . . .* '

I looked down at his face, at the blood smeared over his cheeks and across the floor.

He opened his eyes and looked up at me through his fingers. 'That's right,' he said, some of the sparkle creeping back into his piggy little eyes. 'I bet you haven't told the police you were out there, have you?'

All I could do was look at him, my fist losing focus with each passing moment.

Mervyn began to nod as his grin crawled out from under the blood. 'That's right, so don't think that you can ever hit me again, you *fuck!*' He wriggled away from me and struggled to his feet. 'You'd better just watch what you do, mister, because if you ever try anything like that again I'll hang you out to dry like an old pair of fucking socks.'

'What do you know?' I asked him, and even though the blood was all his I was the one feeling gutted. He was just guessing, I was sure of that, but even his guesses would be enough to bring the whole mess crumbling down on top of me.

'I know enough,' he said, wiping absently at the blood on his face. His nose continued to drip down the front of his shirt.

'What do you know?' I asked him again.

He smiled. 'Do you really need to ask me, Simon?' I stood there, silent. 'No, I didn't think so,' he continued. 'So let's just remember that from now on, shall we?'

I thought for a long moment before I spoke. 'What do you want?'

This time his piggy grin stretched so wide I thought his fat red lips would tear open. 'Surely you don't need to ask me *that*?'

And I guess I didn't—I'd always known what Mr Mack wanted, right from that very first day.

'I'll drop by later in the week,' he said, 'and we can *all* talk about what it is that I want.'

As he walked away from me, I wondered if it wouldn't have been better to just kill him right there. I could have too—I could have been on him in a few steps, and pounded him to paste before anyone could have come to help him.

But I didn't.

I guess we all have regrets.

96

In seventeen days' time I get to take my walk. Seventeen days. I think I can do that, I can hold it together for another seventeen days. That is if Gerald doesn't screw the whole thing up. Though it might be close, and that worries me.

'I met with Agent Hanson,' he said as he sat with me in the little gray interview room.

I sighed. 'And?'

'And I think we've got a chance.'

'Shit.'

Gerald looked at me over the little steel table. 'Are you ever going to tell me why you want to die, Simon?'

'Can't do that.'

'Fine. Then let me tell you what Agent Hanson said, okay?'

'Whatever.'

He spent about half an hour filling me in on all the sordid forensic details. I understood it at the time, but now, as I'm writing, it's hard to recall exactly. Words have always been my thing; science was never my strong point. Suffice to say that the fibby had enough forensic evidence to prove the girls hadn't died the way I said they'd died. That in itself wasn't a huge problem—all it proved was that I'd lied in my confessions about how I'd killed them. The most damning evidence came from Theresa.

'The stab wounds are all wrong,' said Gerald.

'What do you mean?'

'They had some kind of stabbing expert at Quantico take a look at her and he concluded she was killed by a left-handed person.'

I felt my heart sink. 'How did they conclude that?'

'Something about the depth and angle of the wounds.'

'I see.'

'So that means we now have forensic evidence which shows you didn't kill her, because you're right-handed.'

'I held the knife in my left hand.'

Gerald shook his head. 'No, sorry, they already

countered that one. Apparently they can tell from the nature of the wounds whether or not the person is normally left-handed or if they're right-handed and using the knife in their left hand to throw the forensics off.'

'Well, they're wrong.'

'I'm afraid not, Simon. This stuff looks sound. And there's more.'

Something in his voice set off a little ringing somewhere inside me. 'What?'

He paused for a moment. 'They're saying that the stab wounds were more likely to have been done by a woman.'

'That's bullshit.'

'Not according to their expert.'

'Then their expert is wrong.'

Gerald put down his pen and clasped his hands. He took in a long slow breath. 'Juliette is left-handed, isn't she? And she was down there with you.'

I slumped back in my chair. 'Jesus, Gerald, I *stabbed* Juliette, for God's sake. How could she kill that girl with a punctured lung? Hell, she could hardly *breathe*.'

'That doesn't help you, Simon. You could have stabbed her after she stabbed the girl.'

It felt like it was all coming down around me. 'I killed them,' was all I could mutter. 'No one else, just me.'

'I'm taking this stuff to the appeals court at the end of the week.'

'I don't want you to do this, Gerald, all right? I don't want you to do this.'

He smiled. 'So stiff me for the bill.'

'I'm *serious*.'

Gerald leaned forward, and when I saw his eyes I wondered how I could ever have mistaken him for a boy. 'So am *I*. Those girls deserve justice, Simon, and justice is what they're going to get.'

'You don't know what you're doing, Gerald. Let it be—please?'

He gathered his papers together and stood. 'I'll let you know about the appeal, Simon. We should have an answer from the Supreme Court by Friday.'

'There are things you don't understand, Gerald. I'm asking you to let it be. Please, just let it be.'

'Then *tell* me,' he said, suddenly pausing and looking over at me.

The possibility hung between us like a tightrope. But in the end I had no choice. 'I can't tell you.'

'Well, then I guess I'll speak to you after the appeal.'

97

'You look like shit,' Wendall said after the guards had brought me back to my cell.

'Thanks.'

'So what's up?'

I slumped down onto my narrow cot. 'I just got some bad news from my lawyer.'

'Really?'

'It looks like he's finally got decent grounds for an appeal.'

There was a pause. 'And that's bad news?'

'Yup.'

He laughed. 'And you think *I'm* the sick one.'

'You *are* the sick one, Wendall.' I heard him laugh again. 'You sure are happy for someone with only just over a month to live,' I said.

'Tell you what,' he said, 'how about if you do get a

pardon you give it to me. That way you get to die and I get to go on killing. Way I see it, we all win.'

'I don't think so, Wendall.'

'Oh, come on—why not?'

'Because I don't want to go to my grave with the knowledge that you're out there somewhere.'

He chuckled evilly. 'You mean me as well as that pretty wife of yours?'

'Fuck you, Wendall.'

'Just calling the cards as they lay, Simon. You and me both know she was the one who carved up those little bits of skank. You took the rap for her, sure, but she's still out there—and I bet she's starting to get real hungry.'

'Fuck you, Wendall.' I was tired of everyone poking away at me, tired of the questions, tired of having to struggle.

'That's just how it is, Simon. You could have stopped her but you never did. If she does it again, which we both know she will, then it's on your head. Now that don't worry me none, but I bet it sure eats away at you.'

'I don't want to talk about that.'

'Fair enough,' he said, 'but I can't help wondering how come you never stopped her, that's all I'm saying.'

I sighed. 'A long time ago I made a promise and I intend to keep it.'

'And?'

'And now I'm going to sleep for a while.'

'Oh, come *on*. You can't start something like that without finishing it.'

'I'm sleeping now, Wendall.' I lay down on my cot and closed my eyes. He said some other stuff, but I wasn't listening anymore. I was all the way back in

252

that little apartment in New York City where we first made love.

I was with Juliette.

98

I need to tell you about the promise I made to her long ago in that bare little New York apartment, before we started travelling. Don't worry, I'll be brief, but un less you know about it nothing else really makes sense. I've been waiting because I thought you needed to know more about us first.

I woke up that night, and the bed was empty. For a fleeting moment I thought I'd dreamed the whole thing, and then I rolled over and saw her standing looking out the window. She was naked, and the flashing neon street signs painted her red and green in the darkness. I looked at the graceful curve of her back, at the gentle swell of her buttocks, at her long beautiful legs. She was like a painting, a Madonna in filtered neon. Just looking at her made me want her so much my chest ached.

'Juliette?' She turned, and I saw her face was wet with tears. 'What's wrong?' I asked her, suddenly alarmed.

'I hurt,' was all she said.

'What do you mean?' I was worried that I'd injured her somehow with my frantic, clumsied lovemaking.

She walked over and sat down on the mattress. The room was very cold and I could see fine goosebumps on her skin. Her nipples were erect and hard, and despite the fact that I desperately wanted to be sensitive to her distress, the urge to kiss them was almost overpowering.

'I hurt,' she said again, looking at me with eyes stained red with tears.

I put my arms around her and pulled her close. 'What hurts?'

'My life hurts.'

'Your life hurts?'

She nodded.

'Oh, baby,' I said, hugging her, 'don't be sad.'

'I can't help it,' she said as fresh tears rolled down her cheeks and dripped onto her breasts. I bent down and kissed them away. They tasted salty and sweet at the same time.

'What is it that's making you feel like this?' I asked. 'Did I do something wrong?'

She shook her head. 'No, it's not you, it's just . . . '

'What? You can tell me.'

'People have hurt me my whole life, everyone I've ever known. Most times I can deal with it but . . . ' she sniffed and wiped her nose with her hand '. . . but when I meet someone I like, someone like you, it makes me afraid.'

'Afraid? Afraid of what?'

'I get afraid of when you'll hurt me as well.'

I took her by the shoulders and looked her straight in the eyes. 'I will never hurt you,' I said, '*never*.'

And she started to cry again, quiet little sobs that tore at my heart like knives.

'Look at me,' I said as I shook her gently. 'Juliette, look at me.' She turned her eyes up to mine, and when I saw the pain and sadness in them I flinched. 'I will *never* hurt you, Juliette.'

'I want to believe you,' she said. 'I really do.'

And in that cold apartment I made the promise that would damn us all to hell: 'As long as there is breath

254

in my body, and as long as my heart still beats, no harm will come to you. I *swear* it.'

Just like that.

She looked at me, and a sad smile came over her. Impossibly, she looked even more beautiful, a broken queen. She leaned forward and kissed me, a long passionate kiss that pulled me far away from the world and deep inside her.

When I made that promise I made it with all my heart and soul. I made it with everything I was and ever would be. I loved her from that very first time, and as long as I live no harm will come to her. That might seem hard to believe, that I could have said such a thing on the very first night we were together—and more than that, that I could actually have meant it— but I did.

If you understand nothing else about why all this happened, understand this: I loved her *deeply*.

I always have.

99

I left school just before lunch, Mr Mack's blood still drying on my fist. I didn't know at the time that I'd never be back, and even if I had I don't think I would've cared. It had all come so far apart now. There would be no happy endings for me, I knew that with a grim certainty.

I went to the bar I'd been in the other night. I didn't want to go back to my empty house, mostly because the house wasn't empty—it was empty of the living, that was true, but it was overflowing with the dead. So I went to the bar and spent the day getting quietly shit-faced. By the time the sun went down I was well on my way.

'Give me another one,' I said to the barman. It was a different guy tonight.

'Sure thing,' he said and poured me another beer. 'Think it's gonna rain tonight?' he asked.

'I dunno.' At that point I didn't give a flying fuck about the weather.

'The weather guy said it was gonna rain.'

'Really?'

'Yeah, said we might get a couple of inches tonight.'

I just nodded as I sipped my beer.

'Usually those weather guys are pretty accurate,' he said, polishing a glass with a small towel. 'Must be all those satellites they got.'

'I guess it must be.'

'How many of those satellites you think they got up there?'

'I really have no idea.'

He shook his head as he put the glass down and picked up another one. 'I bet they've got a lot of them.'

I have to admit to being a little disappointed in the standard of conversation. In the movies the hero always ends up having deeply cryptic conversations in bars. Maybe I could have with the guy from the other night, but not with this one. All this guy had to work with was the weather. I stayed till closing anyway, and by then I was far enough along the shit-faced road that I didn't care what he was saying.

Just before midnight I went into the men's room for one last piss. As I was standing at the urinal I looked up and saw some urban poet called Dave had scrawled 'Fuck the world' in black marker pen on the wall.

'You got that one right on the button, Dave,' I said

aloud to the empty washroom. 'Fuck the world, and fuck the horse it rode in on.' I tend to talk to myself more when I've been drinking. I'm not an angry-drunk, I'm more a dramatic-soliloquy-drunk.

By the time I got back to the bar the weather guy was turning off the lights and cleaning up. 'Sorry, buddy,' he said, 'I got to close up now.'

I waved a mock salute. 'No problem, buddy. Time I hit the fucking road any old how.' I'd like to think my sarcasm was sufficiently veiled that he missed it, but I'd hazard a guess it probably wasn't. Either way, I don't remember him saying goodnight as I left.

The street was dark and there was a cold wind blowing. A few people were still around, the last dregs of the evening-outers making their way home. I saw her as I was making my way slowly down to the taxi rank. She was standing on a street corner in the same little slut-red dress she'd dropped onto the dirt floor of our cellar four nights ago.

'Hello, Stacy,' I said. She looked at me, then turned and started walking away. 'Hey?' I called out.

'Leave me alone,' she said without stopping.

I ran up to her and grabbed her arm. 'I just wanted to talk,' I said, 'to say hello.'

'Yeah, well, I don't want to talk to you.'

'Why?'

'You figure it out,' she said, pulling her arm away. 'Now leave me alone.'

'Come on, the other night was just a game, that's all.' I knew how lame it sounded, and so did she.

'Some game,' she said as she turned to face me. I could see how angry and hurt she was. 'You think this is *easy*? You think it's *easy* to do what I do?'

'No . . . I mean—'

'Well, it fucking isn't easy, and it doesn't help when

pricks like you get your kicks out of rubbing my nose in it.'

'Stacy,' I said, 'please, I'm sorry. Let me make it up to you? Okay?'

She hesitated and for a moment I thought she was going to give in, but then she found whatever mettle she had left. 'Leave me alone,' she said, and disappeared into the night.

It was probably for the best. I did want to make it up to her, but I wanted to fuck her even more. And I suspect that one would have undone the integrity of the other.

100

I was wrong about one thing—the house wasn't empty. Juliette must have got home some time that afternoon. I knew as soon as I opened the door. The house felt warmer, and I could feel her in there waiting for me. As I got closer to the kitchen I could smell coffee.

She was sitting at the table, her back to the door. I didn't say anything. Instead I got a glass from the cupboard and filled it from the tap. I drank it quickly, most of it sloshing down over my face and onto my shirt. It felt good to be wet.

'Aren't you going to say hello?' she asked.

I filled my glass again. This time I poured it over my head, the cold water splashing over me and puddling on the floor.

'Well?' she said.

'Where have you been?' I asked her.

'I had to go somewhere.'

'Where?'

'That's not important.'

I smiled. 'Is that right? And what about the girls in the cellar? Were they important?'

'Not really.'

It was the utter lack of regard in her voice that got me. I spun round and threw my glass at the wall behind her. '*Christ, Juliette, how can you say that*? You *killed* four people! Jesus, you killed four *children*!'

She didn't flinch. Not when the glass shattered, not when I yelled. She sat as still as old bones. She didn't speak until after I was done, and when she did her voice was quiet and calm: 'Have you finished?'

I just looked at her. I was stunned. Four dead girls in the cellar and that was it—was I finished? We could have been talking about a dent she'd put in the car for all the concern she showed.

I slowly walked over to the kitchen table and sat down across from her. 'We have to talk, Juliette. We have to decide what to do.'

'What do you mean "what to do"?' she said. 'We don't have to *do* anything. We just go on living our lives.'

I sighed. 'Juliette, there are four dead girls buried in our cellar. We have to do something. We can't just pretend they aren't there.'

'Why not?'

'*Because we can't.*'

'Because isn't an answer, Simon.'

I suddenly felt tired, too tired to sit and argue with her about why we couldn't just forget about the fact that she'd killed four people. Maybe I could have done it sober, but there was no way I could do it drunk. 'I'm going to bed. I can't do this now.'

'I love you,' she said.

I looked over at her and saw how much she meant it—even in the middle of all this she meant it. 'I love you too,' I said.

As I walked slowly down the hall to the bathroom I could hear her cleaning up in the kitchen. It took me a while to find the bathroom light switch; I guess I must have been drunker than I'd thought.

And when I did, I wished I never had. I wished that bathroom could have stayed dark forever.

Carol Keenan was splayed out in the shower stall, her blank lifeless eyes staring at me. Pretty Carol Keenan who'd wanted to make a few extra dollars cleaning houses so she could go find God in Hawaii. Her hands were tied to the metal showerhead above her head, and a piece of gray duct tape covered her mouth. She was naked apart from the blood.

And there was *so* much blood it covered her like a shroud.

Her legs were splayed crudely apart and I could see that she'd been laid open by the frenzied attack, cut up so badly her right leg was almost completely severed.

Horror is a hopelessly inadequate word to describe what I felt in that moment as I looked at her, but I can't think of anything else. Nothing really comes close, so that will have to do.

Horror.

101

Juliette brought me cups of lemon tea, that's what I remember the clearest. I went away for a time, somewhere inside, and she brought me cups of lemon tea.

'Drink this,' she'd say as she held the cup to my lips. I didn't like the taste—it was like drinking hot cleaning fluid—and after the tea she'd go away for a while. Occasionally I'd feel her near me, holding my hand, or resting her head on my stomach.

But mostly I was alone.

I slept a lot, and when I did Milly would come. She wouldn't speak, she just stood and looked at me.

Looking back now, I guess I must have gone crazy for a while. If it wasn't insanity then it was something close. It was like being lost in a vast gray space where there are no walls or boundaries, no rules even. Every so often a little piece of reality would leak in, but it would always fade just as quickly as it came.

In the end it was Milly who convinced me I had to go back.

You can't stay here.

'But I want to,' I said to her. We were sitting alone together in the woods on the little cot from the cellar.

You have to go back.

'But . . . but it hurts too much back there.'

She shook her head. *You have to.*

I couldn't look at her, so I looked down at the forest floor. It rippled, like shapes moving under a blanket.

You know what you have to do, Simon.

'I promised her I would never hurt her.'

It has to end.

'I know that, but I promised her.'

A man makes all kinds of promises—promises with his spoken word, and promises with how he lives his life.

I felt her cold hand cup my chin and slowly raise my head. Her milky eyes looked deep into mine.

What about the promises you made to us?

Then she leaned forward and kissed me with her dead mouth. Her cold tongue slid into me, and I tasted dirt. I pulled back from her, shrieking and flailing my arms to escape her icy grip.

And then I found myself sitting bolt upright in my bed, just like in the movies. The light was on and Juliette was shaking me and crying. I was sweating, my body ached, and my mouth tasted foul and gritty.

I was back from the gray land.

Back with promises to keep.

102

It's all starting to pick up speed, I can feel it. I've got a little less than two weeks to go now, twelve days to be exact. I don't sleep much, only a few hours a night, and I pace a lot. Writing and pacing is about all I have left.

I feel jittery and unsettled, like I've been drinking too much coffee. I know that can't be true because the stuff they give us in here isn't coffee—it's more a perversion of coffee.

It's hard to make myself sit down and write. Whenever I do my stomach starts to churn and I have to get up and move around. I write in fifteen-minute bursts and then I have to pace for a while. After fifteen minutes of concentrating on this stuff it's either pacing or screaming. I'll choose pacing any time.

I thought that writing this down would help me, but as I get closer to the end—both the one in the story and the one down the hall—it's starting to feel worse. I'm not scared, not really, but I do feel a kind of restless worry. I don't want to run out of time, you see? I want to finish this. My problem is how to stay focused on one thing when the past and the present seem so interlocked.

Bear with me for a little longer, just a little longer.

103

I think the fibby feels the tick of the clock now as well. As each day passes I think he feels the pressure of knowing that soon I'll be out of his grasp. Not surprisingly his maneuvers have become more direct. Today he brought an old friend in to see me.

'Hello, Detective.'

'Hello, Simon,' Goodlow said as he sat opposite me in the interview room. He looked older than the last time I'd seen him, somehow a little more worn. I guess I shouldn't have been surprised—Goodlow feels his own share of guilt.

'I thought it might be good for you to hear what Detective Goodlow has to say,' said Agent Hanson.

'How are you doing, Simon?' Goodlow asked, and I could hear the genuine concern in his voice. I always respected him for that, he's never tried to bullshit me. Whatever he said was what he was really thinking. Sure he might hold some stuff back, but I always felt I could trust what he did let out.

'I'm hanging in there,' I said.

He nodded. 'Good.'

'We have some news that you might be interested in,' said Agent Hanson. He looked at me with a steady gaze.

'I'm listening,' I said.

Goodlow folded his big hands in front of him on the table. He seemed to be gathering his thoughts. He was a considered man. 'You don't need to say anything, Simon, not unless you want to. Right now I just want you to listen to what I have to say and to think about it.'

'Fair enough.'

'You mind?' he asked as he took out a pack of cigarettes.

I smiled. 'That stuff will kill you one day, Detective Goodlow.'

'Tell me something I don't know.' He lit the cigarette and smoked quietly for a moment. When he did finally speak his voice was low and intense. 'I need to talk to you about your wife.'

I didn't respond, didn't breathe even. Goodlow was so sharp he could read the thoughts on my breath.

'We both know it wasn't you who killed those girls. I always suspected it, and now Agent Hanson here has proved it with his experts up at Quantico.'

'If that's true, Detective, then why am I sitting here in chains staring down the working end of a lethal injection?'

He shook his head. 'I'm not here to talk about how you can save your own skin—it's something much more important than that.'

'More important than saving my own life?'

He looked at me then, with those all-seeing eyes of his. 'I don't think you're all that interested in saving yourself. I think you probably want this to happen about as much as the parents of those poor kids do.' I didn't say anything. It was too dangerous with this man. 'I've sat with a lot of different people in my life, Simon, people who've done all kinds of terrible things, and basically you can break 'em up into two piles: good people who lost their way, and evil people who made their way.' He drew in a long slow breath; the end of his cigarette glowed a sudden radiant orange and I heard a tiny crackle. 'I don't think you're an evil man, Simon,' he finally said. 'I think you just lost your way.'

For some reason I suddenly *wanted* to tell him, I wanted James Goodlow to know it all and to judge me accordingly. He was a decent man, I knew that—I felt it—and I guess a part of me understood that only a decent man could really tell me what the truth was. Wendall said that in the Garden the truth was whatever was convenient, but I knew that with Goodlow the truth would always be the truth.

I wanted to tell him so badly in that moment it actually *hurt*. That's what everyone wanted—Agent Hanson, Goodlow, even me—but I had promises to keep, and twelve more days to keep them. So I said nothing.

'You have to tell us about her, Simon,' Goodlow said. 'It has to stop.'

'It stops with me,' I said, 'in two weeks' time.'

Goodlow shook his head. 'I know you don't believe that, Simon. You're a smart man and you know that it just doesn't work like that. Some things don't stop, they have to *be* stopped.'

'What I believe, Detective Goodlow, is that it *will* stop, in twelve days' time.'

'Did you know any of the girls' parents, Simon?' Agent Hanson broke in. He was good in his own way—not as subtle as Goodlow, but he had a certain way of getting under your skin.

'No.'

'Did you know Milly's dad, Patrick Brown?'

I shrugged. 'I saw him once in a grocery store.'

Agent Hanson reached into his pocket and pulled out an envelope. He tossed it across the table at me.

'What's this?' I asked him, not looking down.

'It's a letter he wanted you to read.' I heard a small crackle as Goodlow inhaled another lungful of cancer. Agent Hanson leaned forward over the table. 'We told him that we think you didn't do it, that you're covering for the real killer. We told him that we thought this other person was going to kill again and again unless we can do something to stop it. Mr Brown wanted you to read this.'

It was grimly ironic—I'd wanted to reach out to Patrick Brown in his suffering, and now here he was reaching out to me in mine. I picked up the envelope and slowly opened it.

I'm not going to tell you what Patrick Brown said in that letter because it was very personal. He told me things about his daughter that he wouldn't want the whole world to know, the private memories of a father who loved his little girl very much. Suffice to say that reading that letter was one of the most painful things I've ever had to do. There was such a deep and abiding sense of sadness in his words that it was almost unbearable. He begged me to tell the police whatever it was they needed to know. He begged me to end it.

I sat holding Patrick Brown's letter for a long time before I could speak. I was thinking about how he'd looked, standing in that store.

And of course I was also thinking about Milly.

I was going to end it, but I couldn't do it through these men. Some roads must be walked alone. If I'd learned nothing else from all this horror, I'd certainly learned that.

'I don't have anything to say to you,' I finally said.

Goodlow sighed. 'She's going to kill again, Simon. We all know that. Do you really want that on your conscience?'

I felt very old, and very tired. 'I'll take whatever's mine with me when I go,' I muttered.

'It's not what's yours that concerns me,' said Goodlow. 'It's what's *hers*.'

104

I have to tell you at this point that I'm not being completely forthcoming with you. There are some things I'm leaving out because I'm worried they may confiscate my notebooks and read them before they kill me. That's why I have to be careful about what I say here. There are some things that can only be said once I'm in the ground. Don't be afraid that you'll miss out though—you'll get to see it all before the end, but not till I'm gone. I've figured out a rough plan, but I'm still working on the details. There are some questions I need to answer first.

And I have to be careful.

105

'We can't put her in the cellar,' I said to Juliette as we sat in the kitchen drinking coffee. It was very early, and the sunlight crept slowly over us as we talked.

'Why not?' she asked.

I rubbed my eyes with the base of my palm. I felt deadly tired. 'There's no room, and besides, I just . . . I can't do that again.'

'Okay,' she said, shrugging her shoulders. 'What about in the garden?'

'The garden?'

'Well, why not? It has to be easier to dig.'

I'd given up trying to hang on to the world by then. I figured I may as well just take my feet off the bottom and let the current take me where it will. 'You don't think the neighbors would get suspicious, what with us digging a grave in the back yard and all?'

She shrugged. 'Well, I don't know.'

'I'm going to take her out into the forest.'

'Herbert Forest?'

It was like we were discussing getting a service for the car. 'Yup.'

Somewhere deep within me I knew what a horror we had become, but I couldn't afford to go there now. Inside that place was only endless, mindless screaming, and there'd be plenty of time for all that later.

You'll have to forgive me if I keep using that word—horror—it's just that my mind seems to keep coming back to it again and again.

'You don't have to do this,' she said.

'Yes, I do.'

She came around behind my chair and let her arms loop around me. 'I love you—you know that, don't you?'

'I know.'

She kissed my ear, brushing it with her teeth and tongue. 'Hurry back,' she whispered and I felt myself getting hard. It's funny how sex cuts across everything, at least it does for me.

'We have to leave, Juliette. Once I've got rid of . . . once I've taken Carol up into the forest we can wait a few days, and then we have to leave.'

'But I like it here.'

'It doesn't matter, we have to leave. After all this . . . ' I sighed ' . . . after all this killing we *have* to leave.' She looked at me and opened her mouth as if she was about to argue, but then she closed it again. 'We're going to go far away from here,' I continued, 'far away from everything, and then we're going to start over.'

I had it all figured out. We were going to go up north, *all* the way up north, to Alaska. Then I was going to swap our station wagon for a four by four and we'd drive out into the wilderness. I'd buy us a cabin that was so far away from the rest of the world that she couldn't hurt anyone ever again. I'd write books, we'd talk, and she would slowly heal. We'd live there together for the rest of our days. It was a simple plan, but it was all I had between me and the mad screaming darkness that pulled at me from all sides. I clung to it, and fool that I was I actually thought it could work.

106

Milly rode with me and Carol out to the forest. I could see her in the corner of my eye. If I looked directly over at her she would disappear, but if I kept my eyes on the road I could see her beside me. She didn't speak, and so we rode in silence.

It had been a job getting Carol into the car. Fortunately she was only just starting to stink, even though she'd been sitting in the bathroom for two days, but she was cold and stiff, and had lost all the beauty she'd once had in life. Now she was as ghastly as any B-grade horror movie prop. I wrapped her in a large roll of black plastic so I didn't trail blood through the house. Everything they ever said about dead bodies is true, she weighed a ton. In the end I slid her down the hall; I couldn't lift her. Then I heaved her into the car, covered her in boxes, and set out for the forest.

It was a beautiful day.

I went all the way round to the other side of the forest this time. It would have been too dangerous to go anywhere near Porter's No. 1. I didn't really think too much about where I was going, I just followed the roads into the forest until they got smaller and smaller. I wasn't after any particular destination, just somewhere quiet. Although it was more than that, I wanted somewhere *secret*.

Eventually I stopped at the bottom of some shitty little dead-end road. It was dark under the trees. It didn't look like the light ever made it down to the ground—which was just perfect for the kind of work that I was engaged in. I sat there for a long time, my hands on the steering wheel, but I can't recall what I was thinking. Dark thoughts would be a safe bet.

Simon.

I looked up and saw Milly standing in the gloom in front of my car, naked and bloody.

You know what has to be done, she mouthed silently.

I opened my mouth to speak, but she was already gone. I guess that was a blessing. I don't know what I would have said to her.

I had to push Carol out the back of the station wagon—she was too heavy to pull. I clambered over her, wedged my back up against the seats, and pushed her out the back with my feet. It was hard work, almost like she didn't want to go. I don't blame her. Who would want to lie out there in the woods all alone?

She tumbled from the back of the wagon and hit the ground with a thump. It was a terrible sound, dead meat and plastic. I dragged her a short way into the bushes, and laid her down at the base of a large tree. There were some yellow wildflowers growing nearby, so I picked a small bunch and placed them on her. It was a pathetically inadequate gesture, but I felt the need to do something. I couldn't just leave her.

Except, of course, that's a lie I tell myself now to

270

make myself feel better, because leave her is exactly what I did.

I stood looking down at her for as long as I could stand it, then I ran back to the car and roared out of the darkness beneath the trees. I didn't slow down till I was halfway back to Bedford.

107

Goodlow has always been there, that's what it feels like. He was in our house when I got back from dumping Carol's body in the forest, and that scared the hell out of me.

'Hello, Simon,' he said as I came into the living room. I'd heard him talking with Juliette when I opened the door.

'Hello, Detective Goodlow.'

'Simon,' said Juliette, 'Detective Goodlow just dropped round to ask us some questions. Apparently another girl has gone missing.'

'Really?' I said. 'That's awful. Who is it?'

'Carol Keenan,' Goodlow replied, his eyes studying me.

'It's just terrible,' said Juliette as she picked up her cup of tea from the table and cradled it in her lap. 'I told the detective how we know Carol. It's just terrible.'

'Yes it is,' I said. 'Do you think she's been taken by the same person?'

Goodlow shrugged. 'It's too early to say at this point, but we're obviously very concerned for her safety.'

'Of course,' I said.

'Come and sit down, honey,' Juliette said as she patted the arm of her chair. I went and sat beside her. 'The detective said they're asking anyone who knew Carol for help in finding her.'

'Well, like I said before, Detective, we'll do anything we can to help.'

Goodlow smiled. 'I'm sure.'

There was a moment of silence. 'Can I get you some more tea, Detective?' Juliette finally asked.

'That would be very nice, thank you.'

While Juliette was out in the kitchen he turned to me and leaned forward. 'We think we know who he is,' he said in a stage whisper.

'Who who is?' I asked, suddenly aware that I sounded like a nervous owl.

'The killer.' He didn't blink. Neither did I, and if Juliette hadn't come back in with the tea I think we would have just kept staring at each other until our eyes dried up and shriveled away.

'Here's your tea, Detective,' she said as she placed it on the table beside him.

'Thank you.'

'So how can we help?' Juliette asked once she'd settled back into her chair.

'Just some routine questions, really.'

'Fire away,' I said.

'When was the last time you both saw Carol?'

'Last week,' said Juliette. 'On Tuesday I think it was.'

'What time was that?'

'Simon took her home about six I think, wasn't it?' I nodded.

'Did you take her straight home?'

'Yes, I did.'

'And she was fine when you left her?'

'That's right,' I said.

'Mrs Chance—'

'Juliette.'

Goodlow smiled. 'Juliette, then. Did Carol say anything to you that you think it might be important for me to know?'

'Such as . . . ?'

'Did she mention any problems she was having? Trouble with boyfriends? Anything that had upset her?'

'No,' said Juliette. 'In fact, she seemed like the picture of happiness from what I could tell. She certainly never talked about anything that was worrying her.'

'I see,' he said, scribbling notes in his little notebook. 'And what about you, Simon?'

'She didn't say anything to me.'

Goodlow raised his eyebrows. 'You mean she didn't speak to you?'

'No, sorry, I mean she didn't say anything that seemed significant to me.'

'Oh, I see.'

'Do you think it's someone she knows?' asked Juliette.

Goodlow looked first at her, then at me. 'Yes,' he said. 'Yes, we do.'

As he was leaving, Goodlow turned to me at the door. 'I didn't want to worry your wife,' he said, 'but we think it's someone local.'

'The killer?'

'Yeah.'

'I suppose we'd better be careful then.'

His smile was so hard you could have broken rocks on it. 'I think you should be very careful, Simon.'

108

'He thinks it's you, doesn't he?' Juliette asked once Goodlow had gone. We were in the living room again.

'Yes, I think he does.'

She frowned. 'Well, he can't prove anything.'

'You think so?'

She came over to me and laid her head on my lap. 'I know so,' she said.

'Oh, my Juliette,' I said, gently stroking her hair. 'It's only a matter of time till he makes his move, and when he does we're finished. There are bodies in the cellar, and I'd guess there's enough trace evidence scattered around this place to convict us ten times over.'

I'd read sufficient crime novels in my time to know that you can't ever completely erase the evidence of a murder. There's always something you forget, a strand of hair or a scratch on a wall. We hadn't even really tried to clean the house. We'd wiped up the worst of it, as you do, but there was still enough death left slicked over the place that they'd find what they needed pretty quickly. A pair of tweezers and a little bit of luminol would be all they'd need to unravel it.

'I won't let them hurt you,' she said.

'That's why we have to leave, Juliette. We have to give it a couple of days, three at the most, and then slip out of town in the middle of the night and disappear.'

'But I like it here,' she said. 'I like the people.'

'I know,' I said, suppressing the urge to shudder, 'but we have to go.'

It was true, she *did* like the people of Bedford—in fact, Juliette had developed a real taste for them.

109

'This time I think we got it,' beamed Gerald from across the table in the interview room. It was lunchtime, and the smell of corn fritters and coffee drifted in from the corridor.

'What do you mean?' I asked him.

'I mean that I've just filed papers with the court to get a stay based on the new evidence. It's taken me a little longer than I would've liked to get it done, but I wanted to make sure it was solid.'

Ten days out from my execution and Gerald still won't quit. He's like a fucking terrier down a rat hole.

'No one's going to grant a stay based on a bunch of scientific mumbo-jumbo.'

'That "mumbo-jumbo" as you call it just happens to be based on the sworn statement of one of the FBI's foremost experts on stabbing homicides. And that carries a bit of weight.'

'I can't believe I'm missing my lunch for this shit,' I said as I pushed myself to my feet. 'Get out of here and stop wasting my time.'

Gerald stood too, his face flushed and angry. 'Sit the *fuck down*!' I'd never heard him swear before. In fact, up until that moment I hadn't known he could, so he took me a little by surprise. I plopped back down onto my stool. 'You *are* going to talk to me, Simon, and you *are* going to tell me what the *fuck* this is all about.'

'I'm missing my lunch,' I said lamely. 'Today's Friday. We always have corn fritters on Friday.'

'*Fuck* the corn fritters, Simon. At this rate you've only got one more Friday left.'

'All the more reason for me to go enjoy my fritters while I can.'

Gerald slumped back in his chair. 'Why can't you just tell me, Simon? Why can't you just say whatever it is that's got you so fired up to die?'

'There are things you don't understand, Gerald.'

He banged his fist on the small metal table. '*God damn it, Simon!* You keep saying that as if I'm just supposed to accept it and let you die!'

'That's right.'

'Well, I can't!'

I sighed. 'Just let it go, Gerald. Pack up your briefcase, go back home to your family, and forget about me.'

'Don't you think I'd like to do that? Don't you think I'd like to just walk away from this whole awful fucking mess and forget you ever existed? But I've had those girls in my head since the first day I read your files. I've seen all the pictures and read all the reports, so don't you tell me to just go home and forget about it. Christ,' he said shaking his head in his hands, 'I even dream about them.'

'What do you dream about?' I asked in a quiet voice.

'They come to me in my sleep, all of them, and they tell me things.'

'What? What do they tell you?'

He looked at me then, and he showed me the depth of his torment for the first time. 'They say the killing isn't over yet. They say it isn't going to stop with your death. That's why I can't just walk away from it.'

I thought for a long moment. Gerald was in this far deeper than I'd ever imagined. I couldn't leave him with that—he was a good man, which is why this has all been so hard for him. 'I'll make you a deal.'

'What?'

'When is it too late to go back? When's the last

chance finally up?'

'I guess that would be when we get word from the Governor about clemency.'

'When does that happen?'

'If we haven't heard by the time we're moving into the last hour then I'll ring him from the warden's office.'

I nodded. 'And if the Governor says no?'

Gerald sighed. 'If nothing else has worked, and the Governor denies clemency, then that's the end of the road.'

'Is there anything else that can make a difference at that point?'

'Barring acts of God, no.'

I smiled. 'I'm not expecting any acts of God.'

Gerald tried to flip the smile back, but second-hand smiles never work as well. 'Me neither,' he said.

'All right, then, here's the deal: You don't ring the Governor until there's less than an hour to go. If he denies clemency, which we both know he will, I'll tell you it all.'

'What do you mean?' Gerald asked, his eyes suddenly sharp.

'I mean that when it's too late to go back—when the execution is a certainty—I'll tell you the rest of the story. I'll tell you the whole truth.'

'What about if I get you a stay before then?'

'I don't think you're going to be able to do that, but if you do then I keep my secrets and the killing doesn't stop.'

'I'm not going to stop fighting.'

'I know.'

He nodded. 'If we get that far down the line, you've got a deal.'

We shook hands, and it was an odd gesture of

honor in this dark little hole. I feel better for having made my deal with Gerald—he needs to know. After this is all over he's going to need to be able to make his peace with it, but not until it's too late for him to do anything to stop it.

110

'Is she coming in to watch?' Wendall asked me that night after lights out.

'Who?'

'Your wife.'

I rolled on to my side on my bunk. 'I don't want her to.'

'Why not?'

'I don't want that to be her last memory of me.'

Wendall chuckled. 'Can I ask her to come to mine?'

'What the hell for, Wendall?'

And he chuckled again. 'I'd like to have a fine woman to look at as I leave this world.'

'Give it a rest, Wendall.' I guess I must have been getting used to his way of talking, because he didn't seem to get under my skin as much now. 'Anyway, why don't you invite your sister along? I'm sure she'd love to watch them put you down, all things considered.'

'Maybe I should invite them both?' he said. 'I'm sure my little sister and your wife would have a lot in common. Hell, they could prob'ly talk for hours about the men in their lives.'

'I don't want my wife having anything to do with you or your sister.'

'Shucks, Simon, I'm hurt by that.'

'I don't think you're hurt by anything.'

He sniffed. 'You seem to be holding a pretty dim view of me, Simon.'

'Dark is more accurate, Wendall.'

He was silent for a few moments, and I'd begun to think he'd gone to sleep when his voice whispered in to me from the darkness. 'Have you worked out what the question is yet?'

'I'm not that clever, Wendall. I don't think I'm going to get it before I go. Maybe you should just tell me.'

'The answer doesn't make sense without the right question a key without a lock is just a hunk of metal.'

'Well, I'm not going to get it.'

'It's not a complicated question, it's a simple one. You just think it has to be real complicated when it's not. People ask it all the time.'

'I don't get it, Wendall.'

'You want a hint?'

'Sure.'

'The answer isn't the answer—you already know that. The real answer is the question.'

'I still don't get it, Wendall.'

He chuckled. 'Keep thinking. You will.'

111

I asked for Father Jack, and because they're going to kill me in just a few days they fetched him promptly. They all want me to be as settled as possible when they come for me. I suspect their conscience takes more convincing when they have to drag us kicking and screaming into the chamber.

'How can I help, Simon?' he asked after he'd settled into the little steel chair the guards brought for him. I was sitting on my bunk.

'I've written my last words and I wanted you to look at them.'

He nodded. 'Of course.'

I passed him a page I'd ripped from my journal. There were two short paragraphs, handwritten. He read them quietly and then looked up at me. 'This looks like a fine way to leave things,' he said.

'It was the best I could do.'

'That's all anyone can ask of you,' he said. We sat for a moment in silence. 'How are you doing?' he finally asked me, and this time I thought I heard a note of real concern in his voice.

'I'm all right, Father.'

'Is there anything you need?'

I smiled. 'The only thing I need is for this all to be over.'

He nodded. 'It will be—soon.'

'Good. I'm growing tired, Father.'

He reached out with one of his large, powerful hands and patted my knee. I nearly flinched. 'We all get tired, son,' he said, and then leaned back in his chair again.

'Can I ask you a personal question, Father?'

'Of course,' he said, but his tone was guarded.

'Why do you do this? Why are *you* here?'

He looked at me with his dark eyes. 'Some things we don't choose, some things choose us.'

'So this place chose you?'

He nodded. 'A long time ago.'

'In Vietnam?'

And when I said the word it was as if his whole body darkened, as if the light was swallowed up by it. 'We're not here to talk about me, Simon.'

'I heard you were kept in a pit for a year,' I said.

His body rippled in the dim light, like a flicker on a television when lightning strikes far off in the distance. 'It's not appropriate for us to talk about that,' he said.

'I'm dying, Father, and I've got secrets I can't take with me. I need to know if I can depend on you when the time comes.'

'You can.'

'I need to know I can trust you with the things I have to say.'

'You can.'

'Then tell me about the pit.'

A long silence stretched out between us. 'Only God and I know about what happened back then, Simon.'

'Let me hear your confession, Father, and then when the time comes I'll give you mine.'

'This is not a child's game, Simon.'

'I'm responsible for the deaths of seven girls, Father. I know it isn't a game.'

He studied me, and I could almost feel his thoughts pushing at me in the small cold space, but he knew what was at stake just as much as I did. 'All right,' he said, and then he did.

Father Jack told me the story of his time in the pit, told me the things that until then had only been known by his conscience and his God. Out of respect for the man I won't repeat his story here, that wouldn't be fair. Some things are meant to stay private. It took him an hour to tell me the whole thing, and he spoke in a quiet monotone, like he was reciting an incantation. By the time he was finished the sweat was dripping from his forehead. I listened to it all.

We sat there together for a long time after he'd finished.

'Now there are three of us who know,' he said.

I nodded. 'But I'll be gone soon, and then it'll just be you and your God again.'

'When the time comes, you have to tell me,' he said.

'Don't worry, Father, when the time comes I'll call for you.'

And I meant it, I will call for him.

112

The night after Goodlow came to our house, Carol's parents made their appeal on the television. They tried to look strong, but that was a lie, and like all lies it quickly dissolved under the glare of the lights. Her mother sobbed, and her father pleaded for her safe return. Like I said before, I fell apart, sobbing and screaming as I ran from one room to the other—unable to listen, but just as unable to turn away. Eventually I collapsed on the floor and curled up into a ball.

It was only Juliette's hand on my cheek that brought me back. 'It's all right, baby,' she whispered in my ear as I cried. 'It's going to be all right.'

I looked up at her through the tears and the snot. 'What have we done, Juliette? What the hell have we done?'

'We did what we had to.'

'But what have we done? She was a *child*!'

'Ssshhh,' she whispered, 'don't think about that now.'

I just lay there, with the memory of her mother's face in my mind. And I thought about Carol, out there alone in the forest, lying at the base of a tree, with a bunch of yellow wildflowers on her breast.

113

I made her promise not to kill anyone else before I went into town for a drink and a phone call. It was like a scene from the blackest of comedies:

'Don't kill anyone while I'm gone, Juliette.'

'I won't.'

'I mean it.'

'I promise.'

'And don't go out.'

She pouted. 'You make me sound like I'm some kind of psycho.'

How could I respond to that? It was the nightmare version of 'Do I look fat?'.

'Just stay in the house,' I said.

'I'll be waiting for you when you get back,' she said, and kissed me on the cheek.

I know it was a stupid thing to do, leaving her like that. I knew what she'd done, and I was scared of her doing it again, but still I left her in the house by herself. That's about as stupid as going upstairs alone when the power goes out in a slasher film. That kind of stuff always irritates me in horror movies—I sit there thinking how stupid it is and how any normal person would get out of the house. No one would do that, I tell myself.

And then I went and left her alone while I went into town. Who can figure? Maybe the truth is that people really do choose to walk into horror. Maybe we just can't help ourselves. Whatever the case, I drove off in a cab and left her. There was a phone call that I had to make.

'Bourbon,' I said as I sat down on a stool in the corner of the bar.

'You're getting to be a regular around here,' said the barman. It was the second guy, Mr Banal.

'I guess so.'

I drank in silence, watching the other people in the bar. There was a younger couple farther down the bar, and two businessmen in a corner booth. The couple were obviously in love. He kept touching her, and she plucked at him with her lips and fingers.

'Young love,' Mr Banal said, grinning at me.

'Yeah, I guess it is,' I said.

'You remember what that was like?' he asked me as he polished a glass.

I looked at the young couple again. 'Yeah. Yeah, I do remember.'

'Me, I been married so long I can hardly remember what that felt like,' he said. 'Seems like the only time my wife ever acts like that to me is when some new Tom Cruise movie comes out.'

I smiled. 'He does drive the ladies wild.'

'You married?'

'Yes, I am.'

'Good for you. She a nice girl?'

It was a complicated question. 'Yeah, she is in her own way.'

He laughed. 'Aint they all? You got kids?'

Mr Banal was full of the tough ones tonight.

I thought of all the girls that were now a permanent part of our dark little family. 'Six,' I finally said.

He raised his eyebrows. 'Man, you been busy for a young fella. Boys or girls?'

'All girls.'

'Well, you sure got my sympathies,' he said. 'Living in a house full of women must be pretty tough.'

I thought of Milly and Carol out in the woods, 'There's only four of them at home now.'

'Still,' he said, 'that's a lot of females under one roof.'

I laughed, and it felt like fingernails sliding over my stomach. 'There sure is a lot under my roof.' From the corner of my eye I saw the young couple looking over at me. I turned to meet their gaze and they looked away again. It seemed I was developing a gift for making people uncomfortable.

'Get you another one?' the barman asked.

I told him he could.

114

At the sentencing hearing they played a tape of the call I made that night. The prosecutor stood watching me impassively as the crackly recording played out in court. The jury didn't look at me, except for a few furtive glances. I think I scared them.

Click.

'Bedford Police.'

'She's in the forest.'

'I beg your pardon, sir?'

'Carol is out in the forest.'

'Would you like to speak to a detective, sir?'

'No, I just wanted to tell you.'

'Are you talking about Carol Keenan, sir?'

'She's out in the forest.'

'Can I have your name, sir?'

'No, she's in the forest, on the other side.'

'I need a name, sir—you can give it to me off the record if you want.'

'She's on the opposite side of the forest to Milly. I

don't know the name of the road but it's a dead end and she's down the bottom, under a tree. She's wrapped in plastic.'

'If I could just have some way to contact you, sir?'

'Goodbye.'

Click.

'Sir? Sir? Holy shit, Marge, I think I just had the killer on the line.'

Click.

'Was that your voice, Mr Chance?' the prosecutor asked me.

I looked at him for a long time before I answered, 'Yes, that was me.'

And even I was surprised at how cold my voice sounded.

115

I hung up the phone and stood in the dark street, my hands shaking. I could feel the end coming. Everything that happened was drawing the police in nearer and nearer to us. I knew that, but there was nothing I could do to change it. It felt like the promises I'd made to Juliette and the promises I'd made to Milly were sucking me closer and closer to the edge of a pit. I couldn't stay, but I couldn't walk away.

I looked up and down the street and it was all but deserted. Save for a few stragglers, I had Bedford to myself. I guess the only ones who felt safe out at night now were the ones who'd made it unsafe in the first place. Without really thinking about it, I headed down towards the taxi rank. I walked slowly, letting the cold night air flow round me. It wasn't till I'd gone a couple of blocks that I realized I was looking for Stacy.

I had no right to look for her—she probably wouldn't even want to talk to me—but I looked anyway. She was the closest thing to innocence I had left. There was a moment when I thought I'd seen her, but as I got closer I could see the woman had brown hair, not black.

'Help you, honey?' she asked. She looked old and tired.

'Have you seen a young girl out tonight? Short black hair, about five ten?'

She shook her head and lit up a cigarette, and in the sudden flare of the match she looked like a Shakespearean hag. 'Sorry, honey, I ain't seen no young girls out here tonight, but maybe I can scratch that itch for you?'

'No,' I said. 'No, thank you.'

She took a long drag on the cigarette and smiled as the smoke leaked out from between her teeth. 'You sure?'

'I'm sure,' I said and walked away. She was making me feel sick. Too much ugliness, too much truth.

In the end I didn't find her, which I told myself was probably for the best. I wouldn't have done anything good for her, just taken some more. All I really wanted was a last quick poke at her in the dark somewhere.

But Stacy was nowhere to be found, so I hailed a cab and went home.

116

The house was dark, and Juliette didn't answer when I called out. In any other house this might have meant something completely innocent, but not here. My senses came instantly awake as I sloughed off the pleasant alcohol buzz like an old skin. In this house darkness was where the bad things happened.

'Juliette?' I called out again, and the silence was absolute. I held my breath so that even the sound of the air moving in and out of me would be gone, and still there was nothing. I took a slow breath, an act of resolution, and made my way into the kitchen. I tried not to think about what I was looking for; in that moment I contented myself just with the knowledge that I was looking.

The kitchen was empty. There were two coffee cups sitting on the table. I had watched Juliette wash our cups from earlier in the night, so I knew they weren't ours. It's odd how your stomach often knows things before your head does, isn't it? My stomach started to sink away from the rest of me the instant I saw the cups; it knew. But it wasn't until I picked the cups up and saw lipstick on both of them that the rest of me figured it out.

Juliette had had company while I'd been out.

I don't know why I didn't turn on any lights—it seems a little odd now, looking back—but I didn't. I moved quietly through the house in the dark. Maybe I was more scared of seeing what the darkness hid than I was of not seeing it.

And it was the silence that scared me the most. Noise would have been far more preferable. Noise meant that things were still moving. I went from one room to the next looking for them, looking for Juliette and her guest, but finding only shadows.

I paused at the bathroom, my hand on the door-knob. It took me a while to build up the courage to slowly inch that door open, and there were a few seconds before my eyes adjusted to the deeper gloom when I thought I saw Carol lying there again, all slashed and bloody. In my mind I saw her lumbering out of the forest, down the dark cold roads, all the way back to the only place she could now call home. I imagined her sitting there waiting for me with her legs splayed out and her insides laid bare. She'd look up, her eyes snapping open, and a demon's smile would split her face in two.

But then the image was gone and there was no one in the bathroom. I stood there panting, my heart beating out the seconds. It was as if the darkness was a living thing, as if it were reaching out, dragging me deeper and deeper into the night, pulling me all the way through to the other side.

As I was standing there I heard a noise from the cellar. A quiet, sliding noise. I turned and walked slowly down the hall to the cellar door. It was slightly ajar, and I could see only darkness through the crack. Whoever was down there, was down in the black. Pausing only for a long shuddery breath, I swung the door open.

Still I didn't reach for the light switch.

'Juliette?' I called out, except my voice was so weak it sounded like the last desperate gasp of a drowning man. In a way it was, I guess.

There was a moan from the darkness below me, and then nothing.

'Juliette? Are you down there?'

Still nothing.

I stepped down onto the stairs. 'Juliette?' And this time I heard something—the whispery hiss of bare feet on the dirt floor. It was such a small noise that if I hadn't been so completely focused I would have missed it. The hackles on the back of my neck prickled at the sound, and I felt my skin literally crawl.

'Juliette?' I whispered. I couldn't have called out if I wanted to; fear had squeezed the voice from my throat. The image of Carol's demon grin came back again, and this time they were all there, dripping dirt from their hair like water as they clambered free of the earth. Shambling across the floor at the sound of my voice, drawn to it like moths to a flame. The dead girls had risen from the clay, and this time they'd come for me.

A match flared in the darkness and I screamed as I reared back against the wall.

'Hello, darling,' said Juliette.

'*Jesus*!' I cursed. 'What the hell are you doing, Juliette? I nearly had a fucking heart attack.'

She smiled up at me as she lit a candle that was sitting on a small wooden box. 'I wanted to surprise you,' she said, taking a seat on the small cot.

As the light took hold in the room I saw that there was a girl tied to the cot. She was naked. There was a pillowcase covering her face, but I could see far enough under it to make out that the girl had short black hair. I could also see a strip of duct tape over her mouth. A slut-red dress lay on the floor beside the cot.

'Stacy,' I said.

'I asked her to come over and play for you this one last time,' said Juliette. Beside her the girl moaned and pulled at the ropes that held her spread-eagled on the cot. Juliette bent down and kissed the girl's stomach, and Stacy's body stiffened at the touch. 'And she said she would. Isn't she a dear?'

'We . . . we shouldn't do this,' I said. 'Just let her up and we can go.'

'Oh, Simon,' she said, 'it's just a game.'

'I don't want to play these games anymore.'

'Yes, you do,' she said.

I looked at Stacy lying naked on the cot, and of course I *did* want to play the game. And I wouldn't let Juliette hurt her, I was certain of that. 'Just this one last time.'

Juliette smiled, and then bent down to the girl. 'Remember that I want you to struggle and fight him,' she said. 'Make it as real as you can and I'll give you some very *special* candy at the end.'

As I walked over to the cot Stacy started to wriggle and moan under the tape. She tried to force her knees together but she'd been roped tightly in place. I remember feeling a far-removed sense of disgust at the taste I'd developed for Juliette's games.

But I remember how much I wanted her too.

117

So much has happened in the last few days. All manner of things are clearer to me now, much clearer than even *I* thought they ever would be. I just have to walk you through it step by step. I said at the beginning of all this that I wanted you along for the whole ride, and I still do, but time is pressing in on me.

I'm writing this in the execution suite, a six-foot square cell with a bed and a toilet. The execution chamber is less than twenty feet from where I'm sitting.

There's just one last door between us now. Failing a last-minute stay, they're going to kill me in just a little under eight hours.

I've said my goodbyes to Wendall. I've taken my last long walk down the row. There's only the dying left. I haven't written much in the last two days because so much has been happening. You're going to have to hold on now, because we need to travel fast. We're headed for the black heart of the thing, and the clock is ticking.

I know now that the killing won't stop; any hopes I had for a different ending are gone. I've sent out two letters via Father Jack in the hope of bringing this thing to a close myself. One was to Juliette, asking her to come to me, and the other I can't speak about yet. Up until a day ago I didn't want her here, but I've learnt things that have changed all that—I finally figured out what Wendall's question was.

She has to come now; it's the only way.

118

Let me tell you the story of my last night on death row. Time seems to have been collapsing in on me. The last few days have passed in a blur that seems both painfully fast and painfully slow. Details jump out at me, mostly visits from Gerald to update me on progress with the appeals. He was still hopeful the last time I saw him, but I can't remember exactly why. He did tell me, I just can't remember the details. All that isn't important anyway. Priorities get a bit jumbled when the concept of a week stops having relevance—now it's just hours and minutes I have to worry about.

It was a strange feeling as I lay on my little cot that last night on death row. The Garden was unusually hushed; all the moaning and crying was still. It's kind of a tradition here that your last night on the row is a quiet one. I don't know what the thinking is behind it—when you're facing an eternity of silence a little last-minute noise is probably a good thing. It didn't bother me though; I had my own stuff to think about.

And I knew that this was the night Wendall and I would finish up whatever it was we'd started. We hadn't talked much over the last day or so. Gerald had come and gone, and I'd paced around, the too-much-caffeine feeling growing steadily worse as the time ticked down. I still didn't feel scared as such, but I did feel stretched as tight as a piano wire.

After lights out I'd lain on my bunk for hours in the silence. I wasn't worried—I knew he'd speak when the time was right.

It was just after midnight when he called out to me. 'You awake, Simon?'

I smiled in the darkness. 'You really think I would have wanted to sleep through this?'

'Sleep through what?' he asked with mock surprise.

'The big ending.'

There was a faint flare of orange from his cell, and then I smelled smoke. 'And what big ending would that be, Simon?'

'The big ending where you tell me what all this has been about.'

'All what?'

I looked around my cell. 'All this.'

He chuckled in the darkness. 'You ready to die?'

'I guess so.'

'You scared?'

293

I thought about it for a moment before answering him. 'I don't know. I don't feel scared exactly, but I don't feel good either.'

'Stuck in the middle again, huh?'

'I guess so, yeah.'

'That's why she chose you.'

'That's why who chose me?'

'You know.'

'You mean Juliette?'

'You do know it was *her* who chose *you*, right?'

I thought back to that bar in New York City from a thousand years ago. She'd appeared beside me and said I looked lonely, and that was as true as anything she'd ever said to me. I had been lonely. I'd *always* been lonely.

'I know,' I said.

'Did you ever stop to think *why* she chose you?'

'She chose me because we were meant to be together.'

He laughed softly. 'She chose you because you live in the middle ground.'

'And how would you know anything about her?'

There was another pause and smoke drifted out between the bars. 'When you work out what the right question is then you'll know how I know.'

I didn't have a clue at that point what his question was, so I went back a little. 'What did you mean when you said that I live in the middle ground?'

'Just what I said, that you live in the middle.'

'The middle of what?'

'The middle of everything.'

I frowned. 'I don't get it, Wendall.'

'It's like this,' he said. 'I live in the dark, always have done; I chose it. But some people live in the dark who didn't choose it, circumstances just pushed them in. Old Father Jack's one of those, and so's that bitch Sondra fucking Hilta.'

'And me?'

'You're deep in the dark now, Simon, but you didn't start out here. You were in the middle when she found you, but she recognized how far you'd go, so she scooped you up and took you with her.'

'She took me?'

'Oh, yeah, she took you all right. It could have been different though. If she'd been some other person you could have ended up living a boring little life in some boring little suburb. It was just your bad luck that she was who she was.'

'So it was just luck then, that's what you're saying?'

'In a way.'

I sighed. 'I don't understand.'

'It was your bad luck that she got you before someone else did, but after she got you everything else you did was your own. She knew that if you had the right reason you'd be strong enough to get the job done, no matter how dirty it was.'

'Thanks for the analysis, Wendall.' I was getting tired of his pop-psychology rambling. Maybe what he said was true, and maybe it wasn't. Either way, it was all academic now.

He laughed. 'You're truly welcome, Simon.'

'What's the question, Wendall? The night's running down and I've got a ways to go before I'm done.'

'Fair enough. Let me tell you a last story and then we'll see if you can't figure it out for yourself.'

And as he began to tell me his last terrible story I felt the darkness closing off around us. It was as if the world was drawing back from us, leaving two damned souls—one to tell the story, and one to listen.

119

'I killed my father when I was fourteen years old,' Wendall said, 'and it was probably the greatest moment of my life.' I knew by now it was best not to interrupt Wendall once he got going, so I just sat and listened. 'We'd spent years travelling round the country bringing God's word to the flock, and my father must have popped enough young cherries during that time to fill a good-sized orchard. I admired him for that, but I hated him too. He had more cunning in him than any man I ever met, but there wasn't an ounce of good in him. He was the cruelest man I've ever known as well.'

There was a few moments' silence, and I heard Wendall's cigarette crackle in the darkness. 'He beat me for years, and I guess I didn't mind all that much, but the last straw was the night he tried to have my sister. I didn't mind him doing all the skank in the towns we passed along the way—hell, it was him who taught me how to hunt in the first place—but I couldn't let him have her. That wouldn't have been right.'

'He tried to rape her?' I asked him.

'You got that right, the asshole. We'd stopped for the night out in the country somewhere, which was unusual for him. He always liked to stop in town so there'd be a good supply of skank around. He'd been funny all day as well, kind of quiet. I knew there was something bad coming.'

'How old was your sister?'

'She was thirteen then, and just starting to develop into a woman. She was pretty, that was something no man could have argued with, and I guess my old man had been biding his time. He wanted her ripe when he plucked her.

'So we pulled off the road and had dinner, and then he sends me out of the truck, tells me he's got some talking to do with her and God. I saw the look on her face as soon as he said it. She knew what he meant—hell, we all did.'

'So did you leave?'

'What sort of a stupid fucking question is that, Simon? Course I fucking left. He would have beaten me unconscious if I hadn't.' There was another pause, and smoke drifted out into the corridor. 'I got up and I walked out into the night. It was dark by then, and the air was still and cold. We were out in the middle of nowhere and so there was no noise apart from what was coming from inside the truck.'

'What did you hear?'

'I remember hearing praying, him at first and then her. Pretty soon it sounded like there was some kind of revivalist meeting going on in there. He was ranting and raving, she was crying—the whole nine yards.'

'So what did you do?'

'I stood there for a while in the cold and the darkness, and I just got angrier and angrier. Like I said, I had no problem with him fucking all those other bits of skank, but it wasn't right him doing that to her. She was his daughter, you know?'

'Yeah,' I said. 'I know.'

'And then he said something to her that was too quiet for me to make out, and it all went silent. She said something back to him and I heard him again. "Take them off," was all he said. She started to cry then, a different kind of crying, a real empty, hopeless kind of sound. That's when I knew I had to do something.'

'What did you do?

'In the end it was a lot fucking simpler than I ever

thought it would be. I just went and got a hammer from the cab of the truck and walked on in there.'

'What did you see?'

Wendall chuckled. 'She was taking off her skirt as I walked in. Her blouse and bra were lying on the ground. She was shaking and crying so much she could hardly undo the buttons. He was already naked and he was standing over her like some kind of hairy fucking ape.

'"What the hell are you doing in here, boy?" he said, and then he saw the hammer. "What are you going to do with that?" he asked me. I simply smiled and hit him.'

'Just like that?'

I could hear the smile in Wendall's voice. 'Yeah, Simon, just like that. He dropped like a fucking dead pig.'

'Did you kill him?'

'I killed him all right, but not with that first blow. That one just put him down for a short time. I knew there was no undoing it from there—he'd kill me when he woke up—so I had to get the job done.'

I was almost afraid to ask him: 'So what did you do?'

He chuckled again. 'I tied the motherfucker up on the floor and sat down to wait.'

'What for?'

'I waited for him to wake up.'

Another pause. More smoke drifting out into the dark corridor.

'And he did after a while. His big stupid eyes fluttered open and he saw me sitting there on his bed. My sister was down the other end on her bed.

'"What the fuck are you doing boy?" he hissed at me.

'"I'm gonna kill you, old man," I said to him, and for the first time in my life I wasn't afraid of him. In my mind he was already worm food.

'"You haven't got the balls to kill me," he said, and then he started to laugh. "You don't have the balls to kill anyone, you little pussy-boy."

'"Is that right?" I said.

'"You better fucking believe it is," he said. "Now let me up and take your medicine, boy."'

Wendall laughed softly in his cell, and it was a bitter sound in the darkness. 'He shouldn't have mocked me, no sirree. I might've killed him quicker if he hadn't, but he did. So I bent down real close to his ear, close enough so I could smell the stink of him. "You really think I don't have the balls to kill you, old man?" I asked him.

'"You don't have the balls for anything, you little faggot," he said. "Now let me up."

'I reached round behind me and picked up the carving knife I'd got from the drawer when he was out cold. "You're right about one thing, old man," I said as I knelt down beside him.

'"What's that?" he asked, and I could see doubt in his eyes.

'"I don't have the balls to kill you," I said, then reached down and grabbed his nuts in my hand and pulled them up hard, "but I can get them easy enough." He screamed and pulled away from me, but he was too slow. I sliced them off him as easy as gutting a fish.'

'Jesus,' I breathed. 'You castrated him?'

'Funnily enough, that's what he said too.' Wendall chuckled. 'Although he wasn't quite so calm about it. Yeah, I castrated him, and then I stuffed his bloody balls into his mouth while he was screaming.'

I felt sick. 'My God, Wendall, what kind of a monster are you?'

'An efficient one,' he said. 'All it took was a little time. He bled out on the floor like a butchered pig. He begged and screamed and prayed, but he died just the same.'

'He bled to death?'

'It took a while, and every so often I'd have to slice another strip off to stop it from clotting, but yeah, he bled to death.'

'What about your sister? What did she do?'

I heard him sigh in the darkness. 'She just lay on her bed with this stupid little red polka-dot pillow pressed down over her head, crying and shaking.'

It took me a moment to realize what Wendall had said, and when I did it felt like he'd hit me in the chest with an ice pick. That's when it all fell into place, when I finally figured out what his question was.

120

If you've been paying attention you'll have figured it out too. All it took was that one detail, the little red polka-dot pillow. Now I knew why he'd been so interested in me, and how come he'd seemed to know so much about us—about her. It was like when you're looking at one of those optical illusions and it all seems to be just a big blurry mess until someone tells you it's a picture of a wolf.

And then you finally see.

121

'Wendall,' I said, my voice shaking and my stomach feeling squeezed flat.

'Yes, Simon.'

'I think I know what the question is now.' I was remembering a long-ago conversation I'd had with Juliette at a bus stop in Philadelphia when she'd told me about hiding her head under a pillow as she listened to her father's dying screams.

'Aahhh,' he said. 'I thought that little story might help you along. What is it?'

I took a long slow breath, and then let the words flow out of me. 'What is your sister's name?'

He laughed and I heard him clap his hands together. 'Well done, Simon. Well fucking done.'

'So?'

'Juliette,' he chuckled. 'My sister's name is Juliette.'

And there it was. That's why he'd been so interested in me, why he'd got himself shifted into the cell next to mine. And that's what all the conversations had been about. Wendall was family.

I found it hard to speak. There was so much to take in.

'I saw her picture in the paper,' he said. 'I hadn't seen her for years, not since she took off on me, but I knew it was her straight away. I'll never forget those eyes of hers. And when I found out you were being sent here—well, let's just say that it made me feel very lucky. I'd been wanting to meet you for such a long time.'

'Wh . . . why?' I stammered.

'Because of what you did for her, and for me.'

'What did I do for you?'

'You took the rap, and because of that she's still out there. I'm gonna die here, I know that, but I'll die knowing she's still out there, still doing what it is that we do.'

I felt numb. Sitting on my cot in the dark I finally understood Wendall's game. I'd always thought he was taking me somewhere bad, and I'd been right. 'What happened that night after you killed your father?'

He laughed. 'I did it myself.'

'Did what?'

'I popped her cherry—what'd you think I'd do?'

The darkness was so thick it was hard to breathe. 'But . . . but I thought you were trying to protect her?'

'I was protecting her—from him. He died, so then I did her myself. How could I not, Simon? Didn't you ever wonder why she is the way she is?'

'Like what?'

'Christ, man, she's a fucking adolescent wet dream! I bet she acts like some kind of weird teenage sexual fantasy, doesn't she?'

I thought about her, about the way she was. I thought about that very first time in New York when she'd just straight out asked me if I'd wanted her. I thought of all the other times too, of the sex we'd had together, and how she was. And what we'd done with Stacy in our cellar. I thought about it all.

'She *is* a fucking adolescent fantasy, Simon,' Wendall hissed. 'She was *my* fantasy.' He laughed then, and in the darkness it was the closest thing to pure evil I've ever heard. 'She was my fantasy, my will made flesh and blood, and when you were fucking her, Simon, you were fucking me as well. We were all in there together.'

I thought for a long time in the darkness as things clicked into place one after another. 'She'll never stop, will she?' I finally said.

'No,' he chuckled, 'she'll *never* stop. Ain't life grand?'

122

I felt like a blind man who'd suddenly had the scales lifted from his eyes—it was all so dreadfully clear. There'd been no stopping her from the moment she'd bludgeoned Sondra Hilta's daughter to death on the river bank all those years ago. Everything that happened in Bedford was always going to happen. The only question now was, what to do?

At first light I sent for Father Jack. I asked to meet him in the interview room: I didn't want Wendall overhearing us.

'How are you doing, Simon?' he asked as he came in.

'I'm doing okay, Father,' I said.

His dark eyes examined me. 'You look tired.'

I shrugged. 'I had a rough night.'

'They won't be coming for you for a few hours yet. Can I get you anything?'

'I need your help, Father.'

'Anything.'

'I need you to deliver two letters for me.'

'All right,' he said. 'Who would you like me to take them to?'

I reached into my pocket and pulled out the two envelopes containing the letters I'd written in the hours since Wendall told me his nasty little secret. Father Jack took them and looked at the name on the front of the first envelope.

'My wife is still in Stanton,' I said. 'That's only a thirty-minute drive from here.'

'I know,' he said. 'And what about this one?' He held up the second letter.

'I think you should find it easy to deliver that one.'

'I'm sure that's true. The question is whether or not I want to.'

'You have to, Father, if you want all this to stop.'

'What are you doing, Simon?'

'I'm trying to end this the only way I know how.'

'I don't know if I can deliver this letter, Simon, not unless you tell me what's in it and why you're sending it.'

'I can't do that, Father.'

He leaned back in the chair and ran a large hand through his hair. 'Then I can't do this, Simon.'

'You have to do this,' I said as I leaned forward and took his big hand in mine. 'You have to do this because I'm in the pit this time. I'm in the pit and I have to find some way to close it up so no one else ends up in here after I'm gone.'

'I don't know,' he said, shaking his head. 'I just don't know.'

'Help me close up the pit, Father, that's all I'm asking.'

He looked at me for some time, his dark eyes probing, and then he stood. 'Very well, Simon. God help me, I'll deliver your letters.'

'Thank you, Father,' I said.

'I'm not sure your thanks are a great comfort to me, Simon.'

I nodded. 'I know, but I thank you just the same.'

123

They came for me just after ten o'clock. A hush had settled over the place. I was ready for them, and heard them before I saw them, quiet deliberate footsteps coming down the row. I saw the warden first, then Father Jack, and behind him the guards.

'Hello, Simon,' said the warden through the bars.

'Hello, Dr Merton.'

We were as cordial as two business associates bumping into each other in a restaurant.

'It's time to move through.'

I smiled. 'I thought as much.'

One of the guards opened the cell door and then the others came in. There was hardly room for me to stand once they were in.

'Are we all set?' I asked Father Jack.

He nodded, and we exchanged a look that only the two of us understood, 'Everything's set,' he replied.

'Good,' I said as I stood and let the guards shackle me for the second-to-last time.

'Would you like to take a book?' the warden asked.

'Yes, I would. I'd like to take my journal if I may?'

The warden nodded. 'Of course.'

And then we shuffled out of my little cell. I didn't look back; I wasn't going to miss it. I paused at the bars of Wendall's cell, and I was dimly aware of the guards tensing behind me, but the warden waved them down.

Wendall was looking out at me, grinning in the darkness of his cage. 'Keep me a seat,' he said and he winked at me.

I put my hand in through the bars of his cell. He

looked at it for a moment, like a stray dog being offered meat, the hunger and fear fighting for control of him, and then he stood and took my hand. It was the first and last time I ever touched him. His skin was hot and dry, and I could feel the muscle and bone underneath.

'Just remember what you said,' I whispered to him as I gently shook his hand.

'What's that, Simon?'

'You said that I was strong enough to do the job.'

He smiled. 'Strong or weak, it makes no difference when they pump their black shit into your arm.'

'Still, I want you to remember it was you who told me that as you sit here waiting to die.'

I felt his hand tighten around mine. 'And I want *you* to remember that she's still out there as *you* die,' he hissed. 'Cos I sure as hell will be thinking about her. She's my legacy to the world, Simon.'

'Oh,' I said, 'didn't I tell you?'

His eyes narrowed, instantly suspicious. 'What?'

'She's coming—I decided to bring her here after all.'

'What are you doing, Simon?' he asked quietly, and I could hear the sudden fear in his voice.

And now it was my turn to smile. 'Just remember that it was you who told me I was strong enough to get the job done, no matter how dirty it was—if I had the right reason.'

'What the fuck are you up to?'

I let go his hand and backed away from him. 'It's like you said, Wendall, I'm getting the job done.'

'*What the fuck are you going to do*?' he yelled, throwing himself up against the bars. The smug killer's smile was gone, the rising panic had stripped it from his face as easily as tearing off old wallpaper.

I smiled at him. 'Goodbye, Wendall.'

I turned and walked away from him. I heard him yelling out to me as I took my last long walk down the Garden, but his was the only voice. No one else said a thing, which was good.

And then we went in through the pink door, and I left Wendall behind.

124

There were some other loose ends I had to tie up before they killed me. Goodlow was one of them.

'Hello, Simon,' he said when he'd sat down outside the execution suite cell on a small chair the guards brought for him.

'Hello, Detective.'

'You sent for me.'

I smiled. 'Yeah, there're some things I have to say to you.'

He nodded. 'I'd hoped we'd get a last chance to speak.'

'It's funny, isn't it?' I said. 'The way things work out, I mean.'

'I don't know about you, Simon, but I don't feel that much like laughing at the moment.'

I smiled. 'I don't mean this, I mean with you and me.'

'How so?'

'I've always respected you, Detective Goodlow, I think you know that.'

He nodded silently.

'And I think that maybe in different circumstances we might even have been friends.' He said nothing. 'Oh, don't worry, Detective,' I said, waving my hands in a gesture of dismissal, 'I don't expect you to respond to that one. I'm a killer and you're the guy who caught me, I know what that means—these are just my final ramblings to the world.'

Goodlow shrugged. 'Anything's possible in the right circumstances.' We sat for a moment in silence before he spoke again. 'What did you want to tell me, Simon?'

'I wanted to explain to you about that night.'

'When the last girl was killed?'

'Yeah.'

He took out a packet of cigarettes. 'You mind?' he asked me. Even after all this time, all we've been through, he still asked me. Like I said, he's a decent man.

I shook my head. 'No, I'm not that worried about the long-term health effects of second-hand smoke.' It was a weak joke, but he smiled anyway.

'What about that night, Simon?'

'I know that you blame yourself for what happened.'

'And how do you know that?' he asked as he lit up.

'Because I know the kind of man you are.'

He looked at me carefully. 'And what kind of man is that?'

'The kind of man who takes it hard when a girl dies that he feels he should have saved.'

'And how would you know what I feel, Simon?'

'Because I feel it too.'

Goodlow smiled. 'You killed her, Simon. How can you feel guilt at not having saved her?'

'We both know I didn't kill that girl,' and I saw his eyes sharpen ever so slightly.

'Is that what you're telling me now? That you didn't kill her?'

'Of course I didn't.'

'And so why now? Do you think this will help you get a stay?'

'Give me a little more credit than that, Detective. There aren't going to be any stays—it's far too late for that. In a couple of hours' time they're going to walk me through that door and kill me. I don't want any stays.'

'So why now?'

'Because I don't want this to prey on you. Any blame here is mine.'

Goodlow's cool eyes studied me. 'And Juliette? What about her blame in all this?'

'Like I said, any blame here is mine. She can't help what she is.'

'And what about all the girls who are going to die because she's still out there?'

'I've taken some steps. I can't tell you what they are, but you won't need to worry about that.'

'What are you up to, Simon?'

'Don't worry about that either. I just wanted to tell you that you weren't to blame for that last girl's death. I was down there with her—I was the only one who could have saved her, not you.'

'So why didn't you?'

I looked at the floor, feeling very tired and very sad. 'That's real complicated, Detective.'

'I'll bet it is,' he said quietly.

Somewhere off in the distance I heard the metallic slam of a cell door closing. 'I need to prepare myself, Detective. I wonder if you'd be kind enough to leave me alone now.'

He looked at me. 'You want me to just walk away?'

'A friend of mine will bring you something after the execution. It's a notebook, and it'll answer all your questions—and your fibby friend Agent Hanson's as well. And, yes, I want you to just walk away.'

There was a moment when I thought he was going to say something else, but to my great relief it passed us by. 'All right, Simon,' he finally said. 'If that's what you want.'

'It is.'

He stood and extended a hand through the bars. I took it and felt his warm strength. 'I never understood you,' he said. 'In all my years of being a cop I never met anyone I couldn't understand except you.'

'When you get the notebook you'll understand.'

'I hope so,' he said.

'Goodbye, Detective Goodlow.'

'Goodbye, Simon.'

125

One by one I'm closing off the books. That's one good thing about knowing the hour of your death—it allows you the luxury of choreographing your closing scenes. If a truck hits you in the street you leave behind all kinds of messy half-finished shit, but if they execute you then you get to finish it all off neat and tidy. Just like in the movies.

126

I'm finding it hard to sit still now, so I'm writing as I pace back and forth in this godawful small space. I wish they'd just do it. All this waiting is driving me fucking crazy. Writing is hard. I feel like I'm going to throw up when I focus on the words, but I make myself. We've come so far together, you and me, and there's only a little bit further to go. But I'm sick of waiting. I'm sick of everything for that matter. I just want it to be over. Wouldn't you?

127

And then there's Gerald. He stuck to his deal and he fought right down to the end. These final few hours must have been hard for him. One by one all his last-ditch maneuvers have come up blank. Of course he never had a chance—there was so much political pressure to kill me that I was never going anywhere but the death chamber. These days the emphasis in capital cases is on getting the job done, not getting it right. It turns out that no one in this great system of ours cares much about new evidence this close to the line, they just want the nuisance gone. It would have saved me a lot of anguish if I'd known that at the beginning of all this.

Still, you live and learn, I guess.

He came to me an hour and a half before the end. 'It's all over, Simon,' he said. 'I just heard back about my last motion. Everybody turned it down. I don't think they even bothered to read it they got back to me so fast.'

'So that's it then?'

He nodded slowly, 'Yup, that's it.'

'What about the Governor and clemency?'

'I'm expecting a call any moment, but I don't think he's going to budge.'

'Good.'

'Can you tell me now, Simon? I need to know what the hell this has all been about.'

'You know the deal, Gerald—when the Governor denies clemency, when there's no going back, I'll tell you it all.'

So we waited together. We didn't say much; mostly we just sat. I found his presence strangely comforting. I don't know why, he just made me feel calmer. Maybe it was the thought that his life would go on after I was gone that did it. Thinking about him living a normal life watching his kids grow up.

Who the hell knows?

The door at the end of the corridor opened and Andy Watson leaned in. 'Phone call for you,' he said to Gerald. 'Governor's office.'

Gerald took a deep breath and stood up. 'Well, here goes,' he said with a thin smile.

'Yeah, here goes,' I said.

Andy stayed after Gerald had gone. 'You know they're not going to grant clemency, don't you?'

'I know.'

'You're a cool customer, Chance.'

I looked at him. 'You think?'

He leaned against the wall and studied me carefully. 'Oh yeah,' he said, 'you're one cool cat.'

'I'll take that as a compliment, Officer Watson.'

He shrugged. 'Take it any way you like.'

The door opened again and Gerald came back in. I could tell from his face straight away what the news was. Andy winked at me: 'See you in an hour, Chance,' he said, and sauntered back down the corridor.

Gerald walked slowly up to the bars. 'The Governor just denied clemency. There's nothing else left.'

I was surprised to see tears in his eyes. 'Sit down,

Gerald,' I said, waving at the little steel chair in the corridor. 'Let's talk.'

Gerald sat down in the chair, but he didn't look at me.

'Hey,' I said.

'What?'

'It's all right, Gerald.'

'I don't understand you,' he said, shaking his head. 'You keep saying it's all right but it feels all wrong to me.'

I took a long deep breath. 'Let me tell you,' I said. And I did.

128

I need to take you back down into our dark little cellar one last time. I need to tell you what I told Gerald, and I have to do it quickly because time is running out. I said I wanted to take you right into the black heart of the thing, so pull a chair up close to the bars and pay attention.

129

'Oh, Simon,' Juliette said to me in the darkness of the cellar, 'it's just a game.'

Stacy lay tied on the cot, naked, her face almost completely covered by the pillowcase except for a few wisps of black hair. She moaned and writhed as if on cue. I told Juliette that I didn't want to play her game, but she knew that was a lie.

'Yes, you do,' she said, and she was right. She knew me better than I knew myself.

'Touch her,' she said as I sat down on the edge of the cot. I reached out and ran my hand over Stacy's stomach. She moaned and drew back from my touch. Her skin was so soft and warm.

'I . . . we should leave,' I mumbled. I could feel my heart beating in my chest.

'Kiss her,' whispered Juliette from the darkness behind me. 'Taste her.'

I leant down and kissed her stomach, licking her with my tongue. She smelt like flowers, and she tasted fresh and clean.

The girl moaned again under the tape that covered her mouth, and she started to cry. I didn't know if it was an act or not, but I couldn't have stopped myself either way. Besides, I could wipe away her tears afterwards—there'd be plenty of time for that later. She was just some junky teenage whore that everybody used, right? What could I do to her that hadn't been done a hundred times before?

I felt hands stripping my clothes from me. Juliette. 'Now take her,' she whispered, and her breath was hot and urgent in my ear.

I climbed onto the cot, feeling Stacy's body go rigid beneath me. I kissed my way up her stomach, over the gentle rise and fall of her breasts, and the sweet scent of her neck. She twisted her head away from me as I started to pull the pillowcase off, but Juliette stopped me.

'No,' she said, 'leave it on.'

Stacy moaned again and struggled underneath me, which only made me want her more.

'Take her,' Juliette whispered, and I heard Stacy sob. Then I pushed myself inside her. There was a moment's resistance, which surprised me, before I slid deep inside her. I felt her whole body tense, and she screamed under the duct tape. All that was just details to me—I was lost in the delicious friction of her. I slipped my hand up under the pillowcase into her hair. It was wet, like she'd just showered.

I thrust and thrust and thrust.

And as I felt it building in me, in the final moments before the need to come took over everything else, Juliette pulled the pillowcase from the girl's head.

And it wasn't Stacy's eyes that looked up at me, but Theresa's. I lifted my hand from her hair and it came away black. Suddenly I understood what had happened. Juliette must have taken Theresa when I was out, then cut her long blonde hair and dyed it black so I'd think she was Stacy.

We locked eyes, Theresa and I, and saw each other for the first time. The tears had made her face wet.

And here's why I must die, because there was an instant before it took me when I could have stopped. It was just an instant, but it was there.

But I didn't. Instead I pushed into her again, telling myself I was confused when all the time it was hellishly clear.

And then it all let go, and I filled her with my selfishness and my weakness. I filled her till there was no more ugliness left in me, and then I tore myself from her and tumbled off the cot onto the cold dirt floor.

'Oh, my God,' I moaned, covering my face with my hands. 'What have we done?'

I felt Juliette's hand on my cheek. 'Now you know,' she said.

I looked up at her, horrified. 'Now I know what?'

She smiled. 'Now you know what it's like to be me.'

I heard Theresa crying on the cot and I pushed Juliette roughly aside. *'Get away from me,'* I yelled at her. I scooped up the red dress from the floor and covered Theresa with it. 'Oh God, Theresa,' I said, gently peeling back the tape from her mouth, 'I'm so sorry.'

She sucked in a deep shuddery breath and turned away from me. 'Please don't hurt me,' she said.

'Of course not . . . I . . . I'm so sorry . . . I didn't know it was you.'

Theresa looked at me then, through the pain and the tears, and we both knew it was a lie. 'I want to go home,' was all she said, her voice choked with the horror of what had been done to her.

'Of . . . of course,' I stammered. I tried to untie the ropes but they were too tight. She was crying as I fumbled at the knots, and I couldn't bring myself to look at her. 'I need to get some scissors to cut these,' I said, 'and then we can call your parents.' It was all nonsense.

I sprinted up the stairs and headed straight for the kitchen, knowing Juliette kept the scissors in there. When I yanked the drawer open everything scattered onto the floor. Dropping to my knees I scrambled for the scissors amidst the mess.

And then I heard a shriek from the cellar that stopped my heart. It was more terrible than any sound I have ever heard in my life, and it trailed off into a series of gasps that sounded almost like coughing.

I knew—in that moment I knew.

I staggered to my feet on legs that had been made useless by dread. As I entered the hallway I heard a banging from the front door.

'Police! Open up!' I dimly recognized Goodlow's voice, but it made no impact. I just knew I had to get back down there.

And when I did I saw that it had all gone to hell. Juliette was standing over Theresa, holding a large carving knife. The girl's body arched violently sideways, trying to twist away while Juliette plunged the knife into her again and again.

Screeching at Juliette to stop, I bounded down the stairs and knocked her away from the cot. She slammed into the far wall just as there was an echoing crash from upstairs.

Theresa's body sagged back down onto the cot. I fell on my knees and held her, sobbing. Theresa was warm and slippery in my arms. She looked up at me for just a few seconds before she died, and it was a moment I can never forget: her eyes were so full pain, so full of fear.

And then she just went blank, almost like someone had turned off a switch. I stared down at her, unable to fully comprehend what had happened. There was so much blood it seemed to cover the whole world.

I heard the sound of running feet upstairs. Juliette began to scream and I turned to see her plunging the knife deep into her own chest.

'*Juliette*!' I wailed.

She just looked at me and smiled as she pulled the knife from her chest and raised it again.

'*Nooo*!' I yelled, lunging for the knife.

We went down together, amidst all the blood and the death. I don't remember much after that. There were lots of policemen, and Goodlow of course, but it all gets blurred for me.

Nothing else mattered anyway. I died when I looked into Theresa's eyes. Everything since then has just been details.

130

Gerald was silent and pale by the time I'd finished.

'Now do you understand?' I asked him.

'Understand what?' His voice was shaking.

'Do you understand why it's right that I die?'

He looked at me. 'But you didn't kill her.'

I shook my head. 'I killed them all, Gerald. Maybe I didn't hold the knife, but I didn't stop the hand that held the knife, which is just as bad.'

'But you didn't actually kill anyone.'

'I raped Theresa.'

'You didn't know it was her. Juliette tricked you.'

'Only for a little while,' I said. 'At the end there was a moment when I knew it was her and it still made no difference.'

'Why are you doing this? Why are you taking the blame for her?'

'I'm not, I'm only taking what's mine.'

'Then she gets away with it, Simon! And she'll do it again!'

I shook my head slowly. 'She won't.'

'How can you be so damn sure of that, Simon?'

'I'm taking care of things.'

He looked around, confused. 'How the hell can you take care of things from in here?'

'You're just going to have to trust me on that one.'

'This is all wrong, Simon, it's all wrong.'

'At last you and I finally agree,' I said, and I smiled at him. 'This whole thing has been wrong from the very beginning, and now it's time to set things right.'

'But you have to tell someone,' said Gerald. 'You can't let it end like this.'

'I can,' I said, 'and I will.'

He shook his head. 'This is all wrong, it's all wrong.'

It was time for him to go. 'Do you love your kids, Gerald?' I asked him softly.

'What?' he said, looking up. 'Of course I do.'

'Then go home to them. You did your best for me and I'm grateful to you, but it's time for you to go home now.'

He looked at me with a grim determination. 'I'm staying,' he said. 'Till the end.'

I smiled and shook my head. 'No, you're not, Gerald—I don't want you here. I want you to pack up your briefcase and go home.'

'But I . . . '

'No buts, Gerald. Go home to your family.'

He started to say something, but then I saw his shoulders slump. He was tired. 'All right,' he finally said. 'I'll do what you ask, but this is wrong, it's all wrong.'

'Thank you, and thank you for all you've tried to do for me.'

He stood, and we shook hands as men do in such moments. There were no last wise words—it was more an uncomfortable and hesitant parting, like he wasn't sure how he should go. Gerald's a good man, and I wish him well in his life.

Before he left I asked if I could have his fountain pen; I told him I needed it to finish my journal because mine had run out of ink. I didn't think the guards would let him give it to me, but to my surprise they did.

I was happy about that. Gerald's fountain pen was one of those space-age ones you see on infomercials. The ones you can stab through a tin can and they still keep writing.

I needed that pen. I still had one last visitor to go.

131

She came when I was still writing up the last scene with Gerald, the one you've just finished. I knew it was her without even looking up—I'd asked her to come and knew she wouldn't let me down.

When I did finally look up she was standing there in the sunlight like a goddess. And despite all that had happened just the sight of her made my chest ache.

'Hello, Simon,' she said, her voice so sweet you could almost taste it.

'Hello, Juliette.'

'I didn't think you were going to send for me.' I could smell her, even amongst the stink of the execution suite I could smell her.

'Of course I was going to send for you.'

She smiled. 'How have you been?'

'I've been okay.'

'Good.'

There was a guard watching us from the end of the corridor, but he could have been a thousand miles away for all I cared. It was so wonderful to see her again. I hadn't seen her since that last terrible night in the cellar, and I'd prepared myself to go to my grave alone.

This moment felt like a gift from God.

I walked over to the bars. 'I just wanted to see you one last time,' I said, clutching Gerald's fountain pen behind my back.

'I know,' she said.

'I have to tell you something.'

She tilted her head and looked at me through the bars, her pale blue eyes catching the light and breaking it up into tiny sparkling chips. 'What?'

I reached out with my left hand and slowly drew

her in close to me, until her forehead was touching the cold steel bars. I saw the guard tense at the end of the corridor.

'There's one last thing I have to do before I die,' I said as I felt the weight of Gerald's fountain pen in my other hand. I imagined how sharp and strong it would have to be to pierce a tin can.

And still keep writing.

'What?' she whispered.

'Close your eyes.'

And she did.

'Do you know that I love you?' I asked her softly. She nodded.

'And do you know that I kept my promise to you, that I have never hurt you?' I could feel myself shaking.

'Yes,' she said and she sighed.

I leaned forward until my forehead was just touching hers through the bars. Her breath mixed with mine. Her smell filled me. My heart was pounding in my chest and I felt the room spinning about me.

'I love you, Juliette. No matter what happens, remember that I've always loved you.'

And then I kissed her. One last kiss for the dying.

And I let her go.

She opened her eyes and looked at me, and for a wonderful moment it was just her and I, Simon and Juliette.

Then she turned and walked away.

132

Did you think I was going to kill her?

Maybe I was, I don't know. I could have. I could

have used Gerald's fountain pen, but in the end I didn't. She was never scared of me; she knew me better than I knew myself. Standing there with her, breathing in her breath, I never had a chance.

Some promises you just can't help but keep.

133

So here we are at the end. In just a few minutes' time the door will open and the warden and his party will come for me. I'm ready for them; I have been for some time now.

Father Jack has been in and I've made my peace with him. I don't have time left to recount our conversation fully, but I gave him my notebook and told him it was my confession. He took it. He asked me if I wanted to accept the Lord as my Savior, but he only asked it half-heartedly. He's gotten to know me fairly well in the last few weeks.

I politely said no thank you. I was careful when I said it—though I'm pretty sure he's a good man he still scares the hell out of me.

I kept only a single page that I ripped from the back so I could write this last aside between you and me. At the beginning of all this I said I wanted to tell you our story in my own way and in my own time. I offer no excuses for what happened; all I want is for people to understand.

That's important to me.

Father Jack was right about one thing though—the closer you get, the harder it is to maintain your resolve.

I am scared.

This has come as a surprise to me, because for

months I haven't wanted anything else but this. Yet still I'm scared. My stomach is churning, and my legs feel weak. My hands are shaking as I write this.

I wish it could have been different. I find myself wishing for so many things in these final moments. Don't worry though, I won't bore you with them.

But I *will* die a good death. I'll walk into the chamber on my own legs, and I'll lie quietly as they strap me down. I'm determined not to wince as they put the needle in, even though I've never liked needles.

I won't say anything that'll add to the girls' families' burden. I'll simply tell them that I'm sorry for what I did, and that I hope my death brings them some small measure of comfort. That's exactly how I'll say it: 'some small measure of comfort'.

And as the poison starts pumping into my arm I'll look only at Juliette.

I did love her so.

Postscript

From "With One Stone" (*Time* magazine, October 1999) by Leonard Raffield:

The execution of Simon Chance at the Eden Hill Penitentiary earlier this week should have brought to a close a story that has haunted the nation for months. Yet the bizarre slaying of Juliette Chance shortly after the execution has ensured it will be some time to come before the ghosts of Bedford can finally be laid to rest.

In many ways Simon and Juliette Chance were the perfect suburban couple. He was a teacher in the local high school, and she played the pretty young wife. Their story should have been a happy one, but as teenage girls began to go missing from the small town of Bedford, police suspicions increasingly focused on Simon Chance. When they finally broke down his door late one night in April last year, they found Chance standing over the raped and mutilated body of seventeen-year-old Theresa Wright. His wife had also been stabbed in the chest. Police discovered the bodies of four more girls buried in the floor of the cellar.

Simon Chance was charged with the murder of these five girls as well as two others that had been dumped in the woods just outside of Bedford. After two mistrials Juliette Chance was acquitted of all charges, despite a flurry of public and political protest. Simon Chance pled guilty to all seven counts of murder and was sentenced to die by lethal injection. His execution was one of the fastest in the history of the state. He spent just under nine months on death row.

Simon Chance died shortly after six p.m. on the

fourth of October with very little fuss. A group of nearly thirty people witnessed the execution, including a number of state officials, the parents of five of his victims, and his wife. Prison sources said that the attending physician had some initial difficulties establishing the intravenous line, but throughout the almost twenty minutes it took them to find a suitable vein to insert the needle, Chance remained stoic and outwardly calm.

However it was the events that unfolded immediately after the execution that have been subject to the most public speculation. As Juliette Chance was leaving the grounds of the prison she was approached by a local woman, Sondra Hilta. Witnesses say that Ms Hilta walked up to Juliette Chance and said, 'This is for Margaret.' She then pulled a handgun and shot Ms Chance in the chest six times. Despite receiving medical aid almost immediately, Juliette Chance was pronounced dead at the scene.

In recent years Sondra Hilta has become something of a celebrity at Eden Hill Penitentiary. She is an ardent supporter of the death penalty and is reported to have attended every execution at the prison since the late seventies. She began attending executions shortly after her daughter, Margaret Hilta, disappeared without trace in 1978.

Police are not commenting on the possibility of a link between the disappearance of Margaret Hilta and the slaying of Juliette Chance, but it is understood that several items were taken from Sondra Hilta at the scene, including a handwritten note from an undisclosed source within the prison . . .